Photography Credits: Jude Dillon

Virginia Nemetz holds a Ph.D. in Humanistic Psychology with a post-doctoral specialty in Jungian Analysis. She works with children and trauma, and has read the 150 original diaries of Anais Nin at the UCLA archives. Honoured to be a 'catcher of dreams', she believes that dreams and journal writing play an essential role in healing the spirit.

Dedication

Alice Munroe, whose words of encouragement stayed with me for many years.

Virginia Nemetz

THE REDEMPTION OF ANAIS

AUSTIN MACAULEY PUBLISHERS™

LONDON • CAMBRIDGE • NEW YORK • SHARJAH

ISBN 9781788487252 (Paperback)
ISBN 9781788487269 (Hardback)
ISBN 9781788487276 (E-Book)

www.austinmacauley.com

First Published (2018)
Austin Macauley Publishers Ltd™
25 Canada Square
Canary Wharf
London
E14 5LQ

Acknowledgments

To my helpful readers Judith Duthie, Nancy Read, and Diane Domonell. They took the time and cared.

To Rupert Pole, who spent hours and days with me, sharing his love and understanding of Anais Nin, his wife.

To Brad, who gives me the space and encouragement to write.

My gratitude to all who have helped in so many ways.

"Have you ever thought," she asked, "how one could be influenced by one's own writing?"

—Nin, Waste of Timelessness

Chapter 1
Yves

Yves listened to a woman's footsteps on the wooden bridge between the quay and his trawler and shook his head in annoyance. Who was she, and what was she thinking to wear high heels down by the water? As she hesitated beside the *Hilaire*, he peered out from the companionway and tried to shake off the effect she had on him. More than beautiful, she was ethereal. There was no mistaking the elegance of the woman.

Fey was another descriptor that came to mind. He stared. She must be lost, he thought. She'd ask for directions next. A woman dressed in a spring green raincoat with matching shoes and brimmed hat, carrying a flowered umbrella, didn't just stroll along the pier. He expected her to turn around any second now and walk away. Instead, she stopped in front of his boat.

"Good morning, *Monsieur*. I'm looking for Yves Gauger."

He tipped his hat.

"At your service, *Mademoiselle*. How can I help you?"

It was obvious to him that he could not keep the surprise out of his voice.

"You have a houseboat for rent and I would like to see it, if it's still available."

She sounded as lovely as she looked, and she looked him in the eyes as she spoke. Her eyes were heather, a bed of soft heather you could fall into, lost forever. He noticed her ring and sighed for the lucky fellow, and thought he caught the scent of perfume as he beckoned for her to follow him. He jumped down from the deck of the trawler and guided her farther down the quay to *La Belle Aurore*. A few minutes later, he left her on board to examine the houseboat, while he waited for her on the *Hilaire*.

Even when Paris had been at its glamorous best, before the war had trodden on the ratio of men to women, when women had worn their lovely clothes on the boulevards and carried parasols, he did not remember such beauty. She would be gone in a few minutes, so he used those minutes to daydream. He couldn't remember the last time he had wanted to daydream about a woman. Though Yves was several inches over six feet, still young enough to dream and handsome in a way that turned heads, he thought of himself as an unimposing fisherman's son. His blue eyes acquired a sparkle of impatience as he paced the deck and wondered what had gotten into the woman to consider renting *La Belle*.

Chapter 2
Anais

It was an hour before she reappeared.

"*Madame*, I hope you found the space to your satisfaction."

"*Oui, Monsieur*. It is perfect, but I have a few requests."

"I cannot change the place, *Madame*. It is too costly and not worth the headache, if you know what I mean."

"Of course, *Monsieur*, but the changes I would suggest I am willing to pay for and have my own workmen construct."

Yves stared at her in astonishment.

"But *Madame*, this is only a rental. Who does such a thing?"

"I do, *Monsieur*."

Obviously, her outer beauty hid a will of steel.

"Well, I'd be a fool to turn down improvements at your expense. What are you suggesting?"

"I will convert upstairs to my own private living space, redo the bathroom, and make a proper bedroom. Downstairs, another new bathroom and a kitchenette-bar. The main room would be converted to an art gallery. Of course, the outside would be repainted. I must check the roof, but the balconies and stairs need to be repaired, too."

"But…it will cost you a fortune! I'll not lower the rent in exchange." He shook his head. "Does this mean strangers will be coming and going all day once the boat is an art gallery?"

"No, *Monsieur*. Its hours of opening will be minimal, and I would be sure to get your approval beforehand."

This was some kind of hallucination. It had the aura of contemporary surrealist art, more fantastic than anything *he* could have imagined. This woman must have money to burn, but who was he to turn away from a bit of good fortune? Since the war ended, he had become unaccustomed to the specter of prosperity and did not easily recognize or believe it. Though it was 1928 the economy had yet to recover from the destruction of war.

They drew up a hand-written contract, and she signed it. Her name, she said, was Anais, an exotic name for an intriguing woman. She used her first name only because she didn't care to involve her banker husband in her mundane affairs, and right there and then she reached into her purse to pay Yves for the first month's rent. He could do nothing less than graciously hand her the keys. According to her, workmen would show up and begin the transformation in a few days. They shook hands, his large and rough grip a contrast to her feminine strength.

She was like an aphrodisiac. As she turned to leave, he watched her hips sway and glide as she left the pier. She was the most graceful woman he had ever met and the rental transaction the smoothest he had ever experienced. Life had suddenly taken on a new dimension, and Yves had no doubt it would soon become more interesting.

It was certainly a day of surprises, for her appearance prompted memories of Paris before the war, of beautiful women and their smell, their walk. One of the most unbearable side effects of the war, as far as he was concerned, was the downtrodden demeanor of ordinary women on the streets. Their downcast eyes, ugly leggings, patched clothes and colorless smiles depressed him. It was as though the soul of the city had seeped away in the tears of its women. Living on the boat in the heart of Paris had taken him as far away from the ugliness of war as he could get. It simply wasn't far enough.

Yves recoiled the mooring line on the deck of his boat. The old fishing trawler wasn't much to look at but it was his free and clear. He once dreamed he would fix the *Belle Aurore* and restore her to the days, when he and his parents and brothers lived on board. Those days before the war seemed like morning fog on the river.

Immediately after the war, when his family was lost to him, Yves had signed up as crew on a boat that had set sail for the Caribbean. As he sailed through warm waters and into unknown ports, his frozen center had thawed until the day he had wanted to return to France. The sound of steel bands that imitated tropical birds, nautical lines that sang in the rigging and his own breath that kept a steady cadence, all these had squeezed into the crevasses of his heart and pried open finer emotions. Once he decided to stop running and decided to feel alive, the decision was made, and not long afterward his old trawler was tied up next to his parent's ancient barge. He had not gone anywhere, since he had tied that knot to the quay. Now, something about this beautiful woman evoked the past, when life had been different. He felt a stir in his chest, as the not entirely welcome thaw threatened to expose feelings that had remained dormant for years.

He had told her to watch her step while he inhaled deeply. This was the Seine, after all, and its deep water moved silently beneath him. He imagined her twirling through the large room on the main floor of *La Belle Aurore* before making her way upstairs. She had stayed for an hour to allow plenty to time to consider her offer while she stood on the upstairs balcony to absorb the ambiance or the river, clinging to it as to a lifeline.

She said she was married to a banker, and he believed her because of the way she was dressed. Few women could dress like a flapper, in the finest fabrics with the latest hairdo and make it seem refined. *Les Années Folles* had come to be called the Roaring Twenties not the refined twenties. Dance clubs and chin-length bobs were in. She had worn a headband of blue and green beads to capture the color of her eyes. Her coat and skirt were short, her stockings silky. He was certain she wore no corset and seemed somehow likely to do whatever struck her fancy in the bedroom. He had heard of Sigmund Freud and wondered about liberated women like her but had never met one. Today was his lucky day. Just because he had never met a sexually liberated woman, didn't mean he was averse to the idea.

Yves' image of the houseboat afloat on the Seine was now superimposed by an image of a beautiful woman, a live bowsprit who lived on board. Details of the image came together in perfect stills. He felt that his brain had processed more than the spring green colors she wore, the beaded headband, or the silk stockings. There was more here than met the eye. He felt the need to step back and see what he was missing. Right now, he was too emotional at the thought of *La Belle's* renovation. He would not, however, forget his impression of the woman. He knew his brain worked slowly, gathering details where shadows fell into depths and nuance. The process appealed to him like a puzzle on which he would muse and arrange pieces that resembled insights. It was Yves' unusual talent, certainly, that had saved him from severe psychic damage, during the war and the days and years since then. He rearranged and coordinated inner images in order to understand their strengths, their importance, and their myriad facets. In his mind's eye the barge had acquired an occupant, and the occupant had turned on a light in the upper window. His original impressions would be re-created slowly in a manner unique to him, that is, without jumping to conclusions.

Chapter 3
Yves

Yves had lost weight lately, forgotten to cook meals for himself and did not look forward to a meal for one. This morning he decided to make an effort to walk to the nearby café where a latté and baguette dipped in hot milk would remind him of better mornings. He might see familiar faces and read a newspaper, say hello to a few old acquaintances and have a conversation with someone who also wanted company. That was one of the remaining wonderful things about Paris. One could always find intelligent conversation, humor, drama and a scent of the art scene. If all went well, one could have a second *latté*. Anyone close to the art scene was familiar with cafés. Artists were performers. Tourists watched them and they watched the tourists. Yves was not an artist, but he was a Parisian, proud of his city's artistic side, the side that dwelled in cafés and the less than glamorous abodes nearby.

He stepped down through the companionway to the galley of the *Hilaire*. Once, she had been a fine little fishing vessel, secure and tough. Most of the other boats on the river had been commandeered during the war, but the *Hilaire* had escaped such a fate. Water was low in her water tank, he noted, so he filled a small basin and took a sponge bath, put on clean clothes and beret and found his shoes beneath the bunk. It would seem that he left the boat open and vulnerable, but he had nothing to steal, nothing to hide. He jumped and his long legs and good balance landed him on the quay where he put on his shoes and headed in the direction of his favorite café on the left bank. He had survived. He was healthy, and dawn had broken full of promise. It brightened his day and sharpened his optimism.

Images, not words, were Yves' entrée to his soul. Had his destiny been different, paint might have been his *métier*, his connection to the world. He might have etched or engraved or used splashes of color that would take him into the future and ahead of his time. He looked at the chipped old paint on the buildings he passed and saw primitive cells and life forms embedded in the walls. History was imprinted in every step he took and shone forth as the sun touched him. Nothing had destroyed his faith in life, its vital force and what he revered. Destiny had put him on battlefields, killed his friends and loved ones, left him bereft of funds and taken him back to the river of his childhood. It had circled him, yet left him whole, while others had been shot or scarred or lost, and he was grateful. War, he considered, could resurrect feelings like appreciation and forgiveness. If he were to choose an image of forgiveness, it would be the boat. The water flowed past, cleansing with every current. With the hum and tremble of the cabin, he felt merged with the river. His little boat was the perfect image of healing. It rested on a respect for the constant flow of the river, aware that his little boat was the perfect image of healing. It rested on the surface of life in the city.

He felt whole this morning as he walked on cobbled stones. Like the spring sun that warmed his shoulders, he carried this wholesome attitude. To witness was to praise or condemn and he chose to praise creation. He reached over and touched a wall as he walked. This morning he felt newly born.

Last night, he had fallen asleep on his bunk, looking up through a porthole to the clear night sky where Venus glowed brighter than any star. He had stared until his eyes closed in sleep and took him where the gentle lights of Paris outlined the whole city. He had felt tired, still exhausted from war and his efforts to recover. Now, he felt reconnected to the beauty of dim streetlights and candlelit windows, the Seine, dark and steely, and his little boat that rocked him gently at its berth. Today, his dreams followed him to the café where he smiled for the first time in a long time. He had money in his pockets, and a beautiful woman was about to move in next door. People with a photographic memory, like his, recalled images after a short instant of exposure. For Yves, images were sometimes connected with sound and the stars nearly sang in mysterious ways.

Yves was no philosopher, but he had had time to review all the tragedies he had seen during the war, to play them over and over in his head and, finally, to come back to the Seine of his childhood. He had once avoided memories of the better times, thinking it would be too painful. Instead, he discovered a fond, selective embrace of the past, and that embrace had become a safe haven, a port. His past had been the old barge, the river, and the soul of Paris. Now, he was glad to be back, alive and whole, but lonely.

Chapter 4
Angela as Hostess

Anais' heels echoed along the empty street. She had hoped to get home before Christolphe who was returning from Zürich this evening and expected her to entertain a few of his colleagues. Frequently, he was called to Zürich for bank business, but hopefully, by the time she got home Camille would have prepared dinner and a fire would be lit in the living room along with candles to welcome the damp spring evening. She planned to look striking in an Oriental caftan while he had a drink in front of the fire and told her anecdotes of his week away from home. She loved it when he was in Paris. He was her friend, her protector and her devoted husband. She, however, was not Anais when she was home. In her mind she was Angela, and the closer she got to home the more she thought like Angela, the more she acted like Angela, the housewife and the banker's adored wife.

To say that she became Angela and left Anais to walk along the empty street is a poor description of a mental aberration whose perimeters had yet to be studied carefully by doctors. The fact remained, however, that Angela had split off a portion of her mind. This rather serious and mostly undetected problem had happened to her during an acute crisis in her life. In effect she had created another personality. Anais had given Angela her name and apportioned to her a segment of her life that would be forever separated from the traumatized Anais. In that way it was Anais who protected the person she called Angela. Yet, Angela knew nothing of the existence of Anais. So Anais knew all about Angela though Angela knew nothing about her.

As she hurried down *rue Monbuisson*, her cloak, that she had changed into at her *pied a terre* in Saint Germaine, was disturbed by the gusts of early spring air. She knew she was late for dinner. If she was lucky, their guests would be enjoying an aperitif. How had it come to this, she asked herself? Late to her own dinner party, an event she had overlooked, if truth be admitted.

The moment the gate closed behind her, she heard footsteps across the street. She had had the sense of being followed all the way from the train station, and it wasn't the first time. Here it was, years after the war, and she was still paranoid. Footsteps on the street after dark, in the evening shadows of alleys and on narrow backstreet sidewalks, still resounded with old war fears and premonitions of disaster. No one had returned to old routines. How much longer would it be before the citizens of Paris could breathe normally, let go and move on? To add to her dismay Anais had accepted employment as a spy.

These days, truth had become a big issue for Angela as well as Anais. Drops of rain accompanied by a lull in the wind softened the air around her. Rain allowed the evening to dampen her disturbed thoughts, as her walk turned into a glide and her cloak whispered around her. She unlatched the wrought iron gate and glanced through the lighted windows on the first floor. Thank God, Camille knew the routine. Angela had told her to organize everything before she left for the day. Quietly, Anais slipped into the garden, entered the house through the kitchen and made her way upstairs.

Several years ago, Christolphe had bought this house in a rundown state. It was only a ten-minute train ride from the city and ten minutes to walk from the station, but it put them outside the tensions of Paris. Though everything about the house had seen better days, Angela had felt inspired when she saw the property. The damp and dreary rooms, the outdated kitchen, the overgrown garden and the neglect that welcomed mice and spiders in from the cold, had driven the price well below market value. Now, three years later, paint and cheerful curtains, a new stove, hours in the garden and her own Japanese style of elegance had created warmth and serenity. It lured visitors and guests from the city on a regular basis. Christolphe loved to entertain in their home, and he loved to showcase his delicate and mysterious wife. His banker friends and colleagues considered it an adventure to take the local train to Louveciennes and walk the ten minutes through the pleasant countryside to their destination. They felt as if they had stepped into an impressionist landscape, far removed from the realities of work. No one ever came out by car. Instead, their metaphorical journey, from the center of Paris to Christolphe's home, gave them a sense of holiday and ritual.

Strange how truth and reality could become so confused. Angela loved to stay at home with walls for boundaries, where life was uncomplicated and the mirrors on the walls reflected nothing more than the view of a room, a face, and makeup applied with care. Christolphe said she was sensitive and lovely, and he wanted nothing more than to protect her gentle sensibilities. She loved that about him and felt cherished.

Angela looked in the mirror. No one had heard her enter the kitchen or take the stairs to her bedroom. She needed to change, repair her makeup and put her mind at peace. Her fears on the walk home had occurred more often in the last month. She'd found herself coming home from the city without any memory of where she'd been. She felt strange. Staring into the mirror did not bring back any memories though she had tried many times. If she didn't hurry, Christolphe would become upset, as he tried to excuse her absence or play the role of host. His attempts to copy her hospitality in the past were less than satisfactory. His demeanor spoke of a staid banker or a conservative and unimaginative businessman. He counted on her to maintain his role as a valuable bank employee while making his home a fascinating place to come to dinner.

The sound of someone following her, her lateness and her lack of recall, frightened her, but being Christolphe's wife helped dispel fears. The role of hostess was something she did well. She was like a sponge that absorbed the talk, the atmosphere, the subtitles and the shadows. After their dinner parties, she squeezed out all the details she could remember into her diary. Its pages had become a receptacle for insights and intuitive observation. Once she had shared her concerns between its covers, she continued placidly about her duties as a housewife.

If there is an art to being a person, Angela wished to practice that art. Fulfillment as a human being was no small ambition. She believed that the effect she might have on others came only from the person she was inside. Before having an effect on the world, she had to be the kind of person she admired. It was the only way she could be sincere, compassionate and non-judgmental. When she was with others, she wanted nothing more than to be immersed in their outlook. Dinner parties were more than random get-togethers, more akin to opportunities to touch others with kindness while looking through their eyes to see new perspectives. She pondered, as she wrote in her diary, whether this attitude had to do with her writer side that sometimes emerged, or her chameleon-like ability to disappear through her relationships. One thing was certain. She loved people and the endless possibility she recognized in them. She saw them and revered what she saw.

***

The talk was unusually subdued until she stepped into the dining room.

"Good evening, gentlemen."

She felt sighs of relief and a stir of interest that meant the bankers yearned to discuss more than bank *chèques* and deposit slips. These days, their conversation was all about debts and overdrawn accounts. Paris was yet to be repaired properly, while her citizens watched helplessly, as money leaked out of the country. It went in the direction of Switzerland or Panama or other foreign countries that accepted hidden assents. It was a slippery business, and a single disparaging comment could bring jobs tumbling, leave tidy offices in chaos and find families abandoned to starvation. Just as her presence soothed and calmed the distracted Christolphe, it did the same for her guests. As a rule Christolphe shared details of his work with Angela until he felt healed of the day and ready to return to his seemingly insurmountable challenges. His guests reacted in the same way and loved their visits out of the mired city, beyond the restrictions of daily habits.

Angela wore a kimono, one she had sewn by herself in front of the fire on quiet evenings. The black silk was lined with brilliant reds and oranges, huge chrysanthemums and delicate green, hand-painted stalks. These patterns could only be glimpsed near the collar of the V-necked wrap, the panel of the skirt and, of course, the unwrapping of the *Kobe* belt. Such vivid details covered the fact that she was naked beneath her costume. Men leaned forward, as though they could imagine the slide of heavy silk against her skin. Yes, they thought, Christolphe was a lucky man.

Of course, he had forgotten to turn on the music. This was typical. Anais considered atmosphere one of the major concerns of the perfect hostess. She realized that a soft oriental ambiance was essential to a sense of well-being. The music she adjusted effortlessly was the exotic and enchanting temple bells that chimed all the notes of a geisha's repertoire. The cook had left many dishes on the buffet, so she began by pouring warm sake, setting a tempura dish at the center of the table and placing miso soup in lovely lacquered bowls before each guest. A few years ago, her dinnerware had been gifted to her on a visit to Japan with her mentor, Roshi. As her substitute father, he had wanted her to have them. He had insisted she accept the fine porcelain because the pieces had been in his family for many years. Tonight, she used them to create a meal that was unheard of in Paris.

This festive evening, Christolphe had invited his boss who had brought a new client. Now that the soup was in front of everyone, a toast was made to health and the recovery of the French economy. Soft bells soothed the frayed nerves of men who felt responsible for the economy of France; conversation hummed with the kind of staid comments that were expected; and Anais was complemented on the unique flavors of the orient. The evening transported them to the Far East to places they could only imagine. They looked to Anais, wrapped in another world and breathed the smells of faraway unknown places. When the doorbell rang, the spell was lifted just enough to admit added excitement and energy to the mix at the table.

"Excuse me. I believe we have a latecomer who will join us. He is our surprise guest this evening."

D. H. Lawrence stepped into the room followed by Anais, who introduced him around the table, as he shook hands and was led to his place. Since he had just arrived in town and had come by for a relaxing evening, he was excused for his late entrance. The fact that he was a writer elevated his status in the room. Few of the bankers had heard his name; no one had read his books; however, he had a new book that had just been released and was in Paris to promote it. Though he was well known to the literati for *Lady Chatterley's Lover,* to the business world he was an artist and a treasure. Everyone present acknowledged that the arts contributed to the betterment of the world. Better the artist than the war mongers whose destruction was still felt in remote corners of France.

Bankers were nothing if not courteous and diplomatic, so with a few revealing comments Anais had them inquiring after the new book and experiences with the international reception of his other books. Intuitively, they knew that this was the kind of dinner party and the caliber of guest that made history. It *was* historic, and they were a part of it. The man was venerable, and the conversation sparkled to rival the kind of repartee that prevailed before the war. It was a dinner that lifted the spirits as nothing else could. How does one explain such moments, when the senses are heightened and the nectar of wisdom overflows into happiness?

Lawrence had read Angela's several attempts at short stories and knew that she had once worked as a newspaper reporter, but his critique of her work was rather harsh. He told her he realized he was being severe but would not bother at all, if he thought she could never meet his standards. It was somewhat discouraging. Nevertheless, she admired his work and insights.

For Angela, the evening was a wild success. Lawrence was at his best, mellow and wise. She remained in the background, serving plates of unusually exotic food, filling glasses with warm sake and changing the music unobtrusively to the sound of a wooden flute, whose notes floated and wove themselves through moments of thoughtful silence.

One day, Angela wanted to write a biography of Lawrence, his life and ideas. She admired him and his insights and wished to understand him as a person, as much as she longed to understand herself as a French woman who had grown up in Paris, left France at age eleven and returned at nineteen. Once, at the beginning of their friendship, after Lawrence had read some of her short stories, he had goaded her into efforts to read and understand Marcel Proust. His prod to understand Proust's work had become her cornerstone and inspiration to write. It had taught her the importance of literary reflection, where all the senses were engaged to describe scenes that brought readers to acute awareness of time to be savored and never wasted. Lawrence was her literary guru, a writer whose respect she craved, and she knew it was important to record their conversations in her diary.

Tomorrow would be time enough to stay at home and remember all the charming moments, the comments and telltale threads that revealed what had transpired in the lives of each person who had been invited to her *soiree*. It was important that her guests had let down their defenses, for the distance from downtown Paris, the presence of someone from the art world and the influence of sake, all conspired to disorient the insular banker and loosen his thoughts.

When the party was over, she sat at her vanity mirror, removed her geisha eye makeup and reviewed the evening's success. Christolphe came and stood behind her to stroke her shoulders.

"Thank you, Anais. That was a special evening. Inviting Lawrence was a stroke of genius. My colleagues will not soon forget this evening. Who knows, I may even get a promotion."

He laughed as he spoke to his wife, the woman he thought he had married, not knowing he spoke to her double as well.

"Oh, I had not heard you were in line for a new position."

"We would not need to move. That would be the wonderful thing about it. If we stay, however, it might involve invitations to more clients than we are used to entertaining."

"But you know I enjoy these evenings, my dear. That wouldn't be a problem, and I love living in Louveciennes."

"That's what I told my boss, *chérie*. But how would you feel, if some of them had been our enemies not so long ago?"

"Well, I suppose I'd feel like a good will ambassador. Peace. Isn't that what everyone wishes for the future?"

Beauty, she thought, created peace. It soothed and ironed wrinkles out of all sorts of sordid situations. She loved to create beautiful gardens, parties, and connections between people. She knew in her heart, for instance, that men and women were equal. She did not believe that aggressive behavior could create anything more than ugly dissention. Her ideas of what created equality for women and peace in the world were unusual and complicated. One might even call them spiritual.

"You've had a long day, my love. I wish you *bon rêves*."

Anais watched him leave her room to go to his own connecting bedroom. Then she gazed at her face in the mirror once again. Tomorrow she would stay in with no visitors. She would reconstruct every moment of the evening in her diary. She walked to the window, once Christolphe had turned off the lights, and gazed down into the garden that was bathed in moonlight.

As she was about to open the window to allow fresh air into her room, she noticed the movement of a shadow in the far corner of the garden near the back gate and felt a chill that was more than the cool air. It was the same chill that had shivered through her, as she had hurried home. Now, she was certain she was being followed. Why would anyone be interested in following her? Or could it be that it was Christolphe who was being followed? Just then, she saw a light go off and on twice in Christolphe's bedroom. Was that some sort of signal? Her peaceful housewife's existence felt suddenly threatened.

Beauty and love: she intuited that her presence somehow contributed to their manifestation. Could those so intent on world power not see that there were as many or more powers for good as for evil? What of the forces of love, the power of beauty? Did they not shine brightly enough? When powerful men left her dinner table, she hoped they would see more love and less evil.

Unfortunately, love and beauty disappear under force. They do not die, but go underground. Was that the reason she was having so much trouble distinguishing between them? This business of day and night, beauty and ugliness, light and dark, created a fog. Try as she might, she could see nothing through such opacity. Everything is lost under the force of war, she thought, and all the important things like love, beauty, limbs and the heart, seek cover.

She sat listening to the wind, then stopped as her pen slowed, and the idea that there might be several truths, intruded. This curious censure that she saw as writer's block, had never happened to her before. Taking a deep breath, she eased her hand on the pen and allowed its flow to continue, unobstructed by fears and criticism.

Later in bed and under the covers, her mind raced. Angela disappeared in the minutes before she fell asleep. Anais' first spy assignment would be under the tutelage of Roshi. She was to create an art gallery and provide a venue where artists would feel comfortable to drop by and voice their concerns. It would be the most natural thing to do while she collected information. Most of them, after all, were her friends. But what could they possibly reveal that might be of interest to national security? Listening with compassion to their problems and concerns was one thing; listening with the intent to pass on information was another.

None of these things dispelled her fears of hollow footsteps or the light that flickered like a signal from Christolphe's bedroom.

"There must be a trip one can take and come back from changed forever. There must be many ways of beginning life anew if one has made a bad beginning."

—Nin, *Waste of Timelessness*

Chapter 5
Angela Is Inspired by the Writing of Proust

In truth, Angela was fragile, exotic and contained. She was like the orchids she grew and placed around her lovely home in the suburb of Paris. She gardened and decorated in a Japanese motif, and she was a construct of Anais' personality. She entertained Christolphe's clients and bank colleagues. They loved her. Their guests were all male, catered to and expertly flattered. Angela was polite and unassuming and treated them with deference and feminine wiles. Perfume, music, color and soft fabrics created an atmosphere of charm, and each man left with his defenses down. It was considered an honor and a treat among Christolphe's colleagues to be invited to dinner, when there was a big deal to close, international clients to woo or a special celebration to acknowledge. Such events were assured success at Christolphe's home. The men went away, whispering to each other of his luck and their admiration for his wife's talents and beauty.

When they left, Angela wrote in her diary. It was the one trait she had in common with Anais. Angela was the perfect name for a cherished, introverted, and protected part of Anais' extroverted personality, one Anais kept track of by occasionally reading Angela's diary. For now, Angela sat quietly, absorbing the dinner conversations. She wrote of gestures and unusual traits, turns of phrase and causes for laughter. By and large it was a serious group unused to frivolous conversation and adverse to jokes. They were bankers, after all, with the weight of post war reparations on their backs and hunched shoulders. She liked to note every detail because she practiced the art of writing and wished to be an author one day. Sometimes, if a character took her fancy, she would write a complete character sketch. On occasion, these had turned into short stories.

Angela's quiet life was lived in solitude and serenity. She made forays to get a few groceries each day, conferred with the housekeeper several times each week, took walks with her little white dog Pepito, who loved her, and spent hours in her flower garden that grew behind the high walls of the yard. When she wrote she could be anyone and take herself anywhere, but she realized she wrote mostly about other writers, the visitors to her home and strangely disturbing adventures in Paris. There were moments, when she wondered where she had come up with some of these adventures and colorful characters, their wild night secrets or the clear portraits of people she was sure she had never met. In the end she attributed them to the gift of imagination and was simply grateful for what she had been given. Her only regret in life was the fact that she had never had a child. She and Christolphe had been married for several years, and children did not seem to be attracted to their path.

***

Last evening, she had hurried to get home. Somehow, she had spent far longer in the city than she realized. Yet, looking back, she could not understand what had kept her so long.

Daydreaming. She must have been daydreaming again. She had done a lot of that lately. Even now, after a lovely and successful dinner party, she was distracted. She remembered how the street narrowed till it was nearly a path that led to her front gate. The housekeeper had left a light on in the foyer, and light glowed obliquely through the old lead glass panes.

The house was old, but she had fallen in love with it and insisted that she was willing to oversee renovations to make it the home it was today. To this end she had applied considerable artistic talent. Now that the house was a home, she loved coming back to it, and it filled her thoughts. As she entered the house, her memory of the day failed her.

But even more than the house, it was the garden that was her pride and joy. In the evening dusk the flowers gave off a scent that filled the air with early roses, forsythia and hyacinths. The roses spread along the wall on trellises, and bulbs covered the ground inside the walls. Each spring she refused to cut the lawn until the primroses disappeared because the profusion of flowers and greenery made her happy. Angela, counted her blessings and considered the article she was writing for a literary journal. It had to do with gardens in literature. Tomorrow, she might ask Christolphe what he thought of the idea. Perhaps her preoccupation with the article was the reason for all her daydreaming and the inner agitation she felt.

Mostly, life was good. It was serene and peaceful and gave her the time she needed to write and garden, to look beautiful for Christolphe and hostess his business dinners. It made her feel like his valuable business partner as well as his enchanting wife. There were moments, when she simply had to pinch herself. Paris was the city that sparked her imagination and spoke to her in a language of deep-seated longing. She loved Paris. There was no doubt about it.

Her Paris was the city of Marcel Proust whose life and writing were inseparable, whose inner life had broken loose of the restraints of history and physical weakness, social structures and boredom. Angela loved the deeply thoughtful work of Proust and read his Swann portraits with persistent study. Over and over she reread his sentences and his habit of staying in the moment as only the best writers do. He was a Zen artist and arranged his words the way she did her flowers for a tea ceremony. She believed he understood landscape and atmosphere the way certain writers understood suspense. She did not think she could ever get that close to a foreign culture, but she admired a writer who could. He was a writer of unique perspective, just as she was. When she wrote, her life came together to resolve a strange and disparate restlessness. Home, her serene garden and her isolation, became a universe of possibilities. Her mind, born in the confines of Paris, mattered more than the brave adventures of mountain climbers or the dark excitement of cabarets. Her favorite flowers and books, her insightful interpretations of musical tones, her relevant memories of voices and her transparent love of beauty: these were all woven in a wreath that she wore like a crown.

Like Proust, Anais relied mostly on memories and glimpses of the world beyond her garden walls. She had been nearly destroyed by a narcissistic father when she was young, just as Paris had been nearly destroyed by the war. She believed that she had raised herself and that her character was strong. She might look frail, but Angela was more than her looks. Writing connected her to inner growth and freedom. Angels protected her every day, as they held her in their protective embrace.

She loved the Parisian community of artists and writers who lived and worked in studios and cramped apartments. It did not matter that she lived a dual life or that most of them did not know her personally. She believed that animosity could be healed on the pages of her diary, or in her garden where a profusion of flowers grew together in joyous color, or in the way she approached life with glad appreciation for each new day.

Anais was told that the Paris of her youth was gone but for her it was alive. The sweet smell of almonds and sugar from the patisserie, the feel of cobbled stones beneath the thin soles of her shoes, the flaked facades of old buildings and the sounds that flowed off her tongue in a language that engaged lips and palate: these lived on in her.

She was told that the war had created terrible divisions and the possibility of more war. It had created spies and secrecy and shadows. In the spring, when apple blossoms filled the air, men who had been wounded by violence walked the streets and inhaled the scent of flowers while unable to smell the scent of fate. It was not the loneliness that was the problem, she realized; it was the inability to recognize solitude or its beneficent nature. She could be herself only by herself. The need for others, she believed, was a need to suffer and overcome numbness. Like Proust, she attended soirees and artistic productions. Diaghilev, Stravinsky, Picasso and Joyce mattered to her. She listened to their music, read their words and daydreamed over their painted images, but it was unnecessary to mingle with them face to face. As for Lawrence, he understood her feminine nature better than she ever could.

Anais believed that great art contributed to the wellbeing of the universe; bad art simply diminished evolution. For her, fame and art were not compatible, and fame created nothing but distraction and social envy. She needed to be alone on the streets of Paris, alone in the cafés, alone as she walked beside the Seine or stopped at La Chappelle to gaze at its rose windows. She needed to sit alone in the Louvre to study the ways of the past; she needed to hear the echoed voices on the crooked footpaths that wound through back alleys. After her walks she returned to her garden as Angela; she sat, wrote and experienced for the second time, the route she had taken, the vital energy that rose up from the streets and the hum of conversations on every corner. Angela knew she would write this way until she could no longer put pen to paper. To write was to reflect; to reflect was to gather experience that could be relived.

What she could not abide was the uneasy dissonance that occasionally entered this idyllic reflection. On occasion, when she felt she was being watched, she stopped, sat on a park bench, or merely glanced over her shoulder. No one was ever there. Was it her over active imagination? At night, when these incidents had occurred, she dreamed dreams of chaotic proportion. Cruelty prevailed. She was reminded of

Artaud's Theatre of Cruelty, of battles and agonizing indecision.

Division. Wholeness. She longed to be whole. Though Angela did not know about Anais she knew something was missing. In her solitude there arose feelings of uneasiness. She attributed to the Great War and its bleak aftermath much of these feelings, but the uneasiness was relentless. She understood that sorrow followed her on the streets and seeped from the apartments and homes she passed. Yet she was one of the fortunate ones, insulated from misery. Wasn't her life like a fairytale? Lovely possessions surrounded her, and her husband adored her. He told her so every day. Her garden was a refuge from ugliness and the mean struggle to survive, while her writing was a source of solace that rearranged uneasiness and returned it to wherever it had arisen.

When uneasiness did escape those confines, she had learned to reassure herself that these feelings would not last forever. They, too, would pass and be replaced by beauty. Meanwhile, she cut flowers and arranged them in formal expressions that refined her thoughts and cultivated an appreciation for the present moment. It brought her back to her good life and reminded her to be grateful.

Chapter 6
Anais

Anais stood still to let the sound of the river and the deep motion of its currents ascend through the soles of her feet. She took off her shoes and slowly made her way around the outside of *La Belle Aurore*. It was an old barge saturated with the essence of all those who had once enjoyed life on the river. There was the aft deck, once a garden that now overflowed with pots and dead plants. The private balcony off the bedroom added to the feeling of spaciousness, and she imagined the room restored to a place where energy from the river would renew her. She thought of the river story told by Kazuko Okamoto that she had grown to love, when she visited Japan with Roshi. The sound of the river flowed through her ears and was absorbed by her thoughts into quiet, motionless music, into colors of loneliness and weeping, into an awakening from deepest sleep. She wanted to scatter apple blossom petals on the ripples and watch, as the moon calmed the water's restless surface. The river created phantoms and put a spell on memories that splashed the edges of the barge and cleaned its sides.

She was Anais and she knew all about Angela, though Angela knew nothing about her. The world outside her head knew them both as Anais, but as Anais she knew she was not truly that gentle and loving persona referred to as Angela. Anais was a fighter, a survivor. She was in love with bright colors and sensual men, secrets and clandestine affairs. She could twist men around her fingers and through her sensuous dark hair. She loved to dance and paint, write sexually explicit stories and flirt with the underworld.

For a moment she stood silently in the doorway to the room that was her bedroom and sanctuary from a cool and lonely marriage to Christolphe. Her beauty glowed in her silhouette. Her gamine appearance: the big eyes, elegant bones, sensuous lips and high cheekbones, spoke of refinement and intelligence. Innocence and worldly wisdom were an unusual combination that she carried in her movements like a wild and willful contradiction. They spoke of her unique inner music.

She awaited the workers who were scheduled to arrive any moment and laughed, as she remembered Yves' reaction to her plans. Like a chameleon, who knew at all times how it was she fit into any environment, she knew, when she was left alone, exactly what she would do with the houseboat. This morning she had arrived early to change into work clothes. She couldn't wait to see the expression on Yves face, when he saw the transformation. She leaned over the balcony and imagined the plants she would use to replace those in the cracked clay pots.

The river's current shifted for a moment and caused her toes to press into the wooden balcony. Spring rain had swollen the currents and dimpled its swift flow and eddies. What she felt was a glorious hum that never ceased, and the longer she stood still the more powerfully the hum spread through every cell of her body. Water was life and energy and clarity for her. It renewed her sense of power, as though she had been plugged into an electrical current. When voices from the past tried to interfere with the future, she needed the river to give her courage. What might cause others to drown, inspired her to go on. She knew this barge would shelter her whenever she needed to recover her own perspective and her own way of being in Paris. The Left Bank was an explosion of pink and white fruit tree blossoms that filled the air as the breeze shifted. Heavenly green leaf buds, her favorite color, sprouted on the trees along the quay and grew as hope. The boat, the river and new growth gave her strength.

Anais considered herself an escape artist, but on this houseboat she felt no need to escape. As she walked across the room that would be her upstairs living quarters, she noted the airy, spacious view in all four directions. The balcony displayed the city on its Right Bank, and the eye-level clerestories faced the pier, the left riverbank and the quay lined with booksellers. She could see Yves on his boat, standing there like he had just awoken, gazing down river. She liked his straightforward manner and honest face. While she could view the river, as it flowed and moved on, she could also see both banks of the river embracing, holding the two halves of the city together.

The room aglow with soft light off the water surrounded her. How was it that no one had rented the place before her? It awaited her careful touch. She intended to emphasize every ray of light to reflect the shape-shifting shadows of the Seine, its hundreds of years of Norman presence, it's undertow of Gaelic journeys and its seamless presence. These nuances captured the essence that gave rise to inspiration. She sat on the upstairs balcony in a pose of meditation. Whenever her heart felt full, she tried to remember to share that sense of rightness and fullness with her physical body. On this balcony, facing the left bank of the City of Lights, it was easy to do.

Anais was a strong woman. She may have looked fragile and exactly like Angela, but she had always been the secure one, the one who got things done. She directed both their lives in matters of survival and practicality. Perhaps that is the reason she sometimes felt the need to rebel, let her hair down and behave wildly. She lived in the moment, as it was meant to be savored or gobbled as the day dictated. *Poor sweet Angela*, she thought, as she slipped into navy blue loose pants and a high-necked sweater, wouldn't be caught dead in such an outfit. Then, she tied a colorful scarf, gypsy style, around her hair and eagerly anticipated a day of hard work, as she stood on deck, facing Yves' trawler, and took a big breath, as she saw him walking toward her.

"*Madame*, good morning."

"Good morning, Yves. It's a beautiful day."

"*Oui*, but what's the rush?"

"I wanted to get here before the workmen and change my clothes. Come by later once they've gotten started, and I'll show you my plans. Oh…I think I see them now."

She waved to two men who stood on the quay with their tools and buckets, looking confused.

"Down here," she shouted.

The woman was full of surprises. He hadn't been able to imagine what she would look like without a Chanel outfit. Today her blue sweater and vivid red scarf did wonderful things for her big eyes. He stopped grinning, when he saw a truck pull alongside the quay, as another two workers jumped out and carried their equipment to join their friends. They tipped their caps jauntily as they passed. This was a good day for them. Paid jobs had been hard to come by since the war ended. These men would put food on the table tonight, and each one of them looked forward to it.

Yves waited an hour before he strolled down the pier to *La Belle Aurore.* He expected to see the workmen busy, but what he didn't expect was the sight of Anais with a mop and pail of soapy water, down on her knees, scrubbing. She had been working alongside the men, and one of them winked at Yves.

"Welcome. Come, I'll show you the plans."

He followed her upstairs, already infected by her enthusiasm and the activity that surrounded them. For a fleeting moment he wondered what all that energy and enthusiasm would be like in bed. Then, he quickly averted his mind and simply watched in delight as she ascended the stairs in front of him.

They stood there in what would obviously be her private living space and surveyed the rubble that looked like a demolition zone. Suddenly, unexpectedly, he felt a great longing wash over him until he felt the need to steady himself. The feeling, long forgotten, resembled hope. She glanced over at him and seemed to know his thoughts and whispered.

"We'll bring Paris back to life, Yves."

Damned, if he didn't know better, he'd swear she could do just that.

To undertake a renovation was to immerse herself in history. She would write about every change that occurred, for the condition of every plank and flake of paint belonged wholly to the past, a true history of the way it was once upon a time. It evoked an image of the irrevocable. Anais knew that her personal experiences had made her older than she was in years, making her thoroughly in sympathy with her own time, unlike many her age who were historically blind. It was a sign of her inner character that she could so fully understand the present in an historical context.

In one sense Anais was fortunate. Unlike Yves, she could put words to the images she saw. Words formed in her mind and spoke to her. Once they had been mere echoes that penetrated her body and became lost sounds. Then, she began to listen. She listened very carefully and heard word structures, then phrases, then whole sentences. She had learned to pay attention. Was it possible, she wondered, to hear the past, a time before her present life, a time she had learned, then forgotten? If she continued to listen carefully, history might whisper into her ears, her inner ears that heard more than she ever could.

Chapter 7
Anais Is the Perfect Hostess

Anais was a friend to the Parisian underworld of painters, musicians and writers. She knew all about Angela, but fortunately Angela knew nothing about her. Angela was considered too frail. She was protected and cossetted by her banker husband and by Anais herself who believed she had enough courage for the two of them. Anais sheltered Angela from unsavory characters that might take advantage of her and, in return, Angela, unknowingly, provided Anais with refuge whenever she needed to retreat.

Since she had recently been recruited as a spy, she had to consider her profile in the art community. She needed to be accessible to her friends yet elusive enough to preserve privacy. The spy business required an unusual balance that she had to learn to accommodate.

***

Today, Anais considered her options and made plans. Once the renovations were finished to *La Belle Aurore*, she decided she would give a party. Yves was right to be astonished by the renovations that were taking place on the houseboat, especially as he had not been asked to contribute a single *centime*. Money, it would seem, was no object. For Anais, a boat, like a tree house or cave or magic carpet, filled a void and replenished a hollow place where imagination might have flourished. She realized that such a place would create memories but also make up for memories that had disappeared. She joked that her lost past had disappeared mercifully, escaped underground. She spent time carefully decorating *La Belle Aurore*, delighting in the fantasy world she would create with fabrics, outrageous colors, textures that caressed the senses, draperies and carpets that would have satisfied Scheherazade, satins, brocades and silks that covered the bed and sofa. Her elegant caftans were hung in the closet and incense filled the air. The rustle of the window coverings evoked mystery, her meditative tea ceremonies tasted of the earth, kept her senses anchored and allowed them to bloom. It astonished her to remember that it was Roshi who made these renovations possible.

Anais intended the party as a celebration to launch her art gallery. Artists were the people she knew best. She believed that if anyone was capable of conquering the malaise and numb disbelief that followed the end of the war, it was the artistic community. She was well acquainted with their starvation and undefeated attitudes. The media referred to the 1920s as the time, when everyone loved to party and dance. Whether it was the foxtrot, the waltz, the breakaway, the Charleston, or the Argentine tango, dance contests had become a fixture of every party. People dated in Paris, a new and novel ritual for sure. Men and women arrived at parties with a date. Fortunately, as a hostess, she did not need a date. However, she did have the brilliant idea to ask Yves to be bartender. To make it a memorable event costumes were a good idea, and the more she thought about masks, the better it sounded. Right now, everyone in the city needed to let down their hair and have fun. She considered it an antidote for which there could be no substitute.

She considered Kiki of Montparnasse and her tendency to come naked to a masquerade. Kiki had lost all sense of artifice and would certainly be on the guest list. She chuckled. Kiki would be delighted to attend a masquerade just to have the chance to remove her clothes.

43

Anais opened her diary to write. She needed to write as much as Kiki needed exposure. This is where she transcended herself. In the diary there was no compromise, no mask; its power was that of a self-portrait whose weaknesses and strengths took her to depths of courage. Like a puzzle or a mosaic, her finished portrait was a revelation. The party, she realized, was the antithesis of experience. It belonged to the world of shadow. As for the diary, it became a fire that must be fed. As she wrote, she forged her shadows into words she branded to her secret center.

From that center sprang energy, vital and feminine.

It was not surprising that thoughts of her diary, where secrecy and complete privacy prevailed, had also prompted her to plan a masquerade party. On some level she wished to give others the experience of privacy. If they did not have her proclivity to create a refuge on paper, then she would provide a venue where secrets were welcome for one evening. With these revelations firmly in mind, Anais concentrated on the guest list, and details for the party began to emerge.

Chapter 8
Lily

Fate decreed that Anais end up back in Paris where she had been born. She had grown up in the Marais, once considered the underbelly of Paris.

The Marais had once been a Jewish ghetto with cheap rents, a place where her father felt he could leave his family, when he disappeared on his concert tours. She and her brothers had been barely tolerated by the man who had fathered them, but she found that music created a connection to the streets and the soul of a city. Anais had grown up as a rough street kid until age eleven, when her family had moved to New York City. The plan was that her father would catch up with them in the land of plenty, but that never happened. Anais had resented the move, the change, the language disruption and the fact that they no longer lived in the Marais.

As she walked toward the Marais, Anais was lost in thought. She couldn't wait to invite her friend Lily to the party. She hadn't seen her in several weeks and imagined how she would take this announcement.

Lily had been her best friend, since she was a street urchin in the Marais. In those days Lily had been her kindred spirit. Her loss to Anais, when she left for New York, was so painful it hurt to think about it. She was Lily of the strawberry hair and pale eyelashes, the despised freckles and toothy grin. Once, they had been inseparable.

Lily was from Ireland though she could not recall much about her homeland. Her parents had always left her in Paris, when they travelled around the world. They left her in the Marais in an apartment with her nanny, who was plump and warm and full of Irish maxims and practicalities. Lily was full of fire and temper and an impulsive drama that made her many enemies, but if she loved you, you were subject to none of that. Instead, you had a faithful friend who fiercely protected your back. It was obvious that someday she would be tall and coltish and strikingly lovely, while Anais would be her counterpart: petite, gamine and equally lovely. During those years, when they had each other, they had little need for other friends. They spoke together, oftentimes, in their secret invented code, and it seemed to Anais, when they were apart for years, that she could hear Lily in her mind, her laughter, her mysterious ways and her smile that adjusted Anais' day whenever she felt sorry for herself; for Lily was an incorrigibly happy spirit.

Anais stepped onto the *rue des Rosiers* and felt memories seep through her shoulder blades. Today, Lily seemed to walk beside her. It was quiet in the Marais and rather eerie. Once kids had played in the streets from morning till dark. She stared at the decorative entryways to apartments that had once been the pride of their occupants. Women used to wash their front stoops with soapy water and iron brushes, then wipe the ornate wooden doors with a damp cloth. Now silence blanketed the past and its streets.

Her cells and pores remembered the shouts of children, playing in the narrow streets where cars were absent. Women in pairs, carrying shopping baskets, might walk as far as Les Halles in the early morning and return in time to begin lunch preparations. She would see Hasidim Jews with their black hats and coats, their locks of curled hair alongside fierce faces. Children ran through the streets, getting up to mischief, and she and Lily had been among them until age eight or nine, when girls were excluded from boys' games. She could hear the doors open, as mothers called their children to lunch or supper, which was the only time children were interrupted from outdoor play. Then there was the sudden silence, when she was left alone. Lily's nanny called for her, but no one called for Anais, as she walked back to her own apartment. She could see her reflection in the shiny glass windows of houses and shops. The families who lived there were poor but proud and caring. So was her mother, who was out working to pay the rent. The other children were fun and friendly, but kids didn't invite each other to lunch in those days. They assumed that she had a mother, making her lunch, and that she needed to get home. Kids are like that, accepting of certain behavior, if it is what they know from their own small worlds.

The day she met Lily, Anais sat on the curb, alone and forlorn. At age six, Lily had recognized the hunched shoulders and downturned corners of a sad mouth.

"My name is Lily, what's yours?" She stopped near the curb and waited.

"I'm Anais."

"Do you want to play?"

They played make believe games all afternoon, and Anais thought the name Lily was the most beautiful name she had ever heard.

"I think we're going to be friends for ever and ever."

"How strange. I feel the same way."

They parted late in the afternoon, each of them knowing they had found a special friend.

Today, the neighborhood was changed. She could smell it in the air, see it in the windows that had not been washed recently. Many non-Jews walked the streets, and the few children who played together were beyond poor; they were unkempt and subdued. Women glanced at her in passing with heads down, and in her bones she sensed unease and fear, and she felt conspicuously out of place, stripped of her chameleon traits.

Lily still lived in this neighborhood. For some reason she had decided it was her true home, and she could not be extracted from it. She loved the old neighborhood, but Nanny was gone, dead of heartbreak, when her only son was killed in the war. Her parents were also gone though, obviously, they had left her comfortable, provided she was careful with her money. Maybe a shortage of money was another reason she chose to stay in this now dreary section of the city.

Or maybe it was simply the fact that Lily had studied to be an artist and felt close to other artists living in this quartier, another reason their friendship had lasted unscathed into the present. Besides, it did not bare thinking about, the fact that they might ever break off their friendship. The only secret Anais had kept from Lily, since she returned to Paris, was the spy business. It was so new to her that she had yet to come to terms with it.

For instance, Lily knew that Anais possessed a dual personality and that she simultaneously lived two lives, the one as Angela, a married woman whose husband was Christolphe the banker, and the one who was known as Anais, the one she had seemingly known since childhood. Lily had never met Christolphe and didn't care to know that side of Anais. She considered herself an artist who rarely crossed over into the world of finance, politics, or travel. That was the world her parents had inhabited. Lily valued security and hated change or loss. It was an odd combination for a flamboyant redhead with an artistic temperament. As far as Anais was concerned, change made life interesting. To her, everyone was unique, and true friendship was one of those rare qualities that was hard to come by.

By keeping Lily safe from the outside world, she was exempt from the traumas of war. Hunger, pain, and death were not for her; they were political, existential concerns. The source and spark within Lily was not reduced by the outer world. It wasn't as if Anais had not heard of the war or that she was too young to understand what was going on in the world around her. She had eyes and ears and a sensitivity that was touched by what she saw and heard, but Anais wrote, then translated her diary conversations to her own reality. She had started out, trying to please her father, but soon turned to immortalize her friend Lily. To be a friend, friendship can grow apace where both friends give and receive while equality is maintained. A diary friendship grows apace and remains one sided only to the limit of imagination. Lily had managed to grow in the diary.

Because of their days as street kids together, the Lily of the past had become the immortal Lily who was full of life's inner spark. She could set fire to pages. Her relationship with Anais had burned brightly on paper where she would never disappear. She was eternal beauty, and their distance apart became insignificant. Beyond truth or beauty was the artistry of re-creation. The diary was a record of everything that must be preserved and saved. Lily, who had once been real, would live forever.

One day, Anais wished to describe Lily in fiction. She would become a character in a story so real that she would remain invincible, and her authenticity would never be questioned. Framed like a painting, Lily would be preserved. Her reality would be the key to unlock part of Anais' childhood, yet keep it safe from harm.

Chapter 9
Lives Lived Through Diaries

When she had first arrived in Paris, so hurt and reclusive, before she had reconnected with Lily, Anais had spent hours, thinking and reading about the life of Marie Bashkirtseff. It could even be said that she had deeply identified with the young Russian who died at age twenty-five. Marie was frail and she, too, had kept a diary. Bashkirtseff was a dreamer with a complex nature who loved life in its many contradictions. She was fearless yet understood that she was not strong; she was ambitious yet tormented within her soul; she admired and longed for true love but analyzed every encounter until it was diminished; she advocated the finite quality of truth but could not resist illusions. She was an artist. Marie's journal orchestrated her words, and her art palette drove her, finally, to hard work and dedication. Her restlessness ceased and her passionate energy found its home. She decided to devote her life to art on canvasses that depicted the tragic contrasts of the streets. Her major flaw was a jealousy that led her to continually compare her work with that of other art students. Perhaps, it was the prod that kept her moving forward at a phenomenal pace toward artistic expression. In the ugly she found beauty; in that which might have been evil she found good. Truthfulness poured into her journal and, while other painters and writers fumbled over the years and the amount of time at their disposal, Marie had nine years to work hard before her death. The vitality of her work gave life to the ugly and insignificant. Her knowledge of languages and her love of books occupied her hours and days, when she was not working diligently and joyously with paint, pen, clay, or music. No moment was wasted. Not one of her life's details was overlooked by the impressionable Anais.

The delicate looks of the tubercular young Marie, the pale skin, red hair, love of dress and feminine vanity reminded her of Lily. Intense Russian grey eyes that flirted with death, growing deafness and the force of her intellect could not interfere with her love of everything around her. In the final days of her short stay on earth, a romance was kindled by the tragedy of death. In the end, one of Marie's greatest achievements was love.

Anais paused in her diary writing to wipe away a tear of recognition and longing. She knew she would not die young; for her, the longer route beckoned. But the same ambitions and strength of will would be needed to overcome adversity. She would take up where this young woman left off and drive herself to love every moment of her life. In a state of dramatic youthful intensity, she would mythologize Marie's intuition and insight. She would defy war and its violence, its dullness and its drag on awareness.

However, Marie Bashkirtseff had not been molested as a small child as Anais had been. She had grown up in privilege and love, pampered, favored and indulged, an educated and well-travelled young woman given every advantage. Of course, she railed against death and used her great strength to overcome despair. This struggle had produced her greatest art. Anais, on the other hand, struggled against disintegration, the separation of parents, and the split of two sides of herself. As such, she was a child of The Great War.

Anais thought of Lily, another victim of war and lost parents, Lily her friend, her connection to the Paris of her childhood. The closer she looked at her friend without the rose-colored glasses of early memories, the more she saw of today's Lily who was aimless, sequestered in her Marais apartment, afraid of change and the future, and very much alone, despite her claims about being part of the art community. She was as much an outsider as Anais because she did not quite fulfill the talent mandate or the self-sacrificial demands of the artist. Truly, she did not share their crazy manifestos and fiery purpose to change the world with paint and a brush. Lily's background was too staid and secure.

Marie Bashkirtseff would continue to be an inspiration. She understood, as few could, what it was like to confide in a diary. Though she had not been trapped in the aftermath of a terrible war she had, nevertheless, been confronted with terrible loss and death. She was a tragic spirit, and Anais identified strongly with her. Throughout her life, she would identify with Marie.

"Writers do not live one life, they live two. There is the living and then there is the writing."

—Nin *Diary: Volume One*

Chapter 10
Roshi and a New Diary

Anais felt most fortunate in that she had two cherished friends in her life. She had heard it said that, if a person had a true lifelong friendship, it meant one was a good person and a good friend as well. To have two such friends, it was said, indicated an exceptional human being. She had never forgotten this folk wisdom.

Lily was her first friend.

Her other friend was Roshi. Truly, he was more than a friend; he was her mentor, her second father, her shelter in any weather and her beloved spiritual inspiration.

They met when she was thirteen and had already lived in New York City for two lonely years. It had been a shock when her parents separated, when her mother had moved them across the water to that crowded city where everyone spoke English and no one spoke French. She hated her new school without Lily and the fact that they were so poor. To be poor in the Marais had been an adventure. To be poor in New York was to be invisible.

To cover her intense hurt, she had refused to speak or write in English. Therefore, in class she was treated like a dunce who was incapable of learning. Anais skipped classes more and more often, wandered the streets while her mother and aunt worked all day and searched through the crowds for a friend to replace Lily.

By a certain undeniable fate she found herself at the New York public library one day and, thereafter, that is where she spent most of her days. Shelves and rows of books surrounded her and drew her into their wonders. Her journal, that she had kept so undefiled in her native French, was filled with pages of longing. In her recurrent dream Anais had a friend, a kindred spirit who knew her unlike anyone ever had. She was a wonderful friend, imaginative and playful, who did not worry. She was brave and kind and did not dwell on the past or the innocence that had been left behind. Her name was Linotte and she stepped from the pages of her diary into her daytime life. As her thirteenth birthday arrived and she became a teenager, she was given a new diary as a gift. This time she switched to English. The frightened little French girl adopted the New York City public library and all the wonders of the English language. She no longer called herself Linotte. She was no longer lovely Linotte, but a young woman who had decided to change. It was then that she decided she would be a writer someday, and it became her plan to educate herself at the library. In this way, she would become mistress of the direction of her life.

Her only other foray in the city was to a French bookstore she had been told about by one of the librarians. It was a lovely place, a sanctuary with comfortable chairs. It served *café au lait*, and the patrons sat, leafing through books they considered buying or speaking in quietly animated French, as they got to know each other. It is where Roshi said he had first seen her, a lovely and shy young woman who sat and read intensely or listened to the occasional conversation. He realized she spoke French as well as English and wondered why she wasn't in school.

One day, at the public library Roshi glanced up from his research and noticed the young woman he had seen several times at the French bookstore. His curiosity piqued, he decided to approach her and find out her story. The library was her safe and second home, so she was not averse to being asked what she was reading by a complete stranger.

He was quite surprised that she was reading poetry, and they took up a conversation about the poet whose work she read. Roshi was astonished at her intelligence and her attitude of maturity. He had not encountered such refinement from young people in America. She was rather old fashioned and spoke with a seriousness that drew attention to the characters she tried to understand through her reading. He also realized that here was a lonely child whose life was lived between the covers of the books she read. For her part there was the intuitive knowledge that she had found a grownup who understood her longing for inspiration and a decent education.

"Where are your parents?" he asked one day.

"Oh, they died a while ago."

He couldn't prove it, but somehow he knew she lied.

"Then who takes care of you?"

"I live with my aunt who has to work all day. She really doesn't care what I do with my time, as long as I keep out of trouble."

He decided to let the subject drop. There was no reason, he decided, why she should tell the truth to a complete stranger, so he changed the subject.

"What are you writing in that book?"

"This is my new diary. I got it for my birthday. Now that I'm a teenager I've decided to write in English, and I'm quite excited about it."

"It sounds like this diary is a good friend."

"It is. It's my best friend."

"Is that your name, Anais? I see you have written on the cover."

"Yes."

"Well, it is nice to meet you, Anais. I'm Roshi, and I was born in Japan. By the sound of, it you were born in France. Now, we both live in New York and are fortunate to come to this amazing library. You know, they have a lovely café around the corner and, if we meet again, I would be pleased to take you for a cup of tea or a *pain au chocolat*. Maybe we'll be library friends."

Anais thought this over for a moment and, with a solemn face, she said, "That might be a good thing to do."

What an amazing child, he thought as he left the library. She was raising herself, a serious little person, bright and lovely with Japanese manners, refined and respectful of her elders.

Roshi knew how the act of writing in a diary could define one's life. To befriend a diary was to hold on to history and memory and to deter loss. It was an ancient spiritual practice at its finest. Every nation and people had those who kept tract of their own development through the written word. For humankind, it was the one media that kept a record of wisdom that needed to be passed on. Despite the many debates about the reliability of fiction or believability of personal documents like diaries and memoirs, those debates did not change the fact that wisdom was disseminated in libraries and tombs. Wisdom was often found in attics, journals or neatly tied bundles of letters. He was impressed by the early age at which Anais had come to understand the importance of her diary. When he met her, it was the single most endearing characteristic he had noticed about her. He could hardly remember being her age, and what he did remember was discipline and hardship. He came from an old and venerable Japanese family that believed in monastic education for the oldest son. Since he was an only son, he had been raised under the tutelage of a great sensei. It was a harsh system, but he had grown to love book knowledge, despite the rigorous methods practiced in order to memorize texts and prayers. Due to his parents' wishes, he was also instructed in languages. Later, he had been sent to Harvard to complete his education, and there he had stayed for many years.

After that day, it came to pass that Roshi and Anais met frequently at the library. They went to the café where Anais ordered hot chocolate, and they sat in the reading room for hours quietly reading. In his subtle but commanding manner,

Roshi was able to direct and greatly influence Anais' reading choices and the sequence in which she read them. His knowledge of history and literature was astonishing, and his wisdom as an educator seemed to come naturally.

Anais had read of monks and Zen Buddhism, and she suspected Roshi had been a monk in another life. He looked like one and acted like one, but he told her he was simply a businessman. It took a liar to recognize a liar, and if he was a simple businessman, she was an orphan. Yet neither one exposed the lies of the other. When they were together, life was uncomplicated. She read voraciously of his literary suggestions, a bit of history, and books in both English and French. Occasionally, she read slowly through a volume in Spanish to acknowledge her lineage. Her parents were Spanish and Cuban and, when they had been together, they often conversed in Spanish. Most of her relatives spoke Spanish, and Roshi told her it was always valuable to speak as many languages as possible. It was a way to expand her sphere of world understanding, since there is no better way to understand a people than to speak their mother tongue. She read *Don Quixote,* as Roshi watched her determination to finish the book. She was certainly a strong-minded young woman.

It was her friend and confident but also her anchor. Maybe it was wrong to say that she had two friends. Besides Roshi and Lily, there was the diary, her constant and most reliable ally, her steadfast and wise friend. Her words anchored her and mirrored back her own light and shadow. It was her life support, but even Roshi was not privy to its contents. She had made a promise to herself to guard its privacy. Not only was the diary her real audience, it was her retreat, her dream world and her own endless story, where she could be the heroine who finds love and heightened awareness. She might be naked, or refined or present images of herself depicted by a lover.

She created word photographs that were seductions, meant to lure lovers into her sphere like a spider entices her partner to impregnate her before she devours him. This act emphasized the spider's feminine power, as she threatened male spiders, fooled them into submission, and destroyed the father of creation.

Anais had come to perfect these portraits. Since the age of eleven, she had tried to seduce her father into loving her, but by age fourteen she understood that he could only love himself. The art of diary writing was the fearless encounter with her most secret self and her father who had abandoned her. Slowly, carefully and patiently Anais observed and discovered truth that was not what it first appeared to be. Her greatest secret and the strongest aspect of Anais' life was her diary.

Chapter 11
Yves Rediscovers His *Belle Aurore*

La Belle Aurore had changed considerably in the two months of renovations Yves had watched the coming and going of workmen in bemusement. Who would spend so much cash on an old and run-down rental? In the past week he noted that a light remained on far into the night in the upstairs bedroom. It would seem that Anais had slept over a few times. He had seen an antique desk being delivered, but only if he stood on the bow of his own boat and leaned out could he catch a glimpse of what he presumed was the new renter at her desk.

Every kind of activity caused him to look out through the companionway passage to watch with astonishment. The old barge had never had it so good. First had come the demolition crew with Anais supervising, when there wasn't a nail or board that escaped her attention. The roof was mended; windows were repaired and cleaned until they opened and closed smoothly; and two new toilets arrived along with the plumber who was inordinately pleased to be installing such modern contraptions on a houseboat. Next, the electrician had added lights and sockets and whatever else was needed to a boat that had never experienced electricity. Yves did not like to snoop, but he had to admit curiosity. The plasterer and painter had come and gone and, finally, the carpenter had arrived with a beautifully ornate, yet somehow appropriate, sign for the entrance and another, identical sign, for the quay. He had also noted colorful posters near the kiosks along the Seine. June was the perfect time to advertise the gallery opening for July. Hopefully, tourists would return to Paris to witness what was taking place right here on the pier.

Cautiously, Yves determined to stroll down the pier. After all, he did own the *Aurore*. It wasn't so odd that the landlord would want to take note of improvements. As he approached the ramp to the boathouse, he noticed that a lovely gate with a small nautical bell had been strategically placed. It invited while firmly asserting privacy and the fact that the occupant did not invite strangers aboard without an invitation. Like the woman inside, there was a subtle sense of mystery attached to the gate. He found something erotic about that mystery but shrugged it off, as if influenced by the mist that was rising from the river. He rang the bell.

A few minutes later Anais appeared. She wore black this time: a high-necked satin jacket and black linen pants. Her shoes were like the cloth slippers he had seen on Chinamen, and her hair was drawn back into a chignon. She wore heavy silver bracelets and earrings with a pendent around her neck that looked Oriental.

"What can I do for you, *Monsieur*?"

"I was hoping to see your changes to the house, maybe take you for a coffee at our neighborhood spot. Everyone is curious. Maybe you'll meet a few neighbors at the café."

"And of course there is your own curiosity, *n'est pas*?"

She smiled graciously. "Come in. You are very welcome to see what I have done."

Much later Yves considered what he had seen. Surprised is not the word he would use to describe the changes. Awed would be more appropriate. The debris and clutter were gone and in its place was serenity graced with splashes of vivid color. The main room had been transformed into a significant art gallery. The north facing windows looked to the water, whose slow churning motion resembled an impressionist painting. Some days, he had to admit, he was so used to the river he forgot about it. But it was given back to him as he stepped inside the gallery. A few magnificent paintings were already hung, but it was obvious there were more to arrive. Their placement was dramatic, yet one was ever mindful of life, the river flow, and a sense of engagement with the surroundings. He wanted to bow down in appreciation. Where had that thought come from?

"*Mais, c'est belle.*"

"So you approve?"

"How could one disapprove of such unique style?"

"That makes me happy."

"It's like the resurrection of the dawn."

They both laughed at his double entendre.

It was the bed with its gauze hangings and elegant satin bedding that had his pulse up. The effect resembled the bedroom of a high-class mistress, not a very feminine and young married woman. He intended to avert his suspicions. He acknowledged to himself that he really knew nothing about this woman. He had noticed a curious detail; she wore a wedding ring, but it was always on a different finger. The desk across the room was the desk of a scholar. Bookshelves lined the wall on either side of the desk and a quick glance revealed works by Proust in French, D. H. Lawrence in English, Cervantes in Spanish and Japanese poetry apparently in Japanese. He did not want to seem too interested in her personal affairs, but it appeared that the books on her desk meant a great deal to her. Several journals were open on the desktop alongside her pen. Obviously, he had interrupted her writing. It wasn't long before he excused himself and politely left, as she said she was expecting a visitor.

"I will leave before I wear out my welcome, *Madame*. Thank you for the tour."

"*De rien, Monsieur.*"

She acted like it was nothing special this resurrection of his parent's home, but to him it was everything. Yves made his way slowly back to the *Hilaire*. This afternoon, and this woman made him feel things he had never hoped to feel again.

Once Yves left, Anais tidied the suite and composed herself. She appreciated his honest reaction to the renovations. This business of renting a houseboat felt perfect. Recently, Roshi had taught her that she must not neglect either side of her being. If she were two people, so be it. She had come to respect her double nature as a gift. There was one important task that she must never neglect and that was the need to keep her two sides alive. To ignore one side was to cause injury to the other side. Roshi respected her duality, and from that foundation he had taught her to learn from her double the life experiences of two women. In this, he had honored Anais who had overcome the traumatic experiences that had led up to her state of disconnection. He emphasized in so many ways how and why she, too, must honor that unique approach to life. It was as if she were in training to become a monk or a witness to the fine art of living life to the fullest. Time, he said, would resolve the mystery of Anais.

How they used to laugh together, when she was just an awkward teenager, and from that laughter they each discovered courage and the willingness to absorb adversity and transform it. Anais would read book after book while skipping classes at her school. Her mother got calls from the school, scolded, then left Anais on her own, while she went to work to pay the rent and put food on the table. Sometimes in the evenings, as she watched her mother sew elegant clothes for wealthy women, she would help by making tiny stitches along hemlines or attaching buttons. They would talk then, sometimes in Spanish, other times in French while her anxious and care worn mother shared stories of her father, how handsome he was, and how he had swept her off her feet. She came to realize that her mother lived in another time, a place of fantasy that had no basis in truth. Her mother's life was an illusion. Her loving husband existed only in her mind. He was a philanderer with a mistress in every concert town and the worst kind of narcissist. The more Anais had written to him, the greater her sense of his absence and abandonment had grown, and the more she had understood that life was a mirage for her mother. It was Roshi who had taught her to see life, to look and see what truly existed. In effect, he became the father she had never had.

She had listened carefully to Roshi's teachings and learned what it meant to be aware of her surroundings and incorporate beauty into every movement. By age fifteen she was already reading Dostoyevsky and agreed with Roshi that beauty could save the world. This shared philosophy had eventually saved her life.

Beauty, however, was illusive. It had to compete with reality. Her diary had become ever more necessary in order to exist with unbearable loneliness. It provided a safe place to escape. In order to live her life she had to re-create it, and in order to re-create it she had to have a place to examine her dreams and breathe. Parents, wars, world politics and other destructive climates were brutal. In her diary she found shelter, where tears were forbidden and dreams encouraged. Beauty could be captured and cultivated through dreams until fears were carefully replaced with finer feelings. The complications of a dual personality became an asset in the diary. Guilt, for instance, was alleviated. With two views of life, reality not only looked different, it could be improved upon.

***

As she waited for Roshi to appear, she glanced over at the *Hilaire* where Yves stood on deck. He stared into the flowing water still bemused by the elaborate renovations, trying to absorb the changes and arrange them into some sort of sense. He was right to be somewhat incredulous. Who simply spent so much money to fix an old barge that did not belong to them? However, she liked the way Yves kept his mind open and his thoughts to himself. She liked his humor, too.

Since being torn from her father at age eleven, Anais had sought a replacement. She did not wish to remember the desperation of abandonment and abuse. Thus, Roshi was invaluable. In his presence, in his role as good father, surrogate to her spirit, she redeemed her inner being that was so crystalline it shimmered and reflected the effort it had taken to learn courage. Roshi had been the teacher who witnessed her efforts to become her own work of art, a masterpiece and an enchantress. Anais was transparent to Roshi; to others she needed to remain hidden.

To the rest of the world, Anais wore a disguise and a costume for every occasion. Each day began with a choice of dress ensemble, dramatic face makeup and painted eyes. Such discipline chased away the chaos of tragedy and suffering. She remained untouched by the daily news and the cracks wherein one might disappear. Visible or invisible was the conflict of being or non-being. A friend, true to the spirit of the soul, gives witness to reality and unreality alike. A friend, by simply standing by, lends credence to all states of being and accepts them, verifies them, validates and solidifies them, without judgment. A double could be a friend.

Chapter 12
Roshi's Visit

Anais tidied restlessly. She glanced out at the balcony beside her living quarters. She had had it painted and varnished a marine lacquer black with a shiny brass railing and had filled new pots with bonsai trees and shrubs. One rose grew among the trees, its placement breathtaking in its solitude. On the floor was a tea table set with a tea service.

A few minutes after Yves had gone, she heard the bell ring, again. She hurried downstairs and out to the gate to formally greet Roshi. They bowed to each other and smiled. She was so happy to see him she could barely contain herself in the traditional Japanese way. She wanted to skip with delight and give him a big hug.

"Welcome to my small sanctuary."

He nodded. "Yes, I'm glad to be here and wish to see what you have done."

They entered the gallery on the main floor.

"You can imagine what a pull this gallery will be to the artists in the city. I suspect much information will enter these doors. Come, I'll show you my private space."

She led him upstairs.

Roshi stood in the center of Anais' apartment and inhaled the scent of Chanel and roses. He was silent, as she observed his movements and the slightest gesture that spoke as loudly as words. He had taught her long ago to listen through her heart. She knew he had caught the scent of her perfume. In the clandestine world of spies scent was a clue that was often dangerous and could draw unwanted attention. Here, in her own space, she had indulged her sense of smell. By his imperceptible nod she knew his thoughts, and they were a reminder that he wanted her to remain alert. They knew each other so well; she knew he would not speak of this lapse, for he knew she understood the warning. Much of their relationship over the years had been silent. He had taught her the power of silence and how much one could learn by simple observation.

Roshi studied the room and its combination of feminine indulgence and scholarly discipline. The white gauzy bed hangings were seductive yet offered privacy. The pale colors were elegant and refined. The room was peaceful, and this made him happy for her. She deserved peace and had surrounded herself with beauty. The desk was tasteful, organized and a container for her literary treasures. Beyond the Persian carpet and opened glass doors, the balcony enticed him to a garden and a tea ceremony. Anais had set out a flower arrangement that had taken patience and thoughtful attention to detail to assemble. The mats were placed correctly on each side of the low table, and the simplicity of the *raku* tea set was stunning. She motioned him to be seated, as they began the time-honored ritual of serving tea while paying homage to beauty. His first comment, when they finally spoke, was of the orchids she had arranged in the gallery.

"You have placed them on an elegant table in the center of the room. They love to be the center of attention and will thrive with the flow of water beneath the boat. They can feel it."

Anais felt delight at his observations.

"But what makes you sad, Anais? You dress in black, so solemn and subdued. Not like your usual energy. Wait a moment before you answer. Listen to that inner voice, and tell me what you feel, my dear?"

"Oh, Roshi, I woke this morning with memories of Joel. You never knew him, but he was such an important part of my stay in Cuba. The memory of him is still so strong it brings me to my knees. On wonderful days like today I grieve for all that talent and joy, all the wonder and excitement of our time together."

They continued to sit in meditative silence. "Keep your feelings for Joel. They're honest and valuable. In sincere emotion there is an acceptance of love. Love never dies, you know."

They stayed silent until Roshi stirred.

"Now we must talk of the present."

She knew that, when they had come to the end of the tea ritual, Roshi would tell her the real reason for his visit. He was never in a hurry, but the patience and self-control needed to be present was something she still needed to practice. She welcomed being at the feet of her mentor, absorbing one more lesson and being given one more opportunity to learn, so she waited quietly.

Today, his request surprised her. He said he wanted her to meet an acquaintance of his who lived in Paris, an American who needed an introduction to the art world because his business was of great concern to France and the free world. This man was to guide her through her next assignment. It had not occurred to her that her written observations were not enough. If writing and observation were all that was needed, it calmed her fears. She never realized that banks, for instance, could or would involve themselves with art collections, thus she had been oblivious to undercurrents and the lucrative reasons so many pretended an interest in the arts. Her accurate and detailed notes provided information that discrete bankers would never have willingly revealed.

"You see, Anais, the world thinks that the Great War was so heinous it could never happen again. That is the newly adopted attitude of the French and particularly Parisians. It has become taboo to think in any other way.

68

However, I am telling you that not only is another war possible, it is probable."

"What has this to do with me?"

"Your vision, your training, your gifts, are those of the true spy; you cover more ground, see more, hear more, and keep your own counsel.

"This man's name is Raphael Dumont. He is an American whose father was French. I have told him all about you and your love of the arts, your banker husband and your many friends in the ateliers of Paris. What you can do is listen to him. If he asks for your help, it is not without reason. I told him you would be willing and able to help him, if what he has to say resonates with your sense of justice. You are not required to help him but, if you do, this will be your next assignment, and I will help you every step of the way. You are, after all, my protégé, and I will be there to watch and help, if you need me."

"I'll meet him, but I have no idea how I will react."

"Something tells me you'll be fine."

He gave her Raphael's address, soon made his farewell bows, and then left the way he came, gliding silently back to the quay, a man of few words and fewer instructions. Yves stepped on deck and watched just as Roshi turned his head and nodded. It was as if he said, "Keep her safe, will you. She is the daughter of my heart."

Yves shook his head. Now that was just fanciful. It was as though someone had switched on an intuitive function in his head that had lain dormant since the war.

Anais climbed the stairs to her private space and stood on the balcony where she could see Roshi walking away. She knew he felt her eyes following him. It had been this way since they met. She trusted him. Until he came along she might never have trusted a man. Her father, she thought, had destroyed that ability. But she was wrong. Roshi had taught her that we can change and be redeemed. We have choices. This day she had decided to meet a stranger and commit herself to something unknown and perhaps

69

dangerous. She knew Roshi would not ask her to do something she could not handle or for which she had no aptitude. Sometimes she thought he knew her better than she knew herself.

On some level it did not surprise her that Roshi had sensed her heartache and had been concerned enough to question her about its cause. Days went by, when she no longer thought of the past or Joel. When her feelings overwhelmed her, as they had this morning, she knew she had more work to do on her psyche, for it was not wise to have secrets from her inner self, especially if she wished to be invulnerable as a spy. What we do not know can harm us greatly, she had learned. Lack of awareness was her worst enemy.

She thought of Angela. Poor Angela. She knows nothing about her own life. But, selfishly, she needed Angela to be where she was. She was that inner room where Anais could go for serenity. She felt selfish, when she thought of Angela's life, but she also felt that Angela was her one defense against pain. She was her safe and protected self. Besides, she rationalized, this had nothing to do with awareness. She was as aware of Angela as she was of her own breath. It was Angela who had the problem with awareness. She was glad Angela would not remember her relationship with Joel, for instance, for it was Anais who lived with the memory of him. To remember would bring nothing but heartache.

When Roshi visited, Anais left the place of loneliness that frequently tormented her. Solidity and oneness of purpose radiated from him and lifted her out of the confusion of dual personalities. The labyrinth of her own unconscious could be seen from a heightened perspective when he was around. He had given her the spiritual tools to see her own mind. Her behavior, he pointed out, created a maze of patterns and dead ends in her brain. There was no need to battle with habits, when they could be seen for what they were; she had simply to identify them and move on. What was not given power gradually weakened and disappeared. Real power came with the recognition of her purpose and actions that led toward its fulfillment. Her acceptance of a second assignment from Roshi liberated her from fear and stepped toward courage. This time she would need to do more than write and observe bankers at dinner parties.

Chapter 13
Anais' Childhood

Before her move to the Marais, when Anais was little and still lived in Paris, she had parents who lived together. There were her two younger brothers, Joachim and Carlo, and there was the regular routine of school. Before her school years she remembered living in the lovely neighborhood of Neuilly where neighbors walked their dogs and shared gossip. She had been shy in those days because she considered herself an ugly child. In fact, her father had told her so.

Most days, when Mama came home from the haute couture atelier, Papa was asleep on the sofa in their Paris living room. Truly there were moments, when she despised Mama for being unable to keep Papa happy. How pathetic. It was so easy really. He once promised to buy Anais a pretty bow for her hair because she had made him so happy. She had made him a promise to never tell anyone about these events, especially Mama, because Mama would be jealous. Anais believed she would grow up to marry Papa, and that would be the end of unhappiness and fighting.

Soon after he left them, Anais, her mother and brothers, had had to move to the Marais because her father was not getting enough concert work, and they could no longer afford to live in Neuilly. Eventually, they had to move to New York City. Aunt Eveline lived there and was willing to take them in as charity.

Life in New York was painful. Papa had promised to write and to join them soon, but he never did. He moved about a great deal, because he was such a great concert artist. Her letters probably never reached him, for he never wrote back.

There were days in New York, when she felt most fortunate that life was bright and happy. Then, the next day, she might feel painfully shy and withdrawn, often following an attempt to make a friend at school. As she came to understand what her classmates discussed in English, she did not let on that she understood. She felt like a voyeur and an outsider. As she listened to their chatter, she knew she was different, very different, from the others. But who would understand? Did anyone else stand in the rain to hear the rain cry? Did anyone else get in the bath and feel hands caress them everywhere, even in places that were completely private? Did the other girls keep a diary? Did their diaries contain messages to an imaginary friend who knew them so well they practically wrote the words for them? She could never describe or explain these profound differences, but she knew she was more grownup than the others.

She knew she had changed as she grew older. There were moments when she was frightened that Papa might not recognize her when he returned; for she hoped he would return one day. Mama said to forget him, but she couldn't. When she had to do housework, she felt like Cinderella: washing, cleaning, cooking, ironing, and caring for younger brothers. Mama still cried a lot, and Anais noted she didn't practice her own advice to forget Papa. It took two years before Anais finally broke down and spoke English at school. The teacher was so surprised; she phoned to speak to Mama who then scolded her for behaving so strangely. That was when she realized that once her secrets were revealed, there was nowhere to hide.

At the same time she suspected that Papa would never return and felt guilty because his memory had gradually faded. Aunt Eveline heard he had found someone to replace Mama. She was told he continued to live in Paris. As much as she wished she could see him again, Anais was jealous and furious. He enjoyed her beloved Paris, the music world, and a Bohemian life, surrounded by friends. That is how she imagined him, and it wasn't fair that he should live in Paris and leave them behind.

These days, when it rained, she was sunk in sorrow and, when the sun shone, she saw rainbows everywhere. It seemed that only her diary knew her. Mama said it was her own fault, if she felt isolated and separated from the kids in school, but she didn't even care if she graduated. Most of the students seemed ignorant. They ignored the important writers and philosophers, and their only common interest was their competition to see who was the most popular. None of them knew a thing about Europe or France while Anais read voraciously. Her education was exactly as she wished it to be.

One day she overheard talk between Mama and Aunt Eveline that sounded like they could no longer afford to live in the city. They discussed where they might go, and one option was the possibility of moving to Cuba. Having found a friend in Roshi, she would now have to leave him behind. To be forced to move to New York, then to be forced to leave, was upsetting. She was no longer Papa's little wife, and soon she would be required to speak Spanish. How could she leave Roshi? The mere thought turned the sun black, as clouds filled the horizon of her future. Surely, such an adventure was impossible to bear.

**

Shortly after the official announcement of their move, she heard that it was sensuously warm in Havana. Flowers and bright gardens, summer clothes and exotic music might not be so bad. In Cuba, Roshi told her, she could better learn Spanish and continue to write in her journal. Now that it was written in English, she suspected it would always be that way. For some reason, perhaps because Papa had betrayed them in French and wasn't coming back, she had dropped the French. English became a part of her new identity. Spanish echoed in her mind as the language in which her parents used to argue. It made her think of the war raging in Europe, and it disturbed her. In Cuba, hopefully, the war would pass them by.

"Aunt Eveline says I will be a great beauty one day," she wrote. "I love to dance and use vivid colors and, of course, write in my journal."

"Yesterday, Mama asked me to go to the drug store. She was packing for Cuba and needed a few necessities. I saw a man with crutches and another sitting on a park bench with his leg amputated. It was ugly. War is ugly. The faces of the two men were hollow, as though their souls had been shot out of them. In Cuba I am told that no one is restless, nor do they think of war. Everyone strolls down the *ramblas* in the spring as the warmth of day subsides, and the warm air hovers for a few hours after dark. They say it smells like cocoa and vanilla beans. I hope the libraries are good down there. I love to read poetry and philosophy, history and literature, and someday I will have artist friends and conversations like *Mme* Récamier did in the great salons of Paris."

"Anais, have you finished packing? Do you have enough books? Be sure to bring anything you might want to decorate your bedroom."

"What makes you think I'll be beautiful someday, Auntie?"

"Genes, my dear. You have beautiful parents."

Anais looked at her careworn mother. A person can dream. She was not so sure her Aunt Eveline wasn't trying to cheer her up while she packed. She owned an old framed photo of her parents together. Should she leave it behind? It was really the only good photo of Papa. Maybe she could cut Mama out of the photo. She quickly stuffed it in the bottom of her suitcase. She needed to find more space for her journals without bringing attention to them because she could never leave them behind. She had taken to recording her dreams in her diary. These daily entries did away with loneliness and put her in a place that was just as alive as Paris, more comforting than Cuba, more vibrant than New York.

Chapter 14
Raphael

Raphael washed his coffee cup at the sink in his third floor walkup. They called it the *deuzieme* in France, making it sound like there were only two flights of stairs to climb instead of three. He loved Paris, normally, but this post war version of the city of light was a travesty of the past. He was sure others suffered more in other times at other junctions in history but, for a city once so immersed in art and cultural affairs, the change was a tragedy.

He stared out the window. It was early spring in Paris, the cold chill wet with promise. He loved it, the time of year, the umbrellas, and the steamy cafés. He was trying to back off to one latté a day, thus the French press and his own brew this morning. He wanted to save the café visit for the loneliest part of the afternoon, when most Parisians indulged in a *cinq à sept* with their mistresses. As for Raphael, he could pass on that. He was a widower with a job that could not accommodate intimate relationships. Besides, today he felt old. He considered taking his accrued pension and heading for the mountains, to his ranch in Montana where intrigue was absent, where coyotes killed voles and rabbits and the sweet grass grew in waves. It was simple and uncomplicated, unless you were caught in a storm the way his wife Caroline had died. He averted his mind.

These days, he meditated and read Buddhist texts. It was peaceful and kept him from dwelling on the beauty of Caroline and the life he once cherished. His girls were off in

University now and that gave him pause. Whatever had gotten into him to accept an overseas assignment with the CIA was a puzzle. He still could not believe he rented an apartment in the Marais, a part of Paris where his father had grown up. His father, the big rancher, had been kicked by a horse several years ago, and Raphael could only be grateful the man's head injury prevented him from realizing his quality of life. Another reason to take this assignment. Someone had to pay for all the medical bills.

That's when he decided to take a walk. One thing he had learned was to move, keep moving, if he didn't want bad memories to catch him. It was time to walk toward new memories, make inroads into his future, and keep in mind that he was in Paris to do a job.

He took out an umbrella and a warm wool pea coat, wrapped a warm scarf around his neck, and put on his beret and gloves. Descending the stairs in his apartment building, he headed toward the Seine, his thoughts settling on the fellow who had just moved in downstairs. He looked German, said he was an opera singer and smelled like a rat. If that guy was in Paris on opera business, then Raphael was Gertrude Stein. This morning, he intended to get a good look at the woman he was told would be working with him on this case. The last thing he needed was a frightened mouse of a woman working with him.

His long legs took him down to the Seine in the time it took to have a few meditative insights until he was pleasantly relieved of thoughts of the past. Such a walk also made him grateful he had not had to serve on the battlefields of the Great War. A widower with two children and a ranch that provided cattle for the soldiers was a greater asset at home. The men on the streets of Paris were walking casualties. If they had all four limbs, they were missing something upstairs. The women looked beaten and neglected; the children looked abandoned. As he stopped on the quay, he noticed an old barge that had been turned into a houseboat, and he stopped. What a fabulous idea, he thought. To live on the river in the middle of Paris was ingenious. The water, on its powerfully quiet journey, evoked strength.

As he stood there, lost in a reverie of all the good things he had ever experienced on the banks of rivers, he saw movement on the upper balcony of the houseboat and the ephemeral shadow of a woman, dressed in black, watering plants. For a moment he wasn't sure, if he had imagined her, then she was gone. Left behind was the image of another woman he had once seen in a dream. He had recently read about the compensatory value of dreams, how they evoked creativity, but he was not exactly aware of how that happened. His native grandmother on his mother's side had once known all about dreams and what they meant. The woman in black disappeared inside the barge, so he turned, left the quay and walked slowly back to his empty apartment. This afternoon, instead of ruminating on an irretrievable past, he might stop by and visit the Buddhist fellow who would be his main contact. His name was Roshi, and he liked the old fellow.

On his way back to the Marais he quietly contemplated life on a river, hoping to stay out as long as possible to avoid the silence of an apartment inhabited by one lonely person. Lately, his friends had tried to match him up at dinner parties and theatre outings, but he had avoided their efforts quite successfully. When and if he wanted a woman to fill the air in his space he would find one on his own. The fleeting image of a woman in black intrigued him. For the first time, since Caroline's death, a longing for the presence of a beautiful woman took his breath away.

***

Anais glanced again at the address Roshi had given her. She was in the Marais close to the apartment she had lived in when she was a child. The Marais was so run down and shabby these days she hadn't dared to dress well. Instead, she had worn an ordinary brown skirt and flat tie shoes, eschewed make up or perfume and pulled an old beret over her forehead.

She rang the bell in the open foyer, but suspecting it did not work, she climbed the stairs to Raphael's apartment. At her knock the door was opened abruptly.

"Goodness you frightened me, *monsieur*. My name is Anais and I was given…"

"I know who you are. Come in."

Raphael's gruff demeanor camouflaged his recognition of the houseboat woman he had seen.

"Please sit. I was just making coffee. Can I offer you one?"

"Yes, certainly. Thank you."

She had elegant manners but seemed timid.

"Your French, it's different."

"Ah, you have a good ear. I spent five years in New York City in my youth."

"So…Roshi tells me you are just the right person for this assignment."

"Yes, but he did not give me any details."

"Sure, I understand. Let's get directly to it. You have rented a place on the Seine. Quite the place. I saw it this morning and it's impressive." He observed his abrupt manner as if from a distance and did not recognize himself.

"I intend for it to attract friends in the art community. Roshi said such a lure would be invaluable, but he did not explain."

"Then let me. You see, we have reason to suspect that the art scene in Paris is being used as a cover for German infiltration. Apparently, the Germans have not accepted defeat in the last war and are clandestinely planning something for the future. Beyond outright war, what that means is uncertain. How it will be financed is also uncertain. We need more concrete information. Roshi has financed this barge restoration, and we think it's a brilliant idea. His agent of choice is you."

He paused, but she merely nodded.

"I must tell you, I am not used to working with a partner. Having a woman partner makes me doubly nervous, especially one as fragile as you."

"Looks can be deceiving, *monsieur.* I am well trained in observation and am a chameleon in social situations. Gathering information with some discernment is what I do."

"I plan to be your escort for the next while. This way we get to know each other, so there will be fewer unpleasant surprises. There are enough of those out there without creating more. Why don't I pick you up at the boat tomorrow? We'll walk along the Seine and go to lunch."

Anais took her leave soon afterwards and walked back to the houseboat. He was a handsome and masculine man, no nonsense and rather severe. He was American, and that explained his impatience as far as she was concerned.

"Writers do not live one life, they live two. There is the living and then there is the writing."

—Nin *Diary: Volume One*

Chapter 15
Reminiscence

Most of all, Anais had missed Roshi when she moved to Cuba. Once he became her mentor, she had become fascinated with the truth. Truth. It was connected to beauty. It was also true that she longed for love. Her senses spoke on behalf of truth, but she was told in Catholic sermons to deny her senses. Once she left her mother's home, she avoided church as much as possible. When she pretended to have a headache on Sunday mornings, her devoutly Catholic mother told her the devil gave her the headaches, and it would go better for her, if she confessed her sins. So what was truth? There were days, especially after she had seen her friend Roshi, when goodness and beauty hovered in the air. Other times, she felt sinful and ugly for no apparent reason. In church she continually heard the phrase, "Lord I am not worthy." This bothered her and made her uneasy. Such thinking caused her to spiral away and down into the darkness. Was it true? How could she know the difference, when these feelings came more frequently after a visit to church? It would seem that conflict surrounded truth.

Her last day in New York City, when she left the library for the café on the corner with Roshi, was an autumn day, and the rain fell gently, wetting leaves on the walk. It was the kind of day that reminded her of Paris. She and Roshi sat side by side and looked out the window, as people hurried by with umbrellas and raincoats. They had talked like two adults. Roshi was impressed by her efforts to become self-educated. He said he had done the same in Japan many years ago. After those early years his education had never stopped. There was so much to learn and so little time to waste. He suggested subjects and authors she had never considered to expand her reading list. He was amazed that she was so young and understood so much. He talked to her about Japanese culture, the way women loved to dress, Noh theatre and flower arranging with graceful, serene motions meant to convey consciousness and the life of Zen awareness. Like a sponge, she soaked up all things Japanese.

She tried to guess Roshi's age but found it impossible. He told her he had been a monk for many years, beginning at an early age, and had experienced both abuse and contentment in the monastery, where his family had placed him to be raised. Placing a son in a monastery was a common practice in Japan, he told her.

Since she had met him at age thirteen, they had taken to meeting often, the mysterious monk and the rebellious teenager, until, as unlikely as it would seem, they became friends. By age sixteen Anais had read voraciously all his suggestions and loved the poetry of other lands.

She would miss him terribly, but he told her absence was not a serious problem. They would meet again because it was destined to be so. He seemed so sure. Yet she remembered Papa saying the same thing, and it had been years, since she had seen him. What intrigued her was Roshi's attitude. Despite the fact that he had been frequently and brutally beaten at the monastery, he said the experience had made him a stronger person. He, too, was an orphan though she didn't believe for a second that his parents were dead; she simply knew that he had allotted them a place in his mind where they could live in peace. He knew her parents were alive, but he told her there was a place for them in her mind. To keep them there was an act of kindness. Could she be so strong? If she could, he told her, she would be a formidable woman someday. It is the mind that lends us character, he taught her, and he wanted her to keep him in a separate box in her mind until they met again. Her task, he told her, was to learn languages because she was so good at it, to continue her studies, and to read from the long list of books he had given her. Somehow, he had become her tutor, her mentor, her friend, and her spiritual advisor.

The written word had fascinated Anais, since she could read. It did not occur to her that spoken words could be equally powerful. Languages. She had not realized she had such an aptitude, especially after her experience in the New York City Public School system. She sat in her room mending stockings, considering the unknown possibilities of language and the opportunity to practice Spanish to gain fluency. Roshi said she would be that much more capable of communicating. She thought of the diary and its secret language. What she created was a consideration of her own strengths and limitations. Even if she was enamored with words, writing held first place in her mind's eye.

Chapter 16
The Past Returns

In Spanish Pablo Neruda wrote, "I will bring you happy flowers from the mountains, bluebells, dark hazels, and a rustic basket of kisses." This sentence depressed and disgusted Anais. It reminded her of her father. Now that she was sixteen and nearly grown up she had come to despise her father. Love and trust can turn to hatred. When she tried to think kindly of him, she imagined cupid and his bow, as arrows of warm fluid filled her and a shiver shot up her spine. Love, beauty, truth: her body could not lie, but it could get confused. Papa, too, had been hurt; she just knew it. Had it been wrong to want to kiss away his hurt, to love him so he would forget his pain? Truth and wisdom are not learned in books, they echo in the body and say, "I will love you always." When she recalled these feelings, guilt echoed in every cell of her body. It was too much to bear.

The other side of truth is the lie. As truth is connected to beauty, so the lie is connected to the ugly and hatred. The end of the diary in French, the language spoken by Papa every day, was her severance of the past. The start of the diary in English was a whole new story. If Papa was put away in a drawer, a closed book so to speak, he might be remembered for his love, the truth of his existence and his vulnerability. Otherwise, he would become an ancient mythic king whose fundamental right to incest with his beloved daughter was taken for granted. He would become the stuff of legend and folklore, great and benevolent. He would remain a heroic figure from the past who could not touch her new life. Therefore, it was imperative that he be locked in a drawer.

**

Once she started to write in English, she felt like someone else as she wrote, an English character in a novel, perhaps, an orphan who lived in an apartment with a maid mother who appeared occasionally with groceries or sewing. In real life her non-heroic mother went off to work each day, where she toiled in the back room of a couturier shop. Occasionally, she brought home sewing, as she moonlighted to pay the bills. While Papa had been so elegant and gallant, such an *artiste,* Mama was a drudge, a Cinderella who had never found her prince.

She tied a lovely bow with a piece of silk ribbon around a finished volume of diary and remembered their apartment in Paris. There had always been the sound of Papa, playing the concert grand piano in the living room. In New York there was only the constant noise of traffic in the background because they had not been able to afford a decent location to live. She thanked *le bon Dieu* that her first diary had been in French. In English, she could more easily shift her thoughts, when they became dark. She remembered that Papa was always so miserable. She had begged him to wait for her to grow up, when she could marry him, and they would live happily ever after. He had liked her so much when she comforted him, and got a dreamy look on his face, as he caressed her. She was small for her age, but she knew he would touch her everywhere, and she would love it. She shivered. Too often, she remembered all the times that Mama would not be home for hours, and Papa would lift her on to his lap. He loved her so much.

Then one day he called her ugly and left. His exit, documented in her first diary that she had locked in a box, was tied with a silk ribbon. She had hidden the box, along with memories that made her feel strange and different. Roshi said it was her wounds that would define her and her mistakes that would give her great wisdom. He had shown her how to store memories in boxes. When she was older, she would put them in a safety deposit box, but for now she retied the ribbon as a detective might do to detect intruders. No one would be able to read these pages, particularly her snooping little brothers.

A web is formed, when truth is ignored. It looks like the convoluted twists and turns of the human brain or the tangled roots of a tree. Pockets and crevasses atrophy after many long years of kept secrets, and people can be seen sitting in chairs in the corridors of nursing homes, as memories disappear along with shrunken brain tissue, shuffling. Suddenly, one is lost in a maze of forgetfulness. Information, remote and lost, become torments in frightening moments of recall. Better that what is remembered be placed in boxes and copied out in her diaries, she thought, than caught in her head in a nightmare of darkness.

***

Roshi sat at his desk in his Park Avenue apartment. Behind him were framed diplomas: Harvard for political philosophy, Tufts for international affairs, Oxford and the Sorbonne. There were also framed photos: Roshi as a monk in Kyoto, his parents at their summer home in the mountains, a reflecting pond in the city garden, the only woman he had ever loved who died too soon and Anais, sitting beneath a reading lamp at the New York Public Library. The images gave him comfort and kept him solidly grounded. He kept them all in this room where visitors were forbidden. The whole room was his private memory box. In this room he was transported to his former life of wealth and tradition, privilege and Samurai honor.

One day Roshi had turned his back on his inherited position in society. Who had he thought he was? His journey had then become a rude awakening and a blow to his pride. His father had spoken frankly to him, telling him he was not suited to a life outside family tradition, that he was not destined to destroy the family and leave it bereft of an heir. His family, but especially his father, had suffered greatly from his decisions. To his father, his beloved son was dead. His mother then faded away to resemble a living ghost. His mind, still overwhelmed by the cruelty of the monks, continued to punish him and beat him into submission. He had not known true suffering, they once told him, so how could he overcome what he had never experienced?

By the time he swallowed his formidable pride, it was too late to return to his family home. Due to the Meiji restoration, his home had become an unrecognizable shell, and his parents had grown old before their time. During an important celebration to welcome him home, he had looked around and pondered whether this was all there was. He obsessed about it until he knew he was close to a breakdown, then decided he had to get on with his life and deal with reality. If this life was the only life he was given, he wanted to use it wisely. When his parents died within a very short time of each other, he knew in his heart that they still blamed themselves for sending him away. They had chosen to ignore his suffering on behalf of tradition. As his father had insisted time after time, the family was, and always would be, Samurai. According to his father, it was not up to an only son to go against the ancestors, for no good would ever come from such a self-centered decision. While he was still little and subject to the wishes of his father, it had nearly broken him. Then, the everyday life of a monk and the years of training had nearly killed him. Looking back, he knew it was not the austerities of the training so much as his inner knowing that the monastery was not where he belonged that caused such agony. He needed gentleness and support. Instead, he was given a small bowl of rice and hot tea. It was not enough for an old soul who was prepared to continue where he had left off in his last life.

Roshi's parents were gone now, but it had taken him years to forgive them. The only woman he had ever loved had left him behind, and then she had died of heartbreak at a young age. Family and the traditional route were not to be his path. Finally, he looked at what he had been given: an inquiring mind, great wealth and health, despite all the beatings and starvation by the monks. These were among his gifts. As well, he was still young enough to travel the world and find whatever it was he was meant to do.

Today, he gazed around the room. He owned a replica of this New York apartment in Paris because it comforted him. After all his travels it was a cocoon from which he liked to believe he could face life with its many challenges. He knew that escape from himself was not possible, yet there were days, when he wondered if these rooms were his ultimate escape. He, too, knew the power of the labyrinthine mind where hidden secrets could fester, and lost memories could die forgotten or neglected. It was a habit of the mind to create tapes of trauma that run over and over.

With the excellent education that he had undergone, he spoke English and French, read German and Western philosophy. The monastery had provided other sources of learning though much of it was mystical knowledge that could not be shared. It took him by surprise, when he was approached by the secret services of several countries while still at Harvard. Few students were in a position to choose their jobs. Even fewer had his unique background. For once, his skills, his languages, and his esoteric knowledge put him in a position where he discovered he was needed.

It was a lonely life he had chosen. Knowing secrets required him to be vigilant. Vigilance was the hidden language of the spy. It was one more thing he had learned before he met Anais. Somehow, he had recognized that she was his spiritual daughter. After all the years and so much study, the need for solitude, and the travel, he had found a kindred spirit in a thirteen-year-old rebellious teenager.

Sometimes, in a mysterious way, it felt that she was wounded deeply. Though she had not told him so, he knew she was the victim of incest. He realized that she had been abused and then abandoned by her father. As for her overworked and miserable mother, there was nothing but shame and the broken hearted knowledge that she had sacrificed her own child for a relationship that had had little chance of survival. Roshi, who never revealed his family name, marveled that the universe had given him one more gift in his old age. He was no longer young but had told several agencies that he was willing to remain in his capacity as consultant for as long as he continued to be blessed with health.

The question now was how he and Anais could maintain their friendship between New York and Cuba? There was the mail, of course, but he would rather keep their relationship private. He knew the family was strictly Catholic, especially the mother and aunt, so now that Anais was of a certain age, he imagined they would keep a strict watch on her. He could only hope that she kept out of trouble. He knew, as well as he knew himself, that she would subject herself to much misery before she came into her own wisdom. He knew it because he had done the same.

Chapter 17
Life in Cuba

As she stood on the deck of the ship that took them to Cuba, Anais felt that her departure was a replica of her departure from the shores of France. Now, however, she spoke English fluently, wrote in English, and had met a second father, someone who knew her as a mature young woman and treated her with great respect. What did that mean? Sometimes she wondered why he never touched her or caressed her, though she knew it was more normal not to be touched by someone who was male and older. Was he a true friend? Time would tell.

As the New York skyline disappeared, she imagined the music and flowers in Cuba. She would not cry or act like the child she was, when she last moved. Mama said she would have to find a job in Cuba because she did not have her high school diploma. Besides, Mama could no longer support them all alone. Learning better Spanish would help to find a job. She had decided she wanted to be a journalist someday, but would she be able to find a job at a newspaper, if she couldn't speak Spanish well enough? She intended to learn quickly.

Mama said it was time to look for a nice young man and get married, but she did not want to get married, ever. What good had it done Mama? When asked, she answered that Anais would never have been born, if she had not married Papa. She still thought of Anais as a child who believed in baby baskets delivered by the stork nine months after a wedding ceremony. In keeping with her belief that it was time for Anais to find a husband, her mother had a photo portrait taken of her in which she looked like an ingénue, yet a complex and mysterious one. It was an intriguing combination.

Roshi had given her his post office box address in New York. She would give it a try and write to him, despite all the letters she had sent to Papa with no reply. Sadly, she already missed Roshi. He had become her best friend, her only friend, really. How in the world had she become friends with an ageless oriental man? She didn't even know what he did for a living, when he wasn't at the library or taking her to museums or art galleries or the library café for hot chocolate. Had she really only known him for a few years? Maybe she had known him in another lifetime. He would surely have been a wonderful father. But she still did not like to think such traitorous thoughts, and she could feel a twinge in her heart like a remnant of guilt or disloyalty. Papa was in a box between the pages of a diary, and she was slowly moving on with her life.

She stood at the railing a long time. If she breathed in a lot of fresh air, she might be able to sleep soundly through the night. When she woke in a few days, she would be starting a new saga in her life. She was certain that this move, while sweet and painful, was worth a tear or two. She cried often, standing alone at the bow of the boat. She cried, beneath the stars and moon and planets, and all of them converged to help her grieve. The heavens were beautiful but cold and far away. It was no use to try to think of poor soldiers, hurt and afraid. She did not know them, and the war was a distant phenomenon. When she tried to imagine those far worse off than herself, it only compounded her grief. Was the whole world just a vat of sorrow and misery? Why were men fighting each other? Boys as young as she was were dying like animals in a slaughter. She could comprehend none of it and wished she were a poet. Truly, poetry must come from the ocean's depths. Dimensions of her inner world stepped up to the ship's rail and turned to tears. The cadence of the sea lulled her senses and, finally, she stepped away, wrapped her sweater more tightly around herself, and returned to her cabin. Once undressed and on her bunk, she took her diary from beneath her pillow and wrote of renewed loss of home and father, language and poetry.

Each evening she stared at the stars and held on to the railing, as waves rose to carry the ship forward into the night. Each night the air was perceptibly warmer, more caressing and soft against her skin, the cold stars closer and the moon brighter. Her tears dried up until she simply ached for a happiness she was not sure existed. Finally, even the ache was gone, as the ship came closer to islands, as it slowed and moved differently and more gently through the water. The ocean, she came to believe, was the greatest of healers. After all, what was a tear or two in a vast ocean of collected tears?

Chapter 18
First Job

Her aunt and her mother spoke only Spanish these days, reverting to their youth, when they had grown up in Havana. Anais had written a letter to Roshi in English with her new address, but there was no answer yet. Yesterday, Mama told her it was time to find a job. She had made her a lovely dress with a short jacket. It was a shade of heather that enhanced the color of her eyes. Maybe, if she found a job, she could afford to buy a second outfit and some eye makeup. For the last three months she had been studying Spanish, trying to understand her aunt and mother who already spoke the language fluently. It was a miserable time for her. Men on the street leered; people were poor; and though the tropical flowers were truly bright and cheerful, it did not seem that people were interested in the beauty of a garden, white curtains or unchipped paint. Poverty, she had been told, gave rise to indifference and even neglect, but she had been poor all her life and found that there was no excuse. Elbow grease, Mama assured her, cost nothing. Luckily, Mama had the pride to clean and scrub and tidy until her surroundings shone.

What was missing here, she suspected, were dreams. When dreams died or were not nourished, then spirit died, too. Could a person dream of that which they did not know? Was it possible to imagine the unknown? How did one rise above an impoverished attitude? Anais thought continually about these big problems and tried to imagine what her own life would be like someday. Her dreams had taken on a vivid hue, since they arrived in Havana. All the decay and humidity, the lush plants and jungle flowers were foreign to her. They seemed bigger than life. Maybe they overwhelmed the life of a person, as they grew in ruthless proliferation. Beautiful children flourished on the streets, but their parents were worn and tired. Heat sapped their strength, insects took their share and unsanitary conditions drained the rest. It was amazing that anyone grew to adulthood in this country. She felt the emotional envy and the disparity between those who had more, so much more that they seemed surreal. She looked, perplexed, at huge haciendas, fat and satisfied men with cigars, wearing suits of the finest linen with Panama hats to top off bald heads. Women who strolled through the lavish parks grew lush in this climate. They let their skin soak up a bit of color, wore their hats at an airy and elegant tilt, removed corsets and allowed their bodies to be arrayed in simple cottons with fewer layers and ankle-length skirts. In her lifetime Anais had expected that she would wear long dresses like Mama, so the many changes were lively and exciting.

Then why had her dreams begun to perplex her? She could make nothing of them. Mama said she had cousins on her side of the family who looked forward to meeting her. They were in Europe at the moment, but they would be back. It gave her an incentive to learn more Spanish. Maybe her dreams had something to do with a brighter future, change, new friends. Who knew?

Meanwhile, she had to find a job, or Mama would insist she follow her to the shop, where she sewed all day. This morning, she walked carefully so as not to sweat in her new outfit; nor could she afford to get blisters on her feet. Last week, she had had a wonderful idea. It had come to her in a dream. Today, she intended to apply for a job on a newspaper. If she was to be a writer, she had to get a start somewhere. From her purse she removed a slip of paper on which she had written the address and checked it once again.

This was it; she was certain. She entered the downtown building and was surprised at the smells: ink, paper, sweat and perfume. It was erotic and almost daunting. At the reception she asked to see Mr. Seaborn and was told to take a seat. She had phoned to make an appointment after she had read a copy of the *New Times* in English at the library and learned that Mr. Joel Seaborn was the editor-in-chief.

When her name was called, she followed the receptionist through a maze of desks where writers sat at typewriters and was shown into the editor's office. Then, she stood there and stared for a moment. He was handsome with an aura of remote control. She wondered how old he was and, for the first time in her life, felt a stirring of romantic interest in a man. Surely not. Her eyes, her best features, leveled on this man who was staring rudely back at her.

"Can I help you, miss?"

"I wish to apply for a job as a journalist."

"You speak English perfectly, I hear."

"Yes, and French."

"Really?" He smiled indulgently. "How old are you might I ask?"

"Just twenty-one." How easy it was to lie. "My birthday was just a week ago." She saw the startled look on his face.

"And your experience?"

"I have brought a few of my short stories for you to read. I am willing to start anywhere in any capacity. This would be my first job, sir. A person must have a first job from which to grow as a writer."

She closed and opened her eyes slowly and dramatically as she had seen done in a silent film. She truly felt twenty-one today. She handed him her tidy portfolio that consisted of two newly typed vignettes.

"Sit for a moment, please." He sat quietly and read rapidly. Then he looked up and nodded.

"This has potential. Is your first language French? There are a few errors in syntax, but you look like a quick study.

You start tomorrow as Jack's assistant. He covers the social beat."

He did not wait for her to answer his questions but picked up the phone and asked his secretary to send in Jack Adams. While they waited, he stared at her.

"You look much younger than twenty-one, but all beautiful women look young. I hope you can pull it off."

Jack walked in, and she faced another handsome man. Were they all like this? She was introduced to Jack, as his assistant reporter, and she thought she caught a smirk on Jack's face. It was done. Her head spun. She had dreamed of getting a real job as a writer, and just like that she was employed. When Jack left, she was told to report for work the next day at 8 AM. She was quoted a salary that was absurd it was so low, but even so she thought it might rival what Mama made while slaving all day. She noted the ceiling fans throughout the pressroom and was shown to her cubbyhole of a desk. She was to be the new social columnist, attend social functions in the city and report on the elite life of its more affluent citizens. Maybe she should take a typing course in her spare time. She could hardly wait to get home to tell Mama and Aunt Eveline and get ready for work tomorrow.

Just like that, a few minutes, an interview and she was a fledgling journalist. This was why dreams were so important. They tended to come true, and they never abandoned a person. When Anais arrived home, the mail had arrived, and there was a letter from Roshi. The brothers were in school; Aunt Eveline was shopping for groceries to make dinner; and the house sparkled from her housekeeping efforts. Mama was still at work, so Anais had the luxury and privacy of sitting there and staring at the envelope. Not even a first job could compete with the anticipation of reading this letter. He had found her, and she was not forgotten. It happened, though seldom, that events that resemble bliss occurred on the same day. Today must be special. Perhaps Venus, the goddess of beauty and love, was transiting her astrological sphere at this moment. After all, she had also met the most beautiful man. She knew he found her very attractive. All French women knew such things, she assured herself.

Roshi's letter was to be savored and saved. She read it over and over, then folded it into her diary to be reread whenever she needed to feel him nearby. As a first letter from her beloved Roshi, she would keep it for years to come.

My Dear Anais,

How are you doing? I am afraid that by the time you are settled at your new address and this letter arrives a long time will have passed. It took your letter six weeks to get to New York, and I know that such a period of time in the life of someone your age may seem like forever. You must be close to seventeen by now. Nearly a grown woman, but I hope this letter will arrive in time to wish you all the best on your special day. Happy birthday, my dear, and I wish you happiness throughout a long life.

I can only tell you that life goes on as usual on Park Avenue. I rarely depart from my routines. The library, the café and the museums are lonely without you. No one else has taken your place.

I hope you will continue with your reading and study of Spanish. It sounds like you are still somewhat longing for New York, but I assure you the winter here is a bit grim this year. You may luxuriate on my behalf in the warmth of an island that many consider a paradise. I would like you to try to reread *Don Quixote* in Spanish. It is worth the effort. Keep with it. Literary figures bow before Cervantes and even Shakespeare, it is thought, revered him. Speak Spanish as much as possible. I know you will not be like most Americans abroad, unable to assimilate a new language. It is your forte. I have included an international money order that may be redeemed at any reputable bank. It is a birthday gift and meant to be used for feminine frivolities that grown women of seventeen must have. Until we meet again, I hope you will not forget our precious friendship.

Your Loyal Friend,

Roshi

When Mama came home, Anais was so excited she could hardly contain herself. When she told her about the new job, her mother was shocked.

"*Mon Dieu.* When they discover your age, you will be fired."

"How would they ever find out?"

"How indeed. We must make you some lovely grown up outfits to wear to the office."

With these words, Anais realized her mother was very proud of her. Soon after, Mama disappeared into her sewing room.

In the morning there was a lovely white blouse, lying across the sofa. Mama was already gone, but there were instructions to hurry and not be late for her first day on the job. From that day Anais would be treated as a grownup who brought home as much money as her mother, which she handed over as her contribution to the household expenses. She was always dressed beautifully because of Mama, and she soon became a welcome figure about the city, where she attended all the important social functions, wrote fact and gossip and, in her new chameleon role, fit in with any group she needed to interview. No one questioned her age.

It was certainly an opportunity to try on a second persona, Anais joked, when she wrote back to Roshi the very evening she received his letter. It was a long and detailed letter that included her excitement over the new job and her chance to be a writer. Roshi was the first to notice the abrupt change from childhood to womanhood. While her salary was shared at home, the money Roshi included in his letters, each time he wrote, would be saved in her own private, but secret, bank account. The private account grew and became a source of confidence, as her new adult personality grew and took on a life of its own.

***

In Europe war had come to an end. It was nothing for a teenager to concern herself about, but for Roshi, who was continually in demand as an advisor to many influential parties, it was a relief. Now would begin the exhausting repairs and the painful recovery from war. It was 1919, and the world had changed. Sadness, greyness, grim survival, and more men with severed limbs appeared on city streets. The government was no better in its crippled depletion. So much and so many had been lost that the big question remained, "Who would pick up the pieces?"

Anais stepped off the bus and strolled elegantly down the main street of the Havana business district. It was Friday morning and the end of a week at work. In her excitement to get to work that morning she had left enough time for a café latté near the office, and her elegant stroll was the confident walk of a successful young woman.

She ordered a roll with butter, jam and coffee, then simply sat, watching the morning rush hour and those who were stressed, those who would rather be anywhere but in an office, and those whose jaunty stride meant something good might happen today. She loved to people watch.

"Will that be all, *Senorita?*"

"Yes, *gracias.*"

She handed over the price of her breakfast and tipped the waiter who counted out change from his money belt. He nodded in appreciation and moved on. She sat a while longer, waiting for her co-workers to enter the building, so she could observe while virtually unseen. Jack Adams approached the main door, looking focused. With his guard down he did not look cynical. Though he wore no wedding ring, it was obvious he was a married man, and there was a certain serious approach to his day. She watched him open the lobby door with determination. Next came Molly, Joel's secretary, who introduced herself to everyone as his assistant. Her skirt was an inch too short, her blouse an inch too tight, and Anais knew it would be wise to avoid her.

Molly had gained a bit of weight quite recently and was beginning to appreciate that her boss barely knew she existed. She hadn't a chance at love, as far as he was concerned, and knew it in her heart of hearts. Anais wondered how long it would take her to look for another job. All this information came from her observation of details. It was a game she and Roshi used to play, when they sat at the café in New York.

"Hi, Anais."

It was the inquisitive reporter whose desk was beside hers. Anais tried to remember her name. Betsy? Was that it? She was the only other woman reporter on her floor and covered the fashion column.

"You look lovely today. I didn't know you stopped here before work. It's my favorite café."

"Oh, I won't be making a habit of it, for sure. My salary doesn't allow for many such indulgences. I am treating myself this morning."

"Good for you. It's nice to have another woman co-worker by the way. Not that the last social page writer wasn't a woman but, you know, someone closer to my own age."

Anais smiled. "Well, I'd best get up there. Can't afford to be late while I am so new on the job."

Anais hurried into the building, leaving Betsy to finish her coffee alone. She was uncomfortable with such mundane interactions, the kind others took for granted, and she hoped she did not appear too unfriendly. Then, she shook her head to clear the image of Betsy with a run in her stockings. She could not tolerate such carelessness. It was as bad as holding a skirt together with a safety pin. Who could live like that? She who had tried so hard to develop her abilities, also wished to be born again as a secure person who did not worry about cracks and run stockings or the fact that the world might simply pass her by. Control. To steer her own fate in her own way was her goal.

Chapter 19
Anais Grows Up and Roshi Moves to Paris

For a seventeen-year-old girl who was a junior reporter on an English paper in Havana there were noticeably more men everywhere: on the streets, in the office, at parties and in her personal social life. Anais was no longer ugly. Her petite and gamine looks were emphasized. The big eyes were bigger with mascara. Her petite form had become delicate and feminine, and she had grown taller. Her flare for style became an asset on the society beat, so invitations to events were a constant. Kind and knowing eyes were a devastatingly attractive combination, and many men seemed to stand as closely as possible at parties. The shy ugly girl had become a *femme fatale*. As a *femme fatale* she gazed directly at whoever met her eyes. She focused her attention and gave the impression that the other, whose gaze she held, was the most important person in the room. It was the perfect disguise, and she knew intuitively that the *femme fatale* was merely a mirror, a woman who ensnared egos.

Roshi read her letters and smiled sadly. Like a good parent, he could see trouble on the horizon. There was nothing he could have or would have done to intervene, however. If, in truth, she had been his daughter, she would have grown up differently. As it was, he knew she was unique because of her past, maybe because of more than one lifetime. Karma is all about debts. He would watch her life and offer unconditional love. It was the best he could do. In the meantime he had his work. The Versailles Peace Conference was still underway. There were so many meetings to attend, he considered moving permanently to his Paris apartment. The conference was not going well in his estimation. He felt urgency and uneasiness. A sixth sense told him these negotiations were an enormous opportunity missed. No one approved of what looked to be an unworkable agreement. They needed to negotiate a better deal. The League of Nations Covenant was drafted, but it merely created the need for more negotiations. To him, it was evident that the outcome would create broken-hearted disagreement in the hands of the wrong people. It was not peace, but an end to peace, and the economy could not hold much longer. He knew people like himself would be called upon to monitor another attempt to repair the current damage. However, what Roshi saw was not peace but the human desire to punish in the form of retribution directed at Germany. It could only lead to more war.

Naturally, there was much anger to be dealt with. Grief settled in the streets of Paris like fog. Victory, he knew, was not a date of surrender; it involved hearts and minds; it was the process of reparation and forgiveness. Responsibility and admissions of wrongdoing, sincere sorrow and the wisdom to know that force was not the solution: these were essential. Defeat was defeat for both sides. Sons and fathers had been maimed or were dead, so understanding had not been an outcome of the conference. Those who did understand realized that German discontent lurked behind every smile. War costs were great and bitterness profound. German superiority and racial slurs had offended the Japanese, and who knew better than Roshi the taint of insult to Japanese pride? Dishonor was no small matter for his people. Inequality would fester until honor could be defended.

When Roshi thought of Anais, he thought of her as a child of the times. She was young, too young to think of herself as a vehicle of despair, but Roshi knew that she had undergone the unspeakable. She did not think of herself as a victim of war because her injuries were invisible and beneath the surface, like so many injuries that had been suffered. When war erupted, she was just coming of age. She had been betrayed by her father and sacrificed by her mother, and now that the war at home was over, she felt free to pursue a new identity. All the ugliness that concealed her hidden beauty, he recognized, had been buried and, he knew, Anais emerged changed. He loved the child he remembered. He also realized that that special child must return one day, if she were to recover her true identity.

From Paris Roshi wrote another letter.

My Dearest Anais,

It is always a joy to hear from you, to hear how you have grown and how you continue to blossom, though there is always my sadness that I cannot be there in person to watch you grow. The journalist job suits you at this time in your life. You need to socialize, to evolve through your writing, and learn about men who are not from your household. I only pray you will not forget your studies and that your natural wisdom will assist you with everyday challenges. Without parents who understand you, guidance must be sought elsewhere.

I refer you to a French writer, though you are right in the center of your Spanish period. Marcel Proust is beyond the comprehension of most young ladies, but you know I have always seen into your extraordinary soul. You will eventually appreciate why I refer you to his heavy tome. Please read him in French.

You may have noticed that my letter has been sent from Paris. I have moved and intend to be located in Paris for some time. I have spent much time here, dealing with the Paris peace talks, and I feel it necessary to stay. Much will transpire in the next decade. If you can find the time in your studies, please read more history. The best way to start would be an overview of European history. You will never regret it.

Arriving soon will be a set of Proust's most famous work. Read slowly. Also there is a credible copy of condensed European history to supplement your studies. Be well in these times of tenuous peace,

Roshi

(If I have missed any of your letters, they will surely catch up with me.)

Anais had never received such a solemn letter from Roshi. If she didn't know better, she would think that he worried about her. Now, of all times, was not the time for worry. Life was good. The war was over. She was surrounded by handsome and fun-loving men who adored her.

As a matter of fact, she had a date this evening with one of the feature reporters in the office. From the very first day at work, he had shown her much attention. Somehow, he managed to have a rose newly cut and in a vase on her desk each week. She knew he must do it in the evening or before she arrived in the morning, but she had never caught him at it. Frequently, there were notes and invitations to lunch from him. Sometimes, she turned him down because she had other invitations, but James was her favorite so far.

The attention was heady. Her paychecks were gratifying, and her exposure to another world where laughter and gaiety prevailed was wonderful. Nevertheless, she was glad that Roshi had put a clever history book in her care package. When people talked about the war, as serious reporters were wont to do, she had kept silent. She could not join in, if she did not understand what was going on. She had heard of the Versailles treaty, of course. That was a good thing wasn't it? She did not wish to be portrayed as all beauty and no brains. She could never settle for being a cliché.

She had worked for a year already. She wished her Spanish was good enough to be a Spanish reporter, but maybe she could keep her eyes and ears opened for a position with more pay and more serious assignments because she was now seventeen and thought she could do better. She was infatuated with her boss, but he had hired her, then basically ignored her. Occasionally, she caught him watching her and wondered, if he was still suspicious of her age. Age seventeen had come and gone, but she could not share her birthday, when she had lied to get her job. Still, there were days, when she considered playing with fire. What would it take for Joel to really notice her? In the newspaper business she had discovered that a rare few men were as attracted to brains as well as beauty. Maybe he was one of them. She would make it a point to read Roshi's history suggestion and start to read the Proust volumes. It might take a while, but in the meantime she could apply for the job of literary columnist. Heaven only knew what a useless writing exercise the social column was.

Fortunately, for the next while she would be too busy to consider a new job. Ernesto and Paulo, her cousins, were to arrive in Havana soon. She had never met these cousins who, for years, had been in boarding school in Switzerland. However, she had been shown photos of two very handsome young men, photos she was told did not do them justice. She wondered, if they were cousins distant enough to date. They belonged to the country club set and knew all the right people, so she would be invited everywhere without the newspaper title as entrée. Havana was a small place, where one needed the proper connections. Between the social page events and her cousins, she expected to be busy and might even need new clothes. Life was more exciting with every year that went by, but it was good that the war was over. Happily, for the most part, the men of Cuba had not been involved.

Anais did not believe in war. She had seen too much of it in her own home while growing up. Anger begot more anger, and an eye for an eye would leave the world blind in the end. She knew this to be accurate because her heart told her so.

She wondered about Roshi in Paris. What was this clandestine work he did that kept him occupied with peace conferences? He seemed more like someone who would work at a bank, but what did she really know about him? He did not sound all that relieved now that the war was over. She believed it was fortunate she knew no one who had had to fight in the war or who had been injured or killed. In her mind Paris existed as a still life, framed the way it was, when she left there years ago. Roshi was a mystery to her, a precious secret that she kept close to her heart, but it was important that he now lived in Paris.

For Anais, unexpected fears or exaggeration might develop without advance warning; it was one of the problems that came with creative inspiration. The abandonment of her father and his supreme indifference had caused an open wound from which she had never recovered. The attention of a surrogate father like Roshi gave her new hope. When she heard from Roshi, the demons of her past melted away. Her soul and spirit came together and gave her reason to want to live authentically. Strangely enough, the kind of attention she received from him was opposed to the fight she normally engaged in with herself. His quiet acceptance, steadfast avoidance of fantasy and powerful presence, was what she could count on; and his friendship had given her a mature view of the world beyond the confines of childhood.

"The song wafted past her and over the hedge, lingeringly.

Inside of her it penetrated sweetly and painfully. Something was worth crying for; something in the song."

—Nin *Timelessness*

Chapter 20
The Cousins Arrive in Cuba

Ernesto and Paulo swept into town, two confident and somewhat superior young men who commanded the ground on which they walked. They had been excellent students, privileged and popular. They excelled in sports, had money to burn and were expected to make the right alliances for the benefit of the family. Anais was from a poor and sketchy background. Her handsome and artistic father had not only been a musician, they were told, but of slippery and unreliable character. Anais was charming and beautiful, they were warned, but not for them. They could play around but not for keeps. They understood. Until the first dance at the club.

She walked in, and the room went still for just long enough to cause a sensation. Everyone wanted to know who she was, her family connections, and her money. It was over before it began, but the boys had been enchanted. She walked like silk sliding off a divan and held herself like a princess. She smiled with a fey and knowing smile that captured their curiosity, and there was plenty of curiosity combined with testosterone in the room. None of these young men had been to war, and their surplus energy was tangible.

Anais heard snippets of conversation as she made her way through the room after her cousins had introduced themselves and brought her a glass of wine. She recognized the same topics that concerned Roshi. The older men were concerned that the peace treaty would not work and debated the consequences for Cuba and Spain. The younger men were overly supplied with hormones. At seventeen, she recognized the differences and felt that she could manipulate any man in the room. Her perception gave her a certain confidence.

It would seem that, except for Roshi, Anais had raised herself. She was her own parent, a young woman who had launched herself into the work world with a savvy beyond her age. The moment thoughts of work entered her mind, she happened to look up and into the eyes of her boss. At work she simply called him sir, when she infrequently had the opportunity to address him at all. She did know his name was Joel Seaborn and that he was first and foremost an American and a patriot. She was told that he came from the East Coast establishment, Boston to be exact. Their meeting at the country club was awkward.

"Good evening, sir."

"It's Joel at a party like this. You are the talk of the evening, my dear, and I'm told those two puffed up young men are your cousins."

Just the use of Joel's first name felt intimate, and she lowered her eyes.

"Distant cousins. This is the first time I have met them. As you know, I grew up in Paris then lived in the United States. Except for boarding schools, I believe my cousins have lived right here in Havana."

"Well, they're both drooling, as are most of the men in this room."

"Does that bother you?"

"I still think you're under age. Tell the truth."

This time she lowered her eyes with a knowing smile.

"Believe me, I'm not too young."

"Really?"

"You know, I've been wanting to talk to you about the possibility of a job change."

"You really are a work of art. I suppose you want a raise or you'll threaten to leave us."

"Actually, I would like to be the literary columnist. I would do a much better job than what passes for a literary column right now."

"Mind you, that wouldn't be hard. Show me a few pieces, and I'll decide from there. This, I must say, puts you in a whole new light."

"How so?"

"Beauty and brains. That's a lethal combination." He looked over her shoulder. "One of your age-appropriate admirers approaches, so I'll just move along."

With that, Joel turned abruptly and was gone. In his place Ernesto towered over her with another drink and a somewhat inebriated smile.

"Let's take in the sights of Havana tomorrow. I have the car, and it's Sunday. You can tell me what you think of this party, and we can even go to the beach. I'll pick you up in time for lunch."

Then he, too, was gone, distracted by the ever louder antics of the party. She wondered, if he would remember the invitation, when he woke up tomorrow. She was glad he was gone because she wished to savor the longest conversation she had had with Joel in months. She wished he was the one who had offered to drive her around the city. She didn't think hers was an over active imagination, but she certainly felt a strong attraction to her boss. Now, she had to get home and write a few sample literary columns. She had done it! She had found the moment and the courage to ask for a job change.

Ambition does not eliminate sincerity. Anais was both sincere and ambitious. She was not a conventional young woman whose past had followed the normal route. Rejection would, however, have been a tragic event in her development. A job change meant a greater acceptance of her writing skills, her talent that attached her to her diary life, which, in turn, attached to the development of a core, a center from which literary roots might sprout and grow.

***

That morning she awoke early and had written of Cervantes' *Don Quixote* until her own head was tilting windmills. The next person she would write about was the upcoming D. H. Lawrence. If she became a literary columnist, her budget would include hardback copies of books she wished to review, and that would be her bonus.

When Ernesto showed up, looking somewhat worse after the homecoming celebration, she was ready with a picnic and a swimsuit. She could sit by the sea and enjoy it like a true water sign. She was a Pisces though she rarely had time for something as frivolous as a day at the beach; she didn't even know how to swim.

She soon discovered it was very different to see Havana by car. Ernesto had a convertible sports coupe with the top down. They wore hats and sunglasses and laughed a lot while she recounted stories about the party. Though he was dashing and sophisticated, she thought of him as young, when he was older than her by a year? He drove a bit recklessly, but she didn't mind. They saw panoramic views of the city and found his favorite beach. Obviously, it was a local favorite, for everyone was there. To think, in a year she'd never known it existed. She had packed a picnic with lemonade and sandwiches on fresh baguettes and had a chance to show off the bathing suit she had never had the chance to wear.

"I can't believe you've never been here in over a year."

"Well, I'm a working girl, you know. I've been with the newspaper nearly a year, I'm learning Spanish, and I try to keep up my studies."

"Why bother? You could be having fun down here. Your Spanish is remarkably good, actually."

They had been speaking Spanish, once Anais realized it was his mother tongue, and he was more comfortable speaking Spanish than English.

"You must have missed Havana, during all those years away."

"I did. Now, I have no intention of leaving. Papa is glad I'm home, too. He needs me at the bank. The Coca-Cola Company is the biggest employer on this island, and he wants to groom me to work with them."

"Is that what you want to do?"

"Sure. Why not? It's ready made. I'm privileged to be here and part of my family again. I'm the oldest now that Juan is gone. He was killed in the war."

Perhaps he was not as young as he pretended to be. A shadow of the Great War crossed the beach and disappeared.

He wanted to teach her to swim, and it was her first time in the ocean, her first swim lesson and the first time in her life, when she could act her own age. It was a strange feeling, and she felt quite unsure. Ernesto laughed at her and called her a little mother. He splashed water at her, and she rolled over and over in the surf, trying to get her footing while sputtering and coughing. They kicked at the sand and joined in a beach ball game. She had never thrown or caught a ball in her life and missed every throw. The men thought she was a doll, and everyone wanted to help her learn to catch a ball, a big pie-wedged colorful ball. For an entire afternoon she was a child, a seventeen-year-old, who had not graduated from high school, whose whole world had been serious while others avoided their studies for sunshine or played after school instead of cleaning house or starting dinner.

Mama and Aunt Eveline had gone off to church that morning, glad they were not at work. Instead, they were in a place where they would kneel to listen to the priest who would inform them that they needed improvement. They worshiped because the Mass reminded them that they were unworthy. Anais preferred to be kicking sand on the beach.

She lay on the blanket, as the sun slowly lowered to the horizon and did not want the day to end. The breeze caressed her shoulders and her nearly dried swimsuit. With her ear down she could feel the ocean waves through the sand, hear the muffled laughter of those preparing to leave the beach, sense the presence of children who never wanted the day to end, and understand parents who did not want to go back to work tomorrow. This is what she had missed growing up. She felt happiness mixed with a great longing for something she had never had, as she watched Ernesto who was sleeping like a child. They had had fun, an experience she had not known until this afternoon. She looked at her cousin, who was truly innocent of her world, and thanked him silently for giving her this gift. He was her cousin and, as far as she was concerned, he was now her good friend, her best friend in Havana.

The next morning, she handed the first sample of a literary column to Joel who glanced up, surprised, as she slipped it on his desk. She went about her work on the social column, and wrote about the country club party. Names were mentioned, clothes remembered and conversations repeated, anonymously. Even the undercurrent of unrest expressed by those older men who never expected to be listened to, such as comments about the Scope's trial in the United States, were included. Everything she could remember was important. The social crowd did not want to appear bubble-headed; the fashionistas did not want to feel ignored; and the society leaders did not want to seem frivolous. She touched on them all with a cleverness that made the party sound like the social event of the year. She handed in her column and prepared to leave for the day.

As she passed Joel's office, she noted he was still there. She wondered, if he was always the last to leave. It occurred to her that, perhaps, this was his whole life. Until this weekend, when she had been a child on a beach, this thought might never have occurred to her. He glanced up and asked her to stop, and for some reason she nearly tiptoed into his office.

"This is damned good." He held up her account of the wandering knight, Quixote. "You've got the job."

"Pardon me?"

"You've got the job." He stared at her. "I could have sworn you were high school age, but you're not, are you?"

She stared back at him. "Thank you."

"You're welcome. You start tomorrow morning, so I suggest we celebrate this evening."

He closed the ledger on his desk, turned off the light, came around to where she stood, immobile, in the doorway, took her arm, then led her down the hallway and out into the gentle warmth of Havana's darkened streets.

It was magical, and it was her first date. At age seventeen she had her own column at work and a promotion. She smelled the sweet smell of overly lush vegetation carried on the breeze, as it infiltrated this exciting city set by the sea. Everything grew here, she noted, and so had she. Maybe leaving New York hadn't been so bad after all. They passed clubs that were warming up for a long riff. Music, slow and jazzy, drifted and enticed. They kept walking. She might be underage, but he was taking no chances.

Another two blocks and he stopped in front of a lovely French restaurant.

"Mademoiselle?"

He let her pass first into a charming, white table-clothed room, and it delighted her. Candles were just being lit at the tables, and only a few customers were there. It was early for dinner in Cuba, but it was already dark, and the candlelight made it seem like their private rendezvous. She knew intuitively that Joel had changed his mind about her. She might still confuse him about her age, but she was now older than he had first assumed. One year could change everything except the lie. Not only was he her first true date, she was with a man, a real gentleman, handsome and brilliant. She thought, looking at him as he studied the menu, "I'm in love."

They talked.

"What do you think of Cuba now that you have been here over a year?"

"It's heady to have a good job, fun and a newfound family. It's so different from New York there is no comparison. And you, do you like it here?"

"Sure, why not? Like you say, it has a tropical island *je ne sais quoi.* A person could get used to it. I don't want to live here forever, but you probably don't want to either. Am I right?"

She nodded. She listened. They laughed together, and she felt more relaxed.

At home that evening, Anais closed her bedroom door and sat on the small balcony alone. It was her own sanctuary, a small space of her own. It had started to rain just as she got off the bus, so she had run the block to their apartment. She didn't have that many outfits for work that she could afford to ruin one. On the balcony it was different; it poured, and she curled up on her chair with a shawl and her diary and thought of her new job description and Joel Seaborn. She listened to the raindrops on the overhead awning and wondered if anyone could have two lives with only one heart. It was a strange thought, but maybe it was the nature of love to indulge in strange reveries.

She loved the way it rained in Havana with a tropical impatience that belied the languorous days of steamy heat. When it rained, it was mostly in the evenings. It left the streets clean, the houses washed, the vegetation revived and the locals energized for hours. She smelled the earth come alive and refreshed as she, too, felt energized. She imagined the street women of the night who would carry on a brisk business this evening. The bars would be crowded and the men on the prowl. For a few moments she tried to imagine what it would be like to be a mysterious call girl, unafraid, free of inhibition and willing to use her body in a parody of love.

She imagined Joel as her lover and nearly swooned with the feelings that overwhelmed her. But one heart, two lives, was that possible? For instance, one life during the day, another after dark. Is that what the thought implied? Was it possible to be so dishonest? Or was such a thought the very purest essence of honesty. Aside from whores, who else might live like this? Now her curiosity was piqued. Was it true that only mischief could occur in the early hours of the morning? These were thoughts that had come out of nowhere, but like a reporter after a story, she stayed with her thoughts and wrote them down. One day she would research the phenomenon of honesty and dishonesty, dual lives and only one heart to share.

She believed like Henry James that the purpose of a novel was to help the heart. To this end she dedicated her life in her writing. If only she could be a writer someday to create order, to overcome inner struggles and to nourish those who read her stories and between the lines. If only she could be graceful and express reality through language that ignored restrictions and flowed beyond convention.

Cuba, she discovered, attracted people whose lives were at an impasse. Death was part of the past and present, the historic and current, night and day. Decay and ruins described both an inner and outer landscape. What she loved about writing was that it could combine all the other forms of art: the painter, sculptor, dramatist, and fortuneteller. The writer was a kind of detective and certainly a voyeur who impersonated what she saw and heard, felt and smelled. Even the rhythm of life could be captured on paper. The only inhibition for her as a writer was the fear of exposure, which is the same as resistance to truth. She aspired to make her future newspaper articles exercises in honesty and revelation.

Chapter 21
Joel

Joel Seaborn was indeed handsome. He was thirty-two years old and had put in his time in France as a news correspondent, during the First World War. He was an American blue blood to the core, whose family had tried to stop him from serving in the war. As an only son with powerful connections, it would have been easy to stay home. Unfortunately, all of his friends at Harvard had waited to sign up the day they graduated, and he had done the same.

Nothing could have prepared him for the endless mud, the trenches, the continual sniping, and the bombs. Traumatized to his core, he would forever remember the severed limbs and the bloody innards strewn from tree limb to bunker wall. Yet, strangely enough, what he would never forget was the absence of trees. The few that stood, barren of leaves, were haunted by the infernal noise, the gases, and the stench. He still took out his camera occasionally, and what he had come home with was photo after photo of trees: trees devoid of color or leaves, trees reaching for the heavens, their limbs imploring that sanity be returned to the earth. In Havana his spare moments were spent in jungle areas, where trees whose names were unknown to him, grew in profusion. Other times he wrote poetry of war heroism. He was no famous war poet, but he understood the cruel beauty in the terrible violence he had witnessed. Like other poets, he searched for meaning in order to understand the senseless struggle that smudged the lenses of his camera. He searched in vain.

He had done such a good job with the photographs he sent back to stateside magazines that he was offered a number of prestigious positions, when he returned, visibly unharmed, from the graveyard that was northern France. He had turned them down in favor of a newspaper editor in a country where trees still grew, uninhabited by terror. Here, no one thought much of Europe. It was quiet, forgotten and forgettable.

Now, he was beset by a young woman with big doe-eyes and ambition. He was cynical enough to believe he was being played for a sucker, but injured enough to wish it were not so. He recognized something in those eyes that reminded him of his own trauma, but he could not put into words what it might be. She was more than just a good actress; what he saw was real. She couldn't be as young as he had first suspected. No teenager could have written of D. H. Lawrence or Cervantes in such depth. He was planning to see her again because, if she was as old as she said, she knew the score. Until now, no woman had tempted him. Empty heads and frivolous pursuits did not appeal to his aesthetics or his post-war emotions. Anais was certainly beautiful, but it was the panache, the spirit and the intellect he admired. Why not? Why not give her a try?

***

Ernesto drove along the coast, alone, with the convertible top down and glad to be home. Though he had been in boarding school, the last few years had held a tension that was hard to shake. The school had emptied gradually, as parents pulled their sons out to return to their countries of origin. It was an international school, and most prominent parents were savvy about the complications of war, how easily a country could get involved and how close Switzerland was to the center of the insane chaos that had struck otherwise quiet towns and cattle-like civilians. Even now, with the peace accord signed, he knew in his bones it was not over. It might take a decade or two, but the war momentum would build again. No, it was not over, but he wished no part in it.

In his heart he was an artist and, god forbid his parents should find out, he was also homosexual. This new discovery had him shaking in his shoes. He had to come to terms with it and kept it a secret, for if his parents found out, he would not be next in line to manage his father's bank. Even his brother did not know, and no one suspected. He had to back off, think, pretend and keep his nose clean. It occurred to him that being seen with Anais might be the perfect foil.

She was a beauty, well spoken, every guy's dream and his cousin. They could be good friends but, if talk about them became messy, they could say they were family and put a stop to speculation. She didn't have to know. She might not know what it meant, even if he were to confide in her. In Cuba, where everyone was Catholic and Spanish speaking, things could go very badly for him, if this were to get out. Even his artistic tendencies needed to be kept under wrap, at least for many years to come. He thought of Damien, the lover who had initiated him to his true self, and he wanted to cry. He had had to be left behind, sacrificed. Their arrangement was that he would try to get back to the Swiss French Alps to ski each winter. Then they would be together. It nearly broke his heart to leave, to warn Damien to never show up in Havana. He was too over the top, emotional and sensitive. Ernesto wished him a good life, but living together was not a possibility.

The more he thought about the details, the more he wondered, if the future for him would be similar to a jail sentence. Time would tell. He drove along until he came to the cliffs, stopped his car, and sat gazing far below at the incoming tide, as waves crashed higher and higher. His current life felt like a leap into the unknown. He felt like a young albatross about to fly, knowing he was not an ordinary seabird, knowing he would be required to hold his wings out and fly for days and miles, miles and months, alone with his heart.

***

Roshi sat in his study on the boulevard de Raspail. It was not the most chic quartier, but his was a vast and rambling apartment. He was not sure why he felt the need for so much space, but it was decorated in classic French décor and provided him with sitting room, library, several guest suites, though he hated having overnight guests, and a dining room fit for a diplomat. In some ways he considered himself an unofficial diplomat. There was enough room in his apartment for secrecy, enough order and beauty to allow his secret intelligence friends some peace of mind, and enough elegance to attract all things artistic and uplifting. He was a great supporter of the arts and felt that art was a need that belonged to the human spirit, that it inspired and freed one from the clutches of chaos and disorder. Beauty, he believed, as had Plato, was necessarily orderly. Mind you, he was also of the same mind as Aristotle, who did not question the experience of beauty but, rather, the understanding of abstract and intellectually sublime beauty. For Roshi, it was not a question of Kantian either/or, but of beauty and order together. He was truly a Renaissance person, his interests vast and his opinions not to be pinned down. The one thing he did acknowledge was that each person was entitled to his or her own opinion, and it was not necessary to flout these opinions or insist that others think in the same way.

He walked quietly through the empty rooms and thought of Anais. He wondered what she looked like now or if she continued her studies. He was quite proud that she had been hired for the new job as literary columnist. It was a step up and more in keeping with the young woman he remembered. Perhaps, he decided, he would have someone take a photo of her to send to him. He continued to wire an allowance that he suspected she banked, sensing that she would save it for something special. She spoke of Joel Seaborn, and Roshi had had his friends check up on his background. Impeccable lineage. If there was a problem, it was the fact that he was socially above Anais and the confines of her world. Certainly, his parents would never find her acceptable. He hated to think Joel might be toying with Anais. At the same time he knew she was bound to make mistakes; no one avoided such things. Roshi was nothing like the father she never should have had, and he sincerely wanted to protect her.

Chapter 22
Christolphe

Christolphe got off the boat and felt a blast of humid air embrace him. He had been to Cuba once as a child and remembered the feeling of being enveloped in a heavy layer of moist warm air. It was reminiscent of winter holidays, when he was a privileged and coddled child. Though they had recently left him modestly cared for, he had grieved until he was so tired of his own grief, he had decided to get on with his life. Christolphe was by nature an optimistic person. He believed it was a genetic inheritance from his parents who had been easy going and very much in love.

What he really wanted to do was make films. Someday. He got off the ship in Havana with an entire trunk filled with his photographic equipment. In the meantime, because he had also inherited a streak of practicality, he would work in a bank. In fact, he enjoyed his bank job and had risen through the ranks to get another promotion. He figured this next position at the bank was an important step. It would prove he was willing to relocate, if asked, and he was still single and free to do so. He knew that, within the next few years, a wife would be an asset most desirable. Therefore, while he was in beautiful Havana, he hoped to find a suitable wife, someone who would support his aspirations. If any of these plans sounded too calculating, Christolphe looked at them somewhat differently. It was not to say that he thought everyone had a responsibility to think his way, it was simply a broader outlook that took up considerable room in his mind. He was often aware that life could be cut short at any moment, despite the fact that he had never gone to war. As an only child with parents to support, he had not been required to do so, therefore he chose not to fight. However, it made him grateful for the opportunity to direct his own life, and he liked to see his efforts pay off.

Representatives of the bank met him, as he disembarked. It was this civilized consideration that he appreciated about his employment. They oversaw the transportation of his trunks and were soon on their way. The apartment that had been leased on his behalf was spacious with high ceilings and elegant old world decorative plaster and chandeliers. A few basic pieces of furniture had been left behind, including a dining room table that could fit enough people to entertain in the manner he wished. Yes, a hostess was his main priority in these next few years. He introduced himself properly to the doorman, Carlo, leaning forward in a stately way to shake the fellow's hand.

"Good to meet you, Carlo. I hope to brush up on some Spanish while I'm here. Perhaps you will tutor me a bit."

He smiled graciously, and Carlo was instantly won over.

"It's nice to meet you, *Senor*. I'll have one of the men help with your luggage while I show you the apartment."

They rode up to the third floor in an open ironwork-scrolled elevator to the top floor.

"I love it. This is perfect. Oh, and the view!"

Christolphe stepped out on the balcony and breathed in the sea air. Hibiscus grew in profusion in pots. Someone had continued to water the plants between occupants, and he had noted the well cared for foyer and hallways.

"Well, Carlo, I must say you do a wonderful job of managing this place. I'm really going to like it here. *Gracias.*"

"Here comes your luggage, *Senor*. Next, we'll have to find you a beautiful Cuban wife."

"Keep on the lookout, my friend." They both laughed.

Christolphe was a poet in his heart. He had once heard it said that the artist was immune to the inner turmoil of the mentally ill. For some reason the brain of the creative person circumvented ordinary cares and concerns with solutions that reached into the limitless reservoir of humanity's pool of answers. Christolphe knew he could be a banker, follow his passions in poetic filmmaking, and still be able to afford a wife. Anything was possible, and he looked forward to every day. Neither boarding schools, parents, nor or a strict and moralistic extended family had been able to curb his optimism.

Chapter 23
Her First Love

Joel was her first love. The fact that he was also her boss never fazed Anais. There were some things that youth could not anticipate, that the bruises of experience would sort out eventually. She was young and indomitable, as youth are meant to be, greatly attracted to him and the fact that he was older. His age only made him more exciting. The fact that she would always chose men who were older never troubled her mind. For now, she was a giddy young woman who had fallen in love, that vat of insanity referred to by Freud and Jung as love psychosis. She was crazy in love.

After their dinner to celebrate her raise in status and increased pay at the newspaper, she went home and dreamed fine dreams. It wasn't until the next morning, Saturday, that she told Mama and Aunt Eveline about her enlarged circumstances. Mama said she would sew her some new clothes in keeping with her new status. Aunt Eveline said it was cause for an elegant new purse and shoes. Even her brothers seemed happy for her. Of course, the fact that she would bring home more money meant that her youngest brother could continue his piano lessons. It seemed that he had inherited both looks and talent from Papa. Both of her brothers would break hearts one day. The two of them spoke only Spanish, now; so between them, her mother and aunt, she was forced to change her orientation at home to Spanish. At times, it made her feel homeless. But today was not the time to think about it. She would write an article for the paper about Marcel Proust. She was in the middle of reading *Swann's Way* and decided her articles for the column could be a series about the life of its author followed by certain volumes that might interest her readers. That way, even if the articles were interspersed with other articles about other books or authors, there would be created a kind of suspense, as readers waited for the next Proustian installment.

As soon as everyone left the house for work or sports, she sat at her little desk in her bedroom and began to write. She had never been this happy. She was doing a job for which she was perfectly suited; she had found a real man, someone who was attracted to her mind, with a chemistry between them that was irresistible. She didn't care about all the Catholic tradition that dictated virginity and double standards of morality. She would let him do whatever he wished with her, as she squirmed at her desk and felt herself melting everywhere just imagining what that might be like. Later today, she wanted to finish another literary article before she had to clean house or run errands. The day was hers to write and dream between household tasks. The evening would be devoted to spending precious time with her diary.

She also wanted to dwell on the strange and wonderful writing of D. H. Lawrence, an author who was little known, unappreciated and even snubbed. His writing had touched her with a desire to free herself from puritanism and validated her own desire to live intensely. She wanted to experience life fully in Cuba, make a name for herself and thrive. In a sense Lawrence had awakened her to herself, and she loved him for it, worshipped his wisdom and hoped, sincerely, that she might meet him one day. It was an unusual focus of hero worship for such a young woman.

***

The next afternoon Ernesto picked her up and they drove with the top down, carefree and happy, to the beach, once again, to watch the sun set as they sat on the sand. They talked of family members, known and unknown to them, and the stories they remembered that had been handed down in the family. Ernesto confided his secret desire to be an artist. Then, he said something that made no sense. It haunted her later.

"My whole life must be a secret."

"Yes, we all have our secrets."

"Not as forbidden as mine."

"You must keep a diary, Ernesto. Some days, when I felt so alone, I am sure my diary kept me alive. It was my best friend."

He nodded to her but said no more about secrets. She sincerely hoped he had not done something so bad it would cause him to feel guilty for the rest of his life. The nice thing was that they were becoming friends. He was easy to be with, and she felt like she could tell him anything she imagined she could tell a girlfriend, except he was not a girl.

It was dark by the time they got home, and the family teased her about having a boyfriend.

"But Aunty, he's my cousin."

"Oh, I wouldn't worry about that. He's what we call a marrying cousin. Many women on this island are married to distant cousins."

"Well, it's not like that. We're friends."

Everyone thought that comment funny.

It wasn't until the following week, when Joel asked her on a date and showed up at the apartment to pick her up that all the fun and laughter ceased.

"He's too old for you, Anais."

"Mama, you are hardly the one to give advice on love matters."

She knew her words were cruel, but it was the truth, as far as she was concerned.

They went to dinner at a place that had a small band. They ate and she had red wine with dinner. Then, they danced for hours. She loved to dance, and he seemed like a different person, when he danced. He laughed and let the music take him to a happier place. She saw another side to him that she was glad to see. He was not serious all the time, and it also meant they had a love of music in common. Women watched him and looked at her with envy in their eyes. They danced in sync, as though they had done so all their lives. They were good together. As they danced they became aware of each other's hips and loins, the movements of their bodies beneath their clothes and the heat of coming together and parting. In their dance talk Anais had the feeling of absorbing her partner and becoming one with him. This was more than sex and more like a state of oneness that made sex feel like an afterthought in comparison.

Back home, he kissed her in the car in front of the apartment. It was her first kiss and rapidly turned into a passionate embrace. She adored every moment of what she later wrote of in her diary, as 'his worship of her body.' His kisses touched her body and soul, and she would have offered him more, if the setting had been more conducive.

At work they were too busy to continue a romance. They restricted their relationship to weekends, but it didn't take too many of those before they became lovers, as she had hoped. She was not yet eighteen, but girls married very young in this part of the world, she rationalized. If he asked her to marry him, she would accept in a second. But he did not ask and never made allusions to the future. When she asked him about his family, he shrugged. There was not much to say. They were Bostonians, the most boring people in the most stuffy city in the world, he told her. Some days she could get him to talk about his studies at Harvard, and she told him she might study at the Sorbonne someday.

"Good for you."

That was his response. How could she do that, if they were married, she wondered? Maybe he had future travel plans in mind, but it made no sense. One day, he said, if he never saw France again, it would be too soon. She loved France, so his off-handed comment gave her a turn. Pieces of her house of cards were slipping. Small hints like the one about France played over and over in her mind, until there was a desperation that entered their lovemaking. Once he cried and said he loved her. It would seem that the little deaths she brought him shook his world.

It must be the spiral path of love, she told herself. Love was not smooth or easy. Everyone knew this. It was a cliché for heaven's sake. But in her tormented heart, Anais knew something was amiss, when her secret eighteenth birthday came and went without an engagement ring. It was time to say something, but first she wrote to Roshi, pouring out her heart about her doubts.

My Dear Friend,

How I hate to burden you with my troubles, but I am beginning to feel desperate. You know about Joel. I have shared with you all I know of his life except for pillow talk. I adore him, and now I wait for him to ask me to marry him, but the subject, I begin to realize, is constantly avoided. He side steps it, and I don't know why. He loves me. What can it be, Roshi? I must confide in you that I am eighteen, in love and pregnant. There, I've said it. I'm sure of my condition, but I truly don't want to tell Joel or force him to marry me. Never that. I do not wish to begin married life with recriminations. As you know, I watched helplessly, as my parents grew to despise each other. I could not bear to inflict such a situation on any child of mine. I feel, that if Joel does not ask me to marry him soon, I must do something desperate.

Meanwhile, I ask your advice though I am afraid, with the slowness of the mail, that I may have to make adult decisions alone. It feels like a terrifying admission price to the world of grownups. Mama and Evaline are hopeless. Do not suggest that I talk to them.

Ever your friend,

Anais

She posted the letter the next morning on her way to work. She had awakened with a plan. She would never go through with this pregnancy, if he did not intend to marry her, so she had to find out. As soon as she arrived at work, she left a note at his desk, asking to see him.

**

They sat at their favorite restaurant that evening in a quiet alcove with a bottle of wine. It was the scene of their first date on the day he had appointed her as literary columnist.

"Do you love me, Joel? I must know because I'm feeling sad and vulnerable."

He hesitated and, in that nearly imperceptible pause, she read rejection.

"Of course I do, Anais, it's just that…"

"What are you trying to say? I'm not too young to hear it, you know. Look around you. Half the girls in Cuba my age are about to be married."

"Is that what you want, marriage?"

"Of course it is. We cannot continue this way. There could be consequences."

"Not as bad as if my parents got wind of our affair. As it is, my mother has heard rumors all the way up in Boston."

"But at your age you can do whatever you want, can't you Joel?"

He bowed his head.

"Don't you understand, Anais? It's more complicated than that. I'm…I'm not well. It wouldn't be fair to you or us."

She felt a shock course through her.

"What's wrong with you?"

"It's all in my head, my dear. Can't you tell? Why do you think this brilliant and promising Harvard graduate, nearly age thirty-three, is moldering in this godforsaken outpost in this nothing position?"

"But you have a wonderful job and…"

"…and you are young and naïve."

"But I love you, Joel. Does that not count for anything?"

"Not enough."

She hadn't meant to say it, but she felt compelled, outside herself, as though she was looking on at a stranger.

"Would it be enough, if I was pregnant with your child?"

"Oh, God, no."

He put his hands to his face, and she knew he cried.

"No, it would be worse. I have been traumatized by war, Anais. It's called shell shock. Do you know what that means? It means my head is full of strange sights and sounds, and my mind is no longer my own. I am a danger to myself, to you and certainly to an innocent child. Get rid of it, Anais. You're too young to end your life."

* * *

So this is how love ended. One minute their fascination was so intense, their imagination, and potential so creative that a child was conceived. The next minute it was rejected, thrown away, and denied. She knew she would never bring a child into this world to be exposed to such hurtful indifference.

She felt sorry for Joel, sorry for herself, sorry for the unknown soul, whose sobs she could hear right next to her heart. She took a handkerchief from her purse and dried her eyes, grateful that they sat in a secluded alcove.

Was it possible for a heart to break in two?

So maybe this is what it meant to have to live with one heart. For one crazy second she considered taking on the burden of an infant, alone and without Joel. Blackness overwhelmed her, and she felt that she was falling into a dark abyss. This option was the last and farthest thought from her mind. Just a few months ago, she had had dreams on a precious evening alone on her balcony. That evening, she had been filled with the sensuous possibilities of a tropical rainstorm and an innocent belief that her thoughts were merely those of an artist. Now, just months later, the realization that one heart might of necessity be responsible for two lives had taken on new meaning.

Her heart was heavy with the knowledge that Joel was sick. She had heard the horror stories of shell shock, even in her sheltered and short life. He said he had horrible thoughts, that violence played in his head and that he was only in Cuba, hiding from the real world, as though this was an inferior post, and he was disgusted with his own mind that could, hereafter, never be controlled.

Yes, she was young, she admitted, and Joel's job had seemed glamorous and important in her eyes. His handsome appearance, his cynical grown-up attitude, his background and education, these had all seemed superior and refined. How could she have had a relationship with nothing more than the shell of a person? How could their lovemaking have not revealed the truth?

That is when she remembered his tears. She had had the delusional thought that they were about her, an outpouring of pure and loving emotion. Now, she saw them as fears. Cynicism was also fear. She saw it clearly now, and though she loved him, she would not subject a child to a father so full of destructive fears. Isn't that what she experienced in her own childhood? She, too, understood trauma, the wounds of abuse along with the numbness and fear that closed off the heart. She felt sorry for his pain and his inability to reconcile his injuries with the person he thought he could and should be in the world. She had had years to deal with her own wounds but, with only one heart, she needed to survive. It was all she could do to survive.

Suddenly, Anais saw herself in the extensive line-up of women around the world whose violation of self was unavoidable. This was the paradox of the dance she so loved. From the oneness of souls came the frightening, inseparable spirit that could only become itself again after being broken. Was there no alternative? She wanted to be whole; instead, she was not. Even the child that lived in her womb felt like a fragment. God, what was she to do?

Chapter 24
Trouble with Joel

They say trouble comes in threes. Without hesitation or second thought she found someone who would rid her of this unwanted child. It was easy to avoid Joel at the newspaper until two months later, when he called her into his office and had the temerity to ask her how she felt.

"What do you mean?"

"Do you not have morning sickness? Nothing? I want to help you with expenses or whatever you'll need when you can no longer work."

She stared at him incredulously. For the last decade in North America, women had held down men's jobs, learned male trades and at the same time learned to stand up, fight, vote and go to school. Here was Joel, sounding like someone from another century. She could barely respond.

"Joel, the baby is gone. It's been taken care of. Your responsibilities are non-existent. Surely, you don't think I was waiting in blind despair while you thought of how to conveniently get rid of me?"

She felt anger well up until she nearly choked. It had been buried with grief and depression, but now it erupted until she looked for something to throw at him.

"I don't need you. I have never needed you, and you have thrown our love away. I would never bring a child into this world under such circumstances."

She left work that day and sought her diary. She took a bus to the farthest point of the city by the sea, and she spent the rest of the day, writing in her journal. She grieved for the child she had never known. She knew it had been a little girl, and she would have named her Celeste. Now she was a spirit in the sky, looking for another woman to call mama, and another body that was willing to channel her small person to begin the long and circular wheel of life all over, again.

"I would not have been a good mother to you," she whispered.

Once she had cried until she thought it was impossible to shed another tear, she took out stationery and wrote once more to Roshi. She told him everything. She had to tell someone who would not judge her for letting Celeste go. It was for the best. She had no doubts about it. But suddenly, life in Cuba was tarnished. Her job was no longer an aspiration.

She did not wish to see Joel's face each day or pine for what might have been. She was tired of trauma. She resented the fact that such a phenomenon existed or that it had spoiled her own life. It was time to leave. It was time to go home to Paris. She missed Roshi, and she missed the beloved city of her birth. Escape was the word she used over and over in her diary that day. She would become an escape artist, and once she had determined the possibilities, she desperately wanted change to enter her life.

She could work in Paris as a journalist. She could go to the Sorbonne and be a normal eighteen-year-old. She could leave behind her dreams of love and babies and the dignity of being a prominent and handsome man's wife. She *could* forget this episode in her life, and that is what she intended to do.

***

Roshi sat in his study and read her letter that was laced with sorrow and the desperate need to escape. He knew

Anais and the true fragility beneath this sorrow and anger as well as depleted self-esteem that leaked from her wounds. No matter how she tried to escape, this aborted child would follow her and compound psychic scars left by her father, wounds that had never been dealt with, wounds that would surface time after time in the years ahead, when she least expected it.

He then made a decision. She could live with him, as the daughter he never had, and he would send her to school. Hopefully, she would experience a needed period of normalcy. He would be a father to her, available for as long as she needed him. It was an enormous decision and commitment for a man who lived like a hermit and liked it that way. The responsibility was frightening for one who had never taken a wife or fathered a child. Normally, he was a man who lived between worlds, a kind of bodhisattva come back to earth to help others. Until now, that help had taken the form of diplomacy, secret assignments and war negotiations.

For the people of his nation, the Japanese people, he had been immersed in that aspect of a peace treaty that would allow a port for Japanese access in the Mediterranean. His was an early voice for sanity and racial understanding. He felt, acutely, the tensions in Europe that gathered slowly and fearfully and took form in a desire to obliterate all races that were not white, blue-eyed, and Nordic. He could feel this closed off and fearful attitude infiltrate polite society in silent pauses and rephrased statements that were supposed to be jokes, unless of course you were the object of those subtle jokes. He didn't like what he felt approaching, so why invite Anais to stay with him? He wasn't certain, but he trusted his intuition enough to know that he had to do this because she needed his protection and benevolence. His mind made up, he put pen to paper to respond immediately to her letter.

***

138

While she waited for his letter Anais went to work. She read James Joyce, his concerns with love and chaos, escape, and continuing confusion in what seemed to epitomize her present life. *A Portrait of an Artist* was suddenly poignant to her, she who had never been to Ireland. She wrote of hints of dissociation, thought of Lily for the first time in years, and read installments of the works of Proust.

In her struggle to survive sadness, she had found a book by a man who had caused a stir in the social sciences. Freud insisted that hysteria and just about any other mental malady that affected women was caused by repressed sexuality. Something he said resonated with her, but she attributed it to the fact that he expressed himself so well. She was particularly fascinated with his *Interpretation of Dreams* and made a note to review it, though it was not officially fiction or literature. Certainly, she knew that babies and sexuality were connected, but could the fact that she had aborted her daughter be interpreted as the ultimate sexual repression. She didn't want to think about it just yet. It made her head ache.

***

One day she entered the office to find nearly everyone gone. Many of the lights were off and only a few of the forlorn sat at their desks.

"What's going on?"

Betsy Stafford worked at the desk nearby. She sat there, blowing her nose as if she had been crying.

"You'd think someone died, it's so quiet in here."

"Oh, Anais, how could you not have heard? Joel is dead."

"What?"

Anais fell into her chair and stared into space.

"Dead? How could that be?"

"You really haven't heard a thing, have you? He committed suicide, Anais. He shot himself last night in his car down by the beach."

She heard her own sobs echo in the newsroom. She saw the few who were still left in the room stare at her. They think I am to blame, she realized. I stopped dating him, avoided him and refused to discuss our relationship. She had never had anyone to share this tragedy with and, though she was devastated, she had been silent. She stood and stumbled for the door, knowing she would never return to this room, ever. The bus, on her way home, was nearly as empty as her heart. At this hour of the morning everyone was heading for the city center, not the suburbs. Alone. She sat alone and felt that half of her was disappearing. Disoriented. She managed to get back to the apartment. Empty. No one was home. Like an automaton she packed her bags. No thoughts. Her mind felt broken. So this is how it happened. One minute life is not easy but not that awful, either, the next moment something breaks inside into two pieces or however many. She wasn't sure. The pieces were scattered. She could hear the echo of a gunshot and jolted, as if she had been wounded. No. She was sitting on the edge of her bed, dry-eyed. She could hear the waves beyond the window, as high tide crashed onto the far off shore in an ever predictable and comforting rhythm. She walked through the apartment, automatically turned on the stove, and made a cup of coffee.

She heard the postman in the hallway, as the letter slot opened to deliver a letter that she knew must be from Roshi. It landed on the floor, and she stood over it, staring and staring. She already knew what it said. Yes, she read, she was welcome to live in Paris at his apartment. They could discuss the details when she arrived. There was an open ticket for the shipping line that still had boats leaving for Europe. She picked up the phone and booked passage for that same evening. Roshi had sent a first-class ticket via one of the world's most luxurious lines.

"No problem, *Mademoiselle*. We will send someone to collect you and your luggage in three hours."

What would she have done without Roshi? She sat down to write notes of farewell to Mama and Aunt Eveline and the boys. Then she wrote a letter to the new editor of the newspaper, whomever that might be, ending her employment. She also wrote to Ernesto. Though she hadn't known him very long, he had become a friend, someone who made no demands on her as a woman. He had come to her rescue after the abortion, but he respected her privacy. That was all. There was no one else to say goodbye to. Two years, a dead baby, a dead ex-lover, a job, and a fluency in Spanish: she reviewed her assets like an accountant, her thoughts automatic and rigid. She was glad she would avoid the tears and histrionics, the farewells and efforts to change her mind. One suitcase held her diaries, her notes for her next column and her favorite books. She walked to the bank and emptied her saving's account, bought necessities for the trip, dressed, and was ready to leave, when the limousine picked her up. They sailed with no delays and, as she watched Havana disappear on the horizon, she felt her inner collapse begin. By the time Mama found and read her note, she would be well out to sea. She determined to speak only French on the ship. She would pretend she could speak nothing else.

Was it true that naked truth was unbearable? If she built a fortress around herself, could she block out all feeling and lose herself in a cocoon of false illusions? Could part of herself have been lost forever in a grave with a man who had chosen the ultimate escape along with their unborn child?

"From now on our travels will have to be inner voyages."

—Nin *Collages*

Chapter 25
Escape to Paris

It was not difficult to stay alone each day. Her cabin suite was luxurious and there were few passengers on board. It seemed that everyone recognized trauma these days. She was not the first to lose someone; she wouldn't be the last. The passengers held themselves like stoics. They stood as though they wore braces. She declined meals at the captain's table and took walks around the deck after dark. The music on board was mostly jazz, a music that had gained more acceptance and some popularity since the war. For some it was too disturbing a sound; others loved the release they felt and the knowledge that the music could reach inside and speak to them. She could hear the saxophone from the deck and sat in the shadows, listening for some kind of reprieve from her brokenness, but it never happened. She tried to think of a new life in Paris, but her mind was a blank.

She could barely remember yesterday. With each passing mile the past took on a cinematic cast. The years seemed to evaporate like early morning mist. Sometimes she took a blanket up on deck and watched the stars, comforted to know that one of those stars belonged to her. She thought the night sky gave her a new perspective. The stars were like the future, the unknown, bright and very beautiful.

One day, she stopped crying, stopped writing in her diary and lived in the soothing moment of the rise and fall of the deck in gentle waters.

In the future she would live as she pleased rather than try to fit herself in to accepted social patterns. Like the jazz she heard playing, she would improvise, and whatever fate she encountered would be the sound of her own hard-won character. Adventure and danger might come with the territory, but she preferred it to that of deadly confines.

***

A limousine awaited her in Marseille, and there she sat as it smoothly took her north, quietly and quickly, along roads that toured through the central heart of the country, through places she had never seen or heard of in a country that, for her, had once consisted of only Paris and its narrow streets. Farmers were hard at work, unobstructed for the first time in years. The country was hungry. Baguettes that came from the once abundant wheat crops were in demand, and there was not a season to lose. In France, as in other war-torn countries, women had been recruited to take the place of men who had been killed or injured. Out in the fields, they worked in any direction she looked. They wore aprons and clogs, sunhats and babies slung over their backs. France suffered from a shortage of men and children. Old people walked from field to field, knowing it would take the next decade to recover. For Anais, this was the first time in her life that war seemed real. Those who walked by with post war strides told her more of their injuries than all the newsreels she had watched. She wondered what her own gait told of her story.

The landscape blurred and receded into the past. How easy it was to pretend it was a hundred years earlier. Villages came and went through the window and exposed a slower life, when farmers came from and went to their fields each day. Horses and carts rolled down the center of dirt and gravel roads, unhurried, in a rhythm that changed only with the seasons. Sun and work, rain and rest: the scenes out the window seemed to make her dizzy, as the dizziness spiraled into a *déjà vu* moment that resembled the one outside the car. She imagined she was young, carefree and loved. The landscape of wheat and vineyards overflowed with joy. One day she would be married, surrounded by her own children and grandchildren whose cradles she would rock and bread she would bake. In her reverie she was beautiful at an advanced age with a beauty that shone from inside.

A pothole in the road caused the car to lurch, as she came out of her reverie, a daydream that was so lucid she wondered if this village had been a part of her past. Was the disruption of that idyllic and pastoral life something she had done to deserve punishment in this life? The innocent and happy young woman she had seen in her vision had most likely raised her children and let them go, perhaps to war or famine or disease. She sometimes succumbed to paralyzing guilt these days but, as the car took her closer and closer to Paris, she was certain she had just stepped onto another path. Her life would soon be unrecognizable.

In Paris, while the chauffeur took her bags to her suite, Roshi embraced her and led her through his second floor apartment. His arm, which she held during the tour, seemed more frail. His normally delicate constitution had grown more refined, and he had continued to age except for his bright eyes.

As a teenager Anais had been slight; now, she had matured into a young woman who was blessed with vitality. Today, she looked wan, and it was obvious she had lost a lot of weight by the way her wrinkled clothes hung on her frame. Yes, she had experienced the loss of a loved one and a dream, and she had made many decisions alone for one so young. Such were the evil effects of war, he reflected. In the near future she would meet many who had been physically wounded and many who would never recover. War did terrible things and, in the aftermath, there was no time for reflection or self-pity. There was too much to be done. Restoration was a concept that carried exhausting responsibilities, yet Roshi was still pleased with his decision to invite Anais to live with him.

He led her to a small suite of rooms that resembled an apartment within an apartment and told her the rooms were hers as long as she lived there. She gazed around in wonder. It was nearly the same size as their whole apartment in Havana, and it was all her own. She walked from room to room: the feminine bedroom, a small study with a desk in the bay window, the books and two armchairs in blue brocade by the fireplace in the miniature sitting room. Blue dominated the apartment. There was a small dressing room with a walk-in closet, where one of her bags had already been deposited.

"Note, there is no kitchen in these quarters. We have our own housekeeper who will clean your apartment and a cook who arrives each morning with croissants, makes *café au lait,* and takes requests for dinner. You are welcome to make other requests. At lunch, *le dejourner,* there is cold salad or anything you require. In the evening, I eat at 9 PM, formally, in the dining room. Often, there are guests, but I will not subject you to them until you are well settled, and only if it is appropriate. Otherwise, cook will bring your tray to your sitting room to that lovely table near the window. You may close your door for privacy throughout the day. You will meet my staff in the morning, and you have already met Jean-Paul who drove you here from Marseille. He fills in and does any miscellaneous chores that need to be done. I suggest you get a good night's sleep; for things always look better first thing in the morning. And Anais, remember, you are safe here and loved."

His voice softened as he bowed to her and turned to leave the room.

She had looked at him with big lost eyes until Roshi wanted to weep. Where was his intrepid girl, the one who was curious and willing to take on any studies that he directed at her? Where was the energy of youth and the resilience of spirit? It would take a long time to heal, that was certain.

"You are my best friend, Roshi. I don't quite know how it came about, but I am so glad you are a part of my life. Thank you."

"You are quite welcome, but we'll talk tomorrow. Right now you need plenty of rest. Tomorrow the world will be put to right again. I'm glad you're here. I've missed you."

He turned and left quietly, walking across the most beautiful Persian carpet she had ever seen. She tried to take in details of the room, of anything, but life began to darken around the edges and get smaller. She dropped her clothes on the floor, crawled between the bed covers, and was asleep instantly. It was a deep and restful sleep, healing and empty.

She awoke, wondering if a spell had been cast, one that dictated she would rest soundly and awaken refreshed. Maybe it was the fact that she felt safe and trusted with Roshi nearby that she had slept the best sleep she could remember. Finally, she admitted to herself that he was the father she had always wished for and, for the first time in nearly a decade, she could think such thoughts without feeling guilty.

***

Anais was met with the smell of coffee, as she made her way to the kitchen, where the heated croissants sat on a plate and the *café au lait* was ready to fill bowls, just as she remembered from childhood. She was hungry and found Roshi in the dining room, reading the morning *Paris Match* while cook bustled about, filling his cup with hot milk and coffee. For the first time in weeks she felt a growling at the bottom of her stomach and nearly smiled.

Roshi looked up from his paper as she stood barefoot, tussled and somewhat better for all that than last night.

"You look quite rested, my dear. Are you hungry?" He smiled kindly.

"Starving."

"*Madame* Sylvan has already set a place for you. *Madame*, this is Anais, and she will be living with us for many years, we hope."

Madame nodded. "Welcome, *Mademoiselle.* You sit, and I will bring more coffee and croissants."

She soon returned with a tray, poured the café and set a basket of croissants on the table.

"*Bon appetit.*"

"Go ahead. I've already finished mine."

Anais bit into a croissant and closed her eyes. The buttery smell was out of this world and brought back memories of living in Paris, as nothing else could have. It is said that a sense of smell is a primitive and most profound access to memory. It carries with it our securities and fears, our survival and comfort. In this case, it was like a secure cradle.

Roshi finished his coffee, as he watched Anais devour three croissants. She drank from her bowl like a true child of France, and they never spoke a word. When she finally came up for air and looked curiously around the room, he thought he caught a glimpse of the young lady he once knew.

"So Jean-Paul tells me you had only two bags. One was filled with rocks, he reports. The other was filled with feathers."

She smiled for the first time since her arrival.

"He's joking. One has my books and diaries. The other has my clothes."

"What did your mother and aunt do, when you said you were leaving?"

"I didn't tell them; I left a note. I explained I was sailing to Paris and told them I would get in touch when I was settled. I also gave them your address. I'm eighteen, a grown woman, now. They would have tried to persuade me to stay, but there is nothing they could have said to stop me. I don't miss them, you know."

"Is there anything you have told them about what has happened in your life?"

"No, they would not have understood and wouldn't want to hear it."

"Okay, I certainly keep everything I hear, know or suspect in this apartment. You are safe here from prying eyes and well-meaning advice. Except from me, of course. If you ask me for an opinion, most likely you'll get one."

She nodded carefully and sighed.

"So how do you feel this morning? Would you like to get your hair and nails done, put on your best and cleanest outfit and leave *Mme* Silvan to unpack and get your clothes in order? We can even go to lunch, if you are up to it."

"*Vraiment?*"

"Truly. Paris still has many places you have never seen, and the shopkeepers need the business. Jean-Paul has already made you an appointment at a lovely hair salon. He tells me it is something all young women have in common, when they wish to put their world right side up."

"He is a wise man."

"Okay, you shower and change. Tell *Mme* Silvan what you choose to wear and she will iron it. Then we will be ready to leave."

***

That day Anais felt like a princess. Her hair was styled in a gamine cut that suited her perfectly. The twenties had exploded in Paris, and women wanted to look bold yet feminine. They wanted to dance, be frivolous and forget the war had ever happened; yet they were savvy and knew they had to get up the next morning to go to the office or some other job outside the home. It was heady and exciting, somewhat too exciting and fearsome for some. She had her nails painted and makeup applied after a facial. She came out of the salon, a small band around her head with a feather

149

tucked into it. She had never seen or heard of this look in Havana, but she was back in Paris and knew Parisian women had a sense of style that was second to none.

They entered a shop soon after she finished at the salon, a boutique where Jean-Paul claimed his wife would give up their first born to shop. The Anais who exited the boutique was no longer a young girl but a mature woman. She wore the newest flapper dress with its dropped waist, fringes and beads. She wore silk stockings and comfortable heels that matched her dress and purse. In her unmistakably new look, they made their way to lunch, an ageless Japanese man, and a young exotic woman who could have been an heiress or a high-class lady of the night. Women stared, and men winked, as they doffed their hats. The outfit was daring, and she had never had this much attention in her life. She rather liked it.

She was home. She had a new father, a place to live, a new look and safety. Their final stop that afternoon was a stationery store. Her welcome home gift from Roshi was a beautiful leather bound diary, and she held on to it, during their drive home, with tears in her eyes. How could he have known that he had returned her best friend to her? For the first time, since she had left France as a child, she had avoided writing in her diary for weeks. It seemed appropriate that, so soon after her return, she would renew her friendship with her other half. She went directly to her room, barely noting that her books were lined up on the shelves in her study or that her clothes were cleaned, pressed and hung neatly in her closet. She sat at her desk in a cozy alcove out over a busy street where the dim light of late afternoon resembled the background of an impressionist painting. Her two worlds were poised for a moment in time, illuminated with inner meaning. Reverently, she opened her new diary and began to write.

"My dear," she began, "Have you ever thought how one could be influenced by one's own writing?

I am like a rainbow, today: the reds and blues and pale lavenders of the French countryside. How lovely. The colors

150

in my world have painted my day. It is a new day, a new world, and I have been blessed. I am grateful, more grateful than I can express, for Roshi's benevolence, his generous spirit and the fact that he has, in effect, adopted me. However have I become so lucky? Perhaps, this abundance has come about as a result of all the wistfulness expressed year after year in my writing, as I mourned the past and longed for a better world. Today, I feel like a creature of limitless horizons. If rainbows spread their arch across the sky, they surely touch on all the potential in the world. Because I am only eighteen, I feel indomitable this day, risen up like a phoenix from the burning fire that was Havana. I can almost see Joel's point of view from where I stand. Almost."

Chapter 26
Recovery

"Blow out the candles, Anais. Blow them out. If you get everyone, you'll get to make a wish."

Roshi saw a shadow shade her eyes, when the wish was made. She was nineteen and touched with the dual trauma of abuse and war. It was March of 1922. So far it was a poor year for wishes or negotiations for that matter. Anais had been with him over a year and in that time Roshi had observed her keenly. Something, he decided, was amiss. Physically, she was beautiful, restored to health, vibrant, an expert with makeup and camouflage. The clothes he frequently bought her suited her. The decade suited her. She was asked on many dates, and he knew from Jean-Paul that the nightclubs and parties she attended were orgies of forgetfulness. He had her watched carefully, despite the fact that she did not overindulge or experiment with drugs. She didn't seem to need them, for only half of her participated in the present moment. When she was home, she was a demure, mysterious and serious student.

This past semester she had enrolled at the Sorbonne, and Roshi had pulled a few strings to get her many prerequisite deficiencies overlooked. It seemed that the party girl and the student were disconnected. Or rather, the party person appeared to know about the student, but the young lady who was a student seemed oblivious to the party girl.

Roshi had become an expert on brain trauma. He realized that her disconnection and depersonalization was an extreme form of escape. He knew about her childhood sexual abuse better than she did. Added to that was the aborted fetus and the suicide of the child's father, her first and true love. The early trauma, though unacknowledged, had caught up with her. When her Catholic values had been disrupted, guilt erupted, and she believed in her own punishment. For the commission of her sins, she believed, she had been the cause of Joel's suicide. The end result was a shutdown of her third chakra that connected the eyes of inner vision with reality. Not only did her psyche feel incapable of looking at these issues, they refused to see them. She became cleverly blinded on the irrational side of her brain from what went on with the rational side. She could, and perhaps would, live the rest of her life with half of her unknown to the other half.

It didn't lessen his great affection for her, but Roshi pondered at length to what means this phenomenon could be put to good use. Otherwise, how would she feel, if she could not contribute her gifts to the world?

He began to formulate a plan. Somehow, he would figure out how to make use of her many talents. Meanwhile, he had only to gaze back over the year, since she stepped off the ship, to see the good changes. From distraught waif to assured young woman who had begun to smile again, she had quite improved.

This year, he had finally asked her, if she would like to hostess some of his dinner parties. Diplomats came and went. For hours, some of them sat behind the closed doors of Roshi's study. There were dinners for a dozen people who sparkled with jewels and seemed to cherish an invitation to his table. They were the decision makers, the policy makers and those who sincerely wished to improve the results of an imperfect peace. The post war decade was now on a solid footing. Her task, he answered, when she asked about her own role, would be to listen carefully at her end of the table, say little and make a charming, feminine contribution by her calm presence.

"Don't forget," he informed her, "most of my guests love to discuss literature."

Anais blew out the candles. It would soon be her birthday, but she could not think about the future clearly enough to formulate one. Life was improved, but the exciting details and plans that she heard others her age discuss were absent. In some way this had led her to believe that fate was a big factor in her life plans. Right now, the moment in which she lived, was the most important time in her life. Beyond the moment was confusion and stress; behind the moment was fear and sorrow. She wanted to help Roshi with his dinner parties simply because she could easily do so and because he had given her so much. It was the least she could do. She recognized that he was busy, important and burdened by world problems, so if she could lighten that burden just a bit she would.

***

The day before her birthday she shopped for a suitable hostess outfit. To her delight and surprise she found a lovely evening dress and jacket embroidered in an oriental design. Beautiful butterflies and cherry blossoms in subtle and exquisite silken shades adorned the bodice and hem. She couldn't wait to see Roshi's reaction. She also bought a new diary with a silk Japanese designed cover and a long hairpin that she intended would decorate her chignon.

She came home to write in her journal that afternoon. "I hardly recognize myself some days. I look in the mirror at an elegant stranger, and I love my new life. There are days, when I try to remember how I got here, but nothing comes to mind." She thought of her flower arrangement teacher *Mme* Sugisaki and the Japanese poetry she sometimes recited as she sculpted a flower arrangement. She often recited the writer Kanoko Okamoto.

"...your birdlike songs died away,
and this fall feels lonely all the more."

or

"...stop crying and sing a lullaby
to an infant child who lies by your side."

Tears came to her eyes, but she brushed them away, wondering where they had come from and why.

That Saturday evening, when she appeared before Roshi, before the first guest arrived, she saw great emotion well up in a man whose mask-like face was immobile in diplomatic circles.

"Exquisite! Where did you find an outfit so perfect? It is as though you have conjured up my homeland."

She smiled graciously in what she imagined to be a most enigmatic Japanese manner.

"You will be a wild success," he assured her. "Would you like a small Pinot de Charent before the doorbell rings?"

They stepped into the dining room and Roshi rang for drinks. While they waited and he gazed at her lovingly, he thought, I would never have imagined a daughter in my old age, but she has blessed my life with her presence.

That evening, when the last guest had gone and Anais said goodnight, he retreated to his study where the fire still blazed in the fireplace and sat staring into its embers. It had been a fine evening. Anais had glowed like a flower. The men were intrigued, the women impressed by gentle manners and a non-threatening demeanor. It came to him in a flash of insight that she was born to such work. He meant to ask her in the morning, if she would consider the study of Japanese at the Sorbonne. He could certainly tutor her whenever she needed help and certainly provide people to give her further instruction. It never hurt to speak another language, and he was convinced that Japan would someday be a worthy power in the world. Anais had quietly represented what he considered the best of Japan this

155

evening. Seeing her, he imagined that other hostesses would adopt the Japanese style of beautiful embroidery, silks and impeccable manners. It was a great step in the enhancement of understanding and appreciation between cultures. Tonight there had been no talk of bank debts or gangs of unemployed workers lining the streets. The talk of flower arrangements, silks and transformation symbols like the butterfly were a welcome change from the often-unpleasant tensions and disagreement about the need of war reparations that often invaded a dinner party. In his opinion his guests had left refreshed and inspired. The women, especially, had been relieved to avoid depressing discussions. For the first time, since he had left Japan, he missed his homeland. Perhaps it was time to make that trip home, take Anais and introduce her to his country. It made him feel decades younger just to consider such a voyage.

While Roshi dreamed of cherry blossoms, Anais tossed and turned in the throes of a recurrent nightmare. She was on the ship that had carried her from Cuba, but it was caught in a dreadful storm that went on all night. The crew appeared frightened and had lost control of the steering. In a state of twilight sleep she feared they would never find their direction.

She awoke the next morning, as the word beauty whispered through her mind. She had heard enough talk of war to understand a bit more of the devastation that had been wrought throughout Europe. War was ugly; it could never be made noble in her mind. The opposite of beauty was the ugly and the way humans behaved to get what they coveted. In this apartment she was free to think of the power of her new world. Roshi, she understood, was a part of the discussions for peace and harmony between those who had fought, killed, and tried to destroy each other. He appreciated refined culture like no one she had ever known.

She entered the breakfast room, expecting to dissect the dinner party. Instead, Roshi bowed to her and pulled out her seat. She was served her usual breakfast and could tell he was nervous. He had something to say and would approach the subject with great care.

"What do you wish to say to me, Roshi?"

"Well, I must begin by complementing you on last evening. I can't remember the last time I thoroughly enjoyed one of my own dinner parties. Your presence was invaluable."

"Thank you."

"So I've been thinking…"

She wondered when he had the time to think.

"How would you like to make a trip to Japan? I don't mean tomorrow or anything like that. I mean in time for next spring. We could be there in time for the season of blossoms. It is the most beautiful of experiences."

She stared at him in wonderment. Was he a mind reader? Her thoughts on beauty, as she woke this morning, were being expressed like part of a living dream.

"I would adore it."

"Just like that? You know you wouldn't understand the language or culture or the Zen religion that is such an integral part of my home."

"I could learn before we leave."

"You could. You could even learn some Japanese before then. What would you think of a Japanese tutor and some suggested reading?"

"I would be honored to have that opportunity. Would I be able to read the work of Kanoko Okamoto?"

Yes, she had been brought into his life for a very special reason. That same day M. Kazuko was hired. He was to give language and culture lessons. The next day Roshi took her into a small room that could only be accessed through his study. It held a miniature temple and led to a small conservatory where orchids and chrysanthemums grew in profusion.

"If you learn enough Japanese, you will be allowed to use this room. I am a Buddhist. I know you have no idea what that means, but if, after your studies progress, you wish to use this place for meditation, just let me know."

That was the opening phase of a new approach to life for Anais. Roshi suspected that such an introduction to the world of the spirit would penetrate both sides of this young woman who was disconnected from half of herself. She was nineteen, and she was a grown woman ready to embark on another chapter in her life.

What did she write in her diary, he wondered. Her diligence, in itself, was an escape from both truth and reality. Her escape was into her own unique version of events and emotions. It had become an expression of 'heightened moments' where she intentionally discarded what she judged to be unimportant illusions. To edit, filter and distill gave her complete control, and her truths, he suspected, resembled the deliberate blur created in meditation, when the eyelids were half opened yet half closed.

Chapter 27
Beauty as an Antidote to Ugliness

Beauty cannot be measured, despite the results of beauty contests. It truly has more to do with the eye of the beholder. Anais fell in love with beauty. That may sound like an unusual way to put it, but it comes closer than any other explanation.

She looked around Roshi's apartment, seeing it for the first time. The patina of age, when dusted with kindness, shone with a lovely face. In the time, since her arrival in Paris, she had survived in a protected cocoon. The best thing was that she had not been pushed or lured out of her cocoon and, now that she had emerged on her own, her vision of life was woven with luminous strands that highlighted everything around her. She sat in the library, enchanted with the poetry of the world's greatest poets. She read Shelly who wrote, "Thy light alone – gives grace and truth to life's unquiet dream." True, she did gravitate to the poetry of the Romantics, but all young and sensitive people have fallen in love with the Romantics.

Roshi noticed her absorption and was content for her. Nevertheless, he found her a gentle tutor and bought her the gracious poetry of Okamoto. He knew the process of translation would help her to learn. He brought in an Aikido master, knowing that her love of dance would be satisfied in the flowing movements of this noble martial art. She learned and spoke two or three new words each day in conversation and, slowly, she began the practice of Zen meditation inside their tiny but sacred home temple. Could this be why she had awakened to beauty? She was surrounded in this apartment by the beauty of ageless objects and manners. Within these walls, self-control and consciousness was a way of life. Virtues had been invited into his home to create rhythm and awareness.

Outside, violence and a lack of order crowded the streets. Repairs, restoration, and healing were the order of the day. People had forgotten to seek the hidden beauty of the moment in their fight for survival. The forests of the Ardennes had been bombed until the tree limbs dripped with the blood of soldiers. Men like Joel, who had seen these brutal scenes through the lens of innocence, carried torment to their graves. The spirits of the dead and severely wounded crowded the streets of Paris, where a person like Joel would have felt confined to hell every day. He was currently banished from her daily memories along with other ugly forms of post wartime. In any case, she preferred to stay indoors to heal while she sealed off exposed wounds. Roshi was not surprised, for she had had a glimpse of Joel's world in her nightmares.

As far as Roshi was concerned, if this healing took place at the expense of wholeness, it was better than the alternative. He knew that she was creating a strong and solid personality, living in his home. Wherever she concealed her other life it was beyond his helpful influence. This way, at least the half of her he helped to heal might someday save her.

Beauty was an integral part of Roshi's birth culture. His quest for beauty had begun in the cradle. Growing up, he had been privileged to have parents who sought inner life in their home. Nature and its examples had been the foundation from which his roots had grown and spread, and he wished to impart such a view of the world to Anais. Surrounded by the emotional impoverishment bequeathed by war, he knew that his outlook was unpopular, but he also knew that the cultivation of the beautiful was more necessary now than it had ever been. Men craved the wholeness of their souls; they yearned for the feeling of awe and inspiration that had disappeared from their lives.

Beauty, in its ordinary and everyday forms can be resurrected with care. The soul, in its search for virtue, clarity and goodness, appears in the most unexpected corners of the mind. On his balcony garden of bonsai plants and trees, he spent precious time, cutting here and there, pruning and smoothing out lines. He trimmed excess, straightened angles and allowed light to reach into darkened corners. His plants thrived and lived in the smallest spaces imaginable, far into old age. They bent and twisted their limbs to create their own aesthetic forms. The characteristics and virtues of his trees were a reflection of his own soul and the patient work he had labored at all his life.

Roshi's world evoked reverence, dignity, and harmony. Thus, he did not interfere with Anais' struggle to overcome her trauma. He offered teachers and books and inspirational surroundings but did not interfere or insist on his way as the best way. The ability to make choices and create the kind of life to which one was personally suited, he reminded himself, was freedom. There would be many instances in which Anais might refuse to do something that he inferred or suggested. The fact that she was comfortable to turn down or turn away from a suggestion pleased him.

Chapter 28
Anais and Lily Meet Again

Anais and Lily met again when Anais signed up for Japanese classes at the Sorbonne.

Anais felt somewhat lost in an environment of hallowed corridors, intimate garden benches, purposeful students who walked briskly to class, and tiered classrooms that resembled performance theatres. She had expected to interact with learned professors and receive guidance in a meaningful and personal context. Instead, she had received a few of her essays back, marked with red ink comments that seemed inconsequential to her. Rather than a close reading of her ideas, she found a critique of her syntax and vocabulary. The professors seemed annoyed at her lack of grammatical dexterity; and she was annoyed at their apparently shallow approach to higher education. She was already a month into the course work and felt that she had learned nothing of relevance to her life.

One day, as Anais walked slowly and reluctantly toward a hated lecture hall; considering whether to go to the library or home instead of class, someone politely avoided her slow forward movement and passed on her left, obviously in a hurry to get to a class on time. She watched the tall figure now in front of her, a lithesome figure topped with a fiery strawberry blond head of magnificent hair. Strangely, it reminded her of Lily. It must be wishful thinking. This is what Lily would look like, she imagined, if they had grown up side by side. Her heart lurched in her chest and she cried out, "Lily?"

The glorious head turned to look over her shoulder, and there were the freckles and the big blue eyes. *"Mon Dieu."*

"Lily? It's me, Anais."

Lily stopped walking while they bottled traffic in the middle of the hallway.

"I know. Give me a moment to get over the shock."

"Lily, I would have recognized you anywhere. You are as beautiful as I imagined you would be."

They embraced like long lost sisters and best friends.

"And you, my friend. I know you, too. We have both grown into better versions of ourselves. Mind you, I still have a lot of these horrible spots all over me."

They laughed.

"Are you a student here?"

"Yes. Art history is my focus. And you?"

"I'm just wetting my feet, fumbling. I take Japanese classes."

"We have so much to catch up on. Let's skip classes, go to a café and get caught up."

"Well, lead the way."

They linked arms just has they had done ten years ago and left the university together. Anais was filled with happiness. How did such a dreary day turn into a highlight in her life? Lily, she had found Lily, and suddenly a great sadness was lifted from her being.

***

The contrast between the two young women was startling.

As they sat at the café on the day of their reunion, Anais looked up from her coffee and repeated, "My name is Anais, what's yours?" Lily looked up in surprise.

"I'm Lily, and I think we are going to be friends for ever and ever."

"How strange, I feel the same way."

They gazed at each other in disbelief.

"Oh, Anais...where did you go? How did you just disappear?"

'It's a long and sad story, my dear. Do you have the whole afternoon?"

And just like that their friendship, once cracked, was cemented and repaired.

Chapter 29
Anais Wishes She Could Be a Whole Person

Anais sat at her desk, staring across the river. Living two lives was not easy. There were days, when it left her emotionally drained. She tried to remember the first moment, when she realized that there was another Anais who knew nothing about her, the Angela who went home to her platonic marriage, to entertain bankers in her lovely home in Louveciennes and dig in her garden. She, too, kept a diary and wrote lovely creative pieces, critiques and articles. She was beautiful, serene and private, and her love of beauty was devout. She arranged the flowers from her garden and sipped tea, read and shopped. The quieter her life, the more she gazed into the reflecting pool in her back garden, the happier she appeared. Sometimes, her husband, the devoted Christolphe, filmed her, when she meditated in one of her Zen states, and those photos and films were evidence to her that she existed.

Anais closed her eyes for a moment and a tear slid down her face. *How could that woman not know about me?* she wondered. On overcast and misty days like today she felt bereft without her. Their lives were so different that Anais did not think of Angela as her other half. She seemed like a sister or a twin. She longed to know her and let herself be known to this other woman. She admired her. All her attempts at meditation, Oriental decorating and serenity, she owed to attempts to copy herself. But one thing she knew of a certainty, she was more whole than that woman who lived in a glass cage, undisturbed and unruffled.

Her own life was full and wildly reckless at times. Angela would never have moved into Roshi's apartment or even left Cuba. She would never have had so many wonderful lovers or the courage to get close to a man. She shook her head and looked over the invitations for the houseboat party, again. She hoped she had not missed someone. The paper was a bright splash of color. That should do it. Let those come to the party who wanted to have a good time. She added to the bottom of the colorful invitation, "Wear a mask."

That afternoon, Anais delivered the invitations. Everyone she talked to was enthusiastic, and word of mouth had already spread by the time she stopped at her last destination. When the deliveries had all been made, she stopped at Café de Flore to relax and catch up with her thoughts, took out her diary to write and reflect on the day and looked around for Sartre or Simone. No one she knew lingered at the other tables, so she was left undisturbed to observe and write. When she had first returned to Paris, there were so many afternoons like this. She had known no one then, and her diaries filled rapidly. To write and fill each little book was a precious endeavor. Someday, perhaps, women would read her written reflections about her days and hours and insights, and they would wonder at her behavior. It might be an awakening for some of them, uncomfortable at times, at times confusing. Some would love her and her observations. Others might hate her for disturbing their comfortable lives. Everything was here: the details, the secret glances, the clandestine meetings, and the force of male and female energy that came together to veil or reveal weaknesses and strengths, dreams and failures, inspiration, beauty and the ugly underside that is the shadow of beauty. She left out nothing, and each diary, as it was finished, was locked in a metal box that she referred to as a safely deposited character.

In the meantime she had to cope with suspicions. She hated the uneasy feeling she had that Christolphe was having her followed. They had an unspoken arrangement that they would not interfere in each other's lives. It was a bit old world to be sure, but it suited them. She did not ask him what he did on his long business trips to Zürich, and he did not ask about their *pied a terre* in Saint Germain. He realized she had artist friends, and it was not uncommon in Paris to have a small place to which one retired from time to time. Otherwise, he was not particularly interested in the Paris art scene unless it benefited one of their dinner parties, and she did not care to open the door to his dark room in the basement. But to have her followed seemed like a violation of those rules of marriage. Why would he risk or disrupt their lifestyle without speaking to her first? Theirs was a good life, wasn't it?

Right now, today, most of what she wrote was a repetitious blur. Insights did not happen overnight. They accumulated. One day and an observation added to the one before that might expose a truth. One might say that all artists were extroverted performers. They wrote, played their music, sang their songs, and painted their canvases to accommodate their world. Once those arts were viewed or heard, they might be appreciated. Until then, those artists absorbed the atmosphere of the streets and the emotions exposed on the faces of passersby. She watched the stride, the sway of hips, the clenched hands with purses. She noted the roam of eyes seeking connections, the stares of the injured and the struggles of those in pain. She wanted to capture it all and keep it preserved, so she sat there and wrote. If Christolphe had become a voyeur because of his isolation with his film work, she could ask to join him on some of his forays to find subject matter. It was not exactly in her sphere of interest, but a writer could turn a photograph into a paragraph. They might grow closer, if they shared more in common.

***

She glanced at her watch. It was Wednesday and only an hour before her appointment at the dressmakers. In keeping with her idea of a masquerade, she had decided to have a costume made. It was, after all, not just any party. It was the introduction of her gallery and perhaps, one day, her salon. A salon could not be artificially put together in Paris. That was not how it worked. A salon grew from its hostess, a certain combination of personalities, and the ability of the hostess to mix and match people and ideas. Right now, in Paris there were three competing salons, and that is what she wanted for her gallery, eventually. The Gertrude Steins of the world had become nearly obsolete. The traditional salon needed an infusion of life and art and character. To that end she paid for her coffee and finished writing her last few observations. There was an idea bubbling in her mind, several really, that would make powerful statements at the party. She knew everyone would be there, but now that the houseboat existed, it felt like a new departure and a time to help glue the art community together. She wanted to connect people, inspire them to persevere and give them a focus in troubled times. Why was it, she mused, that she was certain that war and strife were not over? She thought again of the Marais, the old ornately carved doors and the sense that eyes followed her every move? She paid for her coffee and started the walk back to the quay.

On her walk she thought once more of D. H. Lawrence and the probability that he would not attend the masquerade. He was too somber for a party, but his philosophy of 'livingness' was the perfect theme for a party. His way to reach the spirit was a sexual approach. It was masculine, too. As for herself, she preferred to believe that women in love reach beyond love and partake of a profound quest for truth.

As she walked along the west bank of the Seine, the booksellers prepared for the end of another day. They closed their kiosks and tucked their chairs close to the stalls. Nothing was hurried. The day was like the usual flow of the river at the end of spring. Affluent Parisians were stretching and leaving their mistresses for another evening at home with the wife or, these days, another few hours back at the office. The *heure bleue* had become an addiction, a time to unload anxiety and forget the bills at home. There was unease in the financial world and an acute discomfort with the drastic fluctuations in the stock market. Those concerns were mostly located in the offices on the other side of the river, but the number of tourists on the left bank was always predicated by the traffic on the right bank. Artists and shopkeepers of antiques roamed the streets and worried. This was the world of flowers and cafés, but deep inside everyone knew their prosperity was dependent on those who had money to spend. Who could argue with money, when it put a baguette on the table? Not even the chic new communists objected to food on the table. Turning left to the mooring, she wondered who would show up at her party. What if she invited Christolphe to film the event, to be sure the guests were properly documented and to give her images to study later, when she was free to linger on the event. The more she thought of such a tool of investigation the more she liked the idea.

"People are seeking to live two lives with one heart."

—Nin *Collages*

Chapter 30
An Afternoon Birthday Picnic

That afternoon Roshi planned to take Lily and Anais for a drive beyond the city to visit the old impressionist artist Monet at his home in Giverny. Roshi remembered the enchanting water garden as an unforgettable place where nature was appreciated, and its caretakers worked with reverence. Water lilies would be afloat and open, and the bridge over the pond that is a symbol of the mind would provide a fine spot for a photo of the girls. *Mme* Silvan had packed a picnic, and Jean-Paul drove them in the roadster with the top down. Roshi intended to observe whether Anais had any desire to paint or sketch in ink or to learn more about gardening. It was close to her birthday, and he wanted to make the day special.

Thank God for Lily. She was the perfect friend: lively, intelligent and quite acceptable for his Anais. When Anais arrived from Cuba, he had despaired that she would ever have friends. The day the women had reunited at school was a milestone for both of them. True friendship can build slowly over the years, or it can explode in found interests and a web of mysterious strands that reach out from the heart. Refound acceptance, a smile of reconnection and it continues. He could not truly explain the phenomenon of friendship. It was like a karmic gift, he thought. When they met again, memories of the best days of her childhood had been recovered for Anais, and for that he was grateful.

Lily arrived for their adventure with a large straw hat and a basket of offerings as their picnic. Inside, was her favorite book of poetry by Yeats, a photo of herself as a gift for Anais, and her favorite wine. She wore an elegant but practical cotton poplin dress. Not to be outdone, Anais wore a blue dress of crisp cotton with a matching blue ribbon on her hat. Roshi sat in the front with Jean-Paul and listened contentedly to their conversation.

"Have you heard there will be a marvelous piano concerto on Sunday afternoon? It will be beneath the rose window at *La Chapelle*."

"No, not a word. Where do you hear of such spontaneous events?"

"Oh, I've been hanging around the music scene for years while you have travelled to exotic climes."

Roshi leaned back, happy to hear their voices, the lovely soulful notes of friends in harmony. They talked then of Stravinsky and others of whom he had no understanding. In many ways it was as though the two girls had never been apart. Just the fact that Anais was willing and excited to attend a concert warmed his heart.

The day itself was a balm to his senses. He felt the warmth of the sun touch his shoulders like a comforting shawl. Light fell on flowers and fields, as it sifted out harshness and exposed beauty. Anais announced that she wished to capture some to take home. Roshi thought it should be bottled in a tonic for the poor soldiers who had so recently lived in wet bunkers and sodden foxholes, soldiers who had shivered in soaked uniforms, as they tried to quell their fears. He could still see darkness in their eyes on the streets of Paris and wanted to hand out warm sunshine along with doses of forgiveness. Without such grace, the sins of the fathers would infect many generations of sons. His ancient Samurai family could attest to the effects of violence on the unsuspecting, especially the children. He watched Anais, as he shared his thoughts, but saw no reaction beyond the distant acknowledgement of one untouched by tragedy.

It was that day at the water garden on Monet's bridge of forgetfulness that Roshi realized that Anais had truly split herself in two. Only someone who knew her mind, as well as he did, could detect a person shut off from grief. Most of France was in a state of numb grief. Anais, however, had shaped her lovely Parisian face, smooth as silk, into a geisha face devoid of attachment. Unlike the geisha who had practiced this face and demeanor, hers was not calculated or rehearsed. What he witnessed was a perfect disconnection from pain. It was a state of one side of the mind cut off from the other.

Roshi had yet to see the other side of Anais and could only pray for her sake that it wasn't a destructive or completely ugly side to an otherwise perfect young woman. He looked forward to their trip to Japan, for not only would the best of his culture be showcased, it would be difficult indeed to escape his notice, if a second persona made an appearance.

Chapter 31
A Grand Trip to Japan

He and Anais set sail six months later: a ship across the Atlantic, a train across the United States, followed by a luxury Japanese cruise liner. It took nearly three months of travel before they arrived in Kyoto, but the travel time was well used. They spoke only Japanese, and Anais dressed as a Japanese woman, so she would feel comfortable on their arrival. Poetry was studied and the philosophy of beauty addressed. Roshi made sure that Eastern and Western values were assimilated, but when it came to appreciation of their surroundings, they were in perfect harmony. Bergson and Plotinus were as welcome as *Mme* Okamoto.

Would that it was as easy to come to post war peace concessions. Disappointed, he had left France, knowing that the Port of Fiume negotiations were going nowhere. Racial problems, blatant prejudice and an ignorance of Orientals, would never be settled to anyone's satisfaction. Jews, blacks, browns, and Orientals: everyone, it seemed, was subject to the scrutiny of growing German intolerance. He hoped the voyage would clear his mind and heart. He was not ready to give up on negotiations, but it was rejuvenating to listen to the waves and feel the rise and fall of the boat beneath his feet. Nature was the ultimate healer. Its essence was behind great thoughts and refined being. He spoke often to Anais of the power of nature to absorb the destructive tendencies of man and transform them. She listened carefully, always with

174

the same detachment. She could have been born a Japanese woman in another life.

They created quite a sensation on their travels. Who was this Oriental gentleman who was so obviously wealthy and influential? Who was this white woman who travelled with him like a daughter or, God forbid, a concubine? It fired the imagination of even the most staid and dull passengers. It provided hours of speculation and gossip and guilty talk of the kind that stopped abruptly whenever they approached. She wore a kimono on board, spoke only Japanese, and avoided the other guests. Thus, mystery surrounded Anais, and it suited her quite nicely. Roshi dressed as a Western business tycoon, and they had a standing invitation to dine at the captain's table. Oftentimes, they politely refused, preferring each other's company and the furtherance of her education.

One did not travel all the way to Japan in the 1920s only to turn around and return. Once in Kyoto, they celebrated Anais' twentieth birthday, then toured Mt. Fiji and Osaka in honor of the occasion. Anais felt inspired by the beauty of simple ceremonies, every day routines, and manners that allowed her unique life to blossom. Even her walk had changed. She seemed to glide silently through garden paths so as not to disturb the herons. Wherever she stood, she felt a desire to express the fullness that had entered her soul.

The tea ceremony was her favorite. To sit beside Roshi, as he offered tea to a guest, as they admired the peonies or chrysanthemums she had arranged on the tea table, to sip and appreciate from tiny porcelain cups, the earthy tea, the mist beyond the veranda, and the greatly revered silence, was an experience so new to her, she would dream of it throughout her life. She would let it dwell in that hallowed space of her psyche whenever she needed solace.

The Zen temples were another source of healing. She had not known that she needed such a place in which to practice and refine her gratitude and accept her higher Self. How glad she was to know Japanese, to converse and ask questions. Immersed in all things Japanese, she contemplated her Western life and values. Both were good. Both spoke to parts of her that grew in response to being acknowledged. Perhaps, she *had* been Japanese in another life. She became a sponge that took in both sides of the globe and harmonized those sides deep within her character.

To become immersed in Japanese culture, she cultivated the art of reverence toward the sacred parts of daily life. A cloud, a child's smile, an old and wrinkled hand: these held out to her the opportunity to stir her heart. Since she was not a Japanese woman, Roshi thought of her as a medieval mystic. Beauty, for the medieval thinker, was the beauty of God. To be, was to be wrapped in beauty. All else is forgotten in the presence of such awe. Roshi thought Anais would reach for a paintbrush or a block of calligrapher's ink, instead she reached, once again, for her journal. She wrote and rewrote, as her life force grew stronger. At the top of the first page in her newest diary she copied a quote from Keats, 'Beauty is truth, truth beauty' and that is 'all ye need to know.'

Roshi had miscalculated. He thought that in the silence of coming to know herself, Anais would come in contact with her other half. Instead, she sealed it off forever and turned to the present with all its immediacy. *Fine*, he thought, he would work with the reality that presented itself. She had enough spark in the half he knew to equal as much or more than most whole individuals. After spending so much time together, he had discovered even more about her to love and appreciate.

Chapter 32
While Healing Wounds, Love Enters

She turned twenty-one in 1924, a time when many young women her age yearned to marry. She and Roshi had been back in Paris for several months, and he did not know which way to turn. He did not know any young and marriageable young men. As her surrogate father, he felt responsible and sometimes afraid for her safety and her reputation. Paris was small in many ways. Rumors spread quickly and, although Parisians had double standard in their private lives, they were discreet, and it would not do to have her other life advertised. It had become quite obvious that the demure Angela knew nothing about her other life; perhaps this other Anais had developed slowly, as she sealed off her pain and her past. Roshi was confused and needed to see Anais' other side, so he could know exactly what they were up against.

It wasn't until they were back to Paris that Roshi glimpsed first-hand the other side, the wild and artistic side, the nymphomaniac of insatiable and sensuously dangerous needs. Some would call it the dark side, the ugly and addicted side, the unloved Anais who had been abused by her father and now, unconsciously, intended to punish any man who got too close to her. He was shocked for the first time in years. He had not foreseen such a personality.

Anais was no longer shocked, merely dismayed. She knew she had another personality and had accepted her tormented existence. Some days, she thought of herself as a cancerous disease or as dangerous as a virus. She saw the wholeness in others and marveled at their lack of fragmentation. It made her more thankful than ever for her diary entries, wherein she could recognize characters by their limitations and outlooks as parts of herself that she must keep contained.

The first glimpse came after an afternoon of shopping, when Anais came through the foyer laden with packages. Jean-Paul helped her to carry them from the limousine and winked at Roshi. Winked? Roshi had never been winked at in his life. Anais was flushed and excited and said she'd had a wonderful afternoon shopping. Jean-Paul backed out the door and left them together alone in the foyer. Roshi picked up two of the packages.

"Here, let me help you with those."

She picked up two more packages, and he followed her to her suite.

"*Mme* Silvan is coming with the rest of them."

He perched on the lovely brocade chair in her sitting room. "Show and tell…isn't that what the Americans say?"

"Oh, Roshi, it was one of those days, when everything was so beautiful and fit me and suited me so perfectly. I hope you don't mind. I think I must have spent quite a bit of money."

"Not to worry, my dear. You have the most lovely taste, and anything you have purchased will be well used."

Excitedly, she began to open packages and held up the first item. A red light went on in his brain, as he watched her face."

"But…this can't be mine. I…I must have picked up someone else's packages. Oh goodness…"

The outfit she held up was her size, but it was a bright red and quite risqué. The bodice was sequined and nearly see-through. The length was fashionable, very short and fringed. She touched the other objects in the box. An entire matching outfit suitable for cabaret in a not-so-haute-couture style stared back at her. The headband with black feathers and sequin beading, the black sheer stockings and red heels with a bit of a Mary-Jane strap across the instep were all lovely, but simply not Anais, standing there with a bewildered and dismayed look on her face.

"I shall have to return this to the store tomorrow. Certainly, these are not mine."

A further search through her packages found the most colorful and fun clothes, none of them hers.

"This person must have gone to all the places I stopped. She had the same taste in shops. What a disaster."

She was innocent and confused, but Roshi knew exactly what had happened. He watched her closely, but there was no sign of dissembling.

"We'll phone the shops tomorrow. There is no need to go to all the trouble to return the clothes, Anais. Jean-Paul knows how to return merchandise."

That incident was the first of many close calls, unveilings and exposures. It was as if the wild side was taunting her, wanting to be known and accepted. But the refined side became more quiet, closed off, and as Roshi watched closely, more determined than ever to live in denial. This side was the one most hurt and most in need of camouflage. The quiet side continued in her classes at the Sorbonne; occasionally wrote articles on literature for literary magazines, and acted as hostess for the dinner parties that had once again begun in earnest.

The League of Nations struggled to become effective, but the French had occupied the Ruhr, when the Germans failed to make war reparation payments. There was also a treaty signed with Turkey that became known as the Treaty of Lausanne. Roshi made many trips to Switzerland by train and, occasionally, Anais went with him. He had come to worry too much about her to leave her home alone.

***

179

The romance happened while Roshi sat in endless conference talks in Geneva, and Angela took herself outdoors to sit at her favorite café by the lake. She sat alone each day, writing in her diary. That morning, she was somewhat confused. After reading several diary entries of detailed, fantastic outings, clandestine meetings with unknown men and sexual encounters, the hairs on her head were raised and she felt a chill. She normally recorded her dreams, but these were dreams so lucid as to feel real. Lately, there had been more than a few of these unwanted dreams and Angela, who was so good at dream interpretation, was somewhat perplexed.

"May I take this seat?"

"Yes, it's free."

To take a seat at a table that was already occupied was common in Switzerland. It made sense to offer up an empty seat. There was a certain protocol for privacy while in the most crowded spaces, and only the briefest of small talk was allowed.

"Lovely day."

She nodded in an acceptably friendly manner while she studied him through her sunglasses.

"I've never seen you here before. Do you live nearby?" he asked.

"I live in Paris."

"Ah, Paris. Someday, I shall live there."

She was intrigued and suspected he was American. When she remarked on his British Public School French, she realized they had already spoken more than was acceptable.

"That's good, very good. How did you figure that out?" He joked, "You must be a spy."

She laughed. "I've been told I have an affinity for languages."

"I'll say! It's quite the talent. Do you speak any other languages?"

She answered in English. "English, Spanish, Japanese, and French, so far."

"So far? You intend to learn more?"

"Well, these days it might be wise to speak German."

"True."

They fell silent until the waiter finished taking his order.

"And you. What other languages do you speak?"

They fell into a conversation of the type that is often relied upon by strangers. But there was an underlying attraction. She was charming and beautiful, and he succumbed to the eyes of a doe, the smile of a geisha and the taste of an elegant Parisian. She thought of him as handsome, serious about his work and kind. She seemed kind. No, he had not fought in the war. He was a student, when the war began and just finished with his studies, when it ended. He was also an only child whose father was gone, which provided a valid reason for him to be excused from war conscription. Truthfully, he said, he was not a man who was drawn to war or violence as a way to settle grievances.

She thought Roshi would approve.

It was an hour before he left her table, and they exchanged addresses. She had a smile on her face, when she picked up her pen to describe him in a character sketch. She was improving her writing skills and had decided that she adored short stories. She felt inspired, when a title appeared in her mind. She would write about a woman whose heart was closed off from its own separate chambers. Perhaps she would have four lovers, one for each compartment. Soon, she must do something about the barrage of story images in her dreams. That's the reason for my dreams, she concluded. It was meant that she write a short story or perhaps a novella. These written styles were terribly popular right now, and the idea of writing in such a cohesive manner appealed to her.

When she had finished her character sketch, Anais hugged her diary to her chest. She had created a man in her imagination who was good and kind, who loved her to distraction, who bought a house in Paris with a garden, a dog and a lovely privacy wall around it. He took her to black tie and diplomatic functions on his arm like a princess. She was the envy of women and admired by important men in his circle. Her fantasy included the personal style she would develop, the clothing she might wear and the perfect children they might have who would be under the care of a British nanny.

She did not mention a word about Christolphe to Roshi until they were back in Paris. Instead, she started to write a story that got longer and longer until it became a novella, and the title she gave it was *The Four Chambered Heart*. Then, she tucked it away in a drawer, where it was forgotten for some time.

One day, a letter arrived from Christolphe. He would be in Paris in two weeks' time and would love to meet her parents with their permission, then take her to dinner.

That evening she told Roshi about Christolphe. She would write to him that evening, she said, because she would really love to have Roshi meet him and allow him to take her to dinner. It was agreed, and Roshi took her letter to the post office the next morning. That same afternoon he hired a detective to investigate Christolphe, for Roshi would be the first to acknowledge how much of deception and evil went on in Europe these days. Caution was, after all, the Japanese way. But Christolphe proved to be the genuine article. Tall and handsome with American and French parents, he intended to make a lifelong career in banking and, after Harvard undergraduate and business school degrees, had accepted a job in Cuba followed by a promotion to a major Swiss bank. This in itself was unusual because the Swiss chose mostly Swiss employees. Christolphe spoke German as well as French and intended to live in Europe permanently. His hobby was photography, but his upbringing was far too staid for him to have ever considered an artistic career. Had Roshi known, he would have realized that Christolphe was, on the surface at least, much like Joel Seaborn. There was only one factor about

Christolphe that gave Roshi pause. Some sixth sense told him that Christolphe might have a tendency to fall in love with another man rather than Anais. But his investigation found nothing untoward, and Roshi chastised himself for even imagining such a thing. He even laughed at himself for appearing to be an overprotective father. In his work deception came from every direction, and he would never take for granted a simple chance meeting that involved someone close to him. Anais had no idea what situations he dealt with or the complications of his work. She appeared blithely unconcerned about war and the ramifications of war. So far, he believed, she remained unaffected, at least in the persona he so carefully nurtured and wished would heal.

In reality, Roshi had at his command a score of agents, the crème de la crème of agents from various allied organizations. These were the only ones he knew who worked in harmony, unconcerned with praise or promotions. He had hand selected these men himself, and each one of them, no matter how well trained they appeared, when they arrived on his doorstep, were carefully trained in his own methods and attitudes. Intolerance and other signs of corrupt attitudes were weeded out, powers of observation were examined closely, and loyalty was encouraged. These men often worked in pairs, so he considered it of the utmost importance that they be compatible.

In Roshi's opinion no one had ever learned much from violence and hatred.

Since July fourteenth, 1919, when the victorious allied troops, to commemorate victory, marched down the *Champs Élysée* to rest the French Unknown Soldier in his grave under the *Arc de Triomphe*, Paris continued to increase its population. Housing shortages were dramatic. In contrast, trees still lined the grand boulevards, but booksellers crowded close to the river. Street musicians flourished, and the *Cité Universitaire*, founded in 1921, was filled with students. Construction continued to replace destroyed edifices, which camouflaged the disintegration of the city. The Opera House, the *Place des Vosges*, and one of the oldest quartiers known as the *Marais*, where silk merchants once prospered and Victor Hugo wrote his famous tomes, where the Bastille was stormed and the infamous *Boulevard de Crime,* caused many to laugh and weep before it was destroyed: these and other magnificent locations struggled to survive and repair themselves. In a city bursting with history, Paris would be remembered for its freedom fights, its independence and its spirit of inquiry. As Roshi knew, history was prone to repeat itself. He loved this country and its indomitable *esprit*. The behavior of the French peasant and the man on the street was inconceivable in Japan. Roshi knew the difference and had an outsider's appreciation for that which locals sometimes took for granted. What one generation fought and died for in the thousands, quickly became history, the past or forgettable unlearned lessons. Therefore, he chose carefully, when he trained his agents. Tolerance was a rare commodity, following war, and a virtue he valued above many other characteristics.

As for Anais, her apparent unconcern for her emotional surroundings was merely camouflage. There was no question that the effects of war had contributed to her divided life. In effect, she personified the signs of the time. Who she was and had become were inseparable from post war Paris.

Chapter 33
Marriage

They were married in 1927, the year Christolphe was assigned to a bank in Paris and Anais turned twenty-four. His Paris relocation was part of a promotion. Roshi could find no objection to the handsome young man, as he and Anais were the right age for commitment. No mention was made of a double personality. As a matter of fact, it had subsided after that year of lucid dreams, just after Christolphe had come on the scene. It would appear he was good for her.

Roshi spared no cost for the wedding that took place at St. Madeline. Four-hundred people attended. Those in certain circles knew and respected Roshi, and an invitation to the church ceremony was coveted. Anais knew none of these social climbers, but a princess needs a kingdom, and that was exactly the impression she gave, as she walked down the aisle on Roshi's arm and shared a smile with Lily who was her maid of honor. Christolphe was astonished at Roshi's generosity. People on the streets speculated whether they were royalty, wealth or well-known film stars. They could be no less. Anais did not finish her university degree, but that fact seemed to be of little concern to her. She was substantially more educated than her classmates and would continue the tradition of self-study throughout her life. Christolphe was well launched in the business world, his only regret that his mother would not be there to see them married. She had died the year before, lonely and longing to join his father who had died some years previously. She did, however, leave her entire estate to her only child. For that Christolphe was grateful. It had given him the courage to propose at age twenty-eight. He was quite a traditional and methodical fellow, and marriage was a state he took seriously.

To Anais he was a storybook prince: handsome, smart, ambitious and successful. She thought any woman would be lucky to find him, and she was right.

There was not much fault to find, and on the surface they were the perfect couple whose perfect courtship would go on to be the perfect marriage. Here, life met the illusion of what it should be. Roshi had the wedding party catered for a select few at the apartment. It was her real home, and he was her father who gave her away at the altar. The typical father, he was proud and sad and just a touch worried that something unforeseen would go wrong.

As for Christolphe's new job and promotion to a Paris bank, it was generally acknowledged that his connections were the right ones for advancement. He was not European though he thought like one. He held no Swiss passport, but he was nonpartisan, spoke French, English, and German, and carried himself like a diplomat. It did not hurt that he was Roshi's son-in-law, a coup indeed. It seemed that Roshi's name opened and closed doors. Only those in inner circles knew of his power and the integrity with which he kept secrets. Roshi was nearly a caricature of the inscrutable Oriental, and for that reason and many others his advice was greatly sought after.

Angela moved out of Roshi's apartment after the wedding. Their generous gift from him was their honeymoon that they spent in London, a city well known to Christolphe. If their intimate relationship was somewhat awkward or Angela's state of non-virginity questioned, it was not discussed. Suspicions lay dormant. She could not openly compare Christolphe to a man with whom she had become pregnant, had an abortion and loved with every fiber of her soul. That person did not exist. He could not be sure she withheld secrets and did not want access to his secrets, either. Thus, they started their married life in a conventional, convenient, and undisturbed manner.

In the way of tradition they looked for and found the house on *rue* Monbuisson. They rented in the city while paint and dust settled with the necessary renovations, but as soon as they could, they moved to the suburbs with its ten-minute train ride and another ten-minute walk from the station. They were typically happy newlyweds. Angela stayed home, sewing curtains, arranging new furniture, and planning meals for Christolphe. She could understand why the Swiss loved him; she could set her clock by his arrival home each evening. His manners and his dignified bearing inspired confidence and contributed to a sense of security that she had sought since childhood.

Life continued in this idyllic vein for the first year. Nothing ruffled their routine; nothing intervened with future promotions, more frequent dinner parties or soirees in the city. Angela dressed and acted her part while Christolphe played his newly wed happiness card so well he received commendations from his superiors. It seemed he and Angela had become an example of the way France was returning to life and recovery in the post war era. His excellent attitude on behalf of the bank was duly noted.

Then one morning, as was bound to happen, Angela awoke to nausea and the instant suspicion that she was pregnant. She did not question her inner knowing or remember another time, when she had been pregnant. She was a married lady and rarely did one question the natural progression of events that created children. She dreamed for a month of the presence of a child in their lives before she finally told Christolphe. He was delighted, he told her but, superstitiously, they agreed to wait for a few more months to make an announcement.

However, once they had decided to stay quiet on the subject, Angela began to have frightening dreams. War, abuse, torture and mayhem created nightmares that left her exhausted and haunted her days.

Unknown to Angela, her other half, the wild Anais, was in a rage. She did not want this child. She was adamant. How could she be free; how could she have lovers or live the life of a Bohemian artist? For some time, she had rented a small studio *pied a terre* near the Sorbonne, crowded with art types who communed about the meaning of life and death, and there she spent stolen time. She was an existentialist to her fingertips, and she was coming to dislike the Angela who never stepped out of line, who seemed to have no thoughts unless they came from her husband's head and no backbone unless it was laced into a corset. She had sacrificed much to get to the awareness she cherished and refused to take ten steps backward with regard to rights as a woman. As an artist and a thoughtful human being, she decided it was time to step in and make decisions before they became impossible.

First, she decided to have an abortion; she had done it before, and it was easy to arrange; second, she would tell Christolphe she had miscarried; and third, she would tell him she needed to keep her *pied a terre* in the city to recuperate and to think about life. This way she could use the small apartment more often without having to find excuses to be there. She might even tell him she could have no more children.

With her decision made, she had the abortion immediately. It was not one of her long-thought-out decisions. The next thing she did was automatic. She found herself standing on Roshi's doorstep.

***

He answered the door himself that day. On one level he was not surprised to see Anais; on another level he was

188

deeply surprised. Standing in the doorway was the Anais he had never met.

"Come in, my dear."

"You know who I am, don't you?"

"I believe I do."

She was dressed in an exotic cape. Her makeup was almost too much, but it suited his image of who she might be."

"Let's go to my study. There is a nice fire there, and Jean-Paul can bring us a cognac."

"At least you haven't offered me tea."

"No, I believe that would have been rejected."

She saw a look of recognition from Jean-Paul as he set the cognac before them. She nodded, and he discreetly left the room.

"So Jean-Paul knows who you are as well."

"Yes, I believe so. He's a bit like you after all these years of employment."

"He has been trained to notice such changes. But let's get down to the reason you're here. By the way, I am delighted and honored to meet you, finally."

She seemed a bit taken aback by his forthright admission that he had actually been aware of her existence for some time.

"Did you think I did not know of your other half? Poor Anais."

He paused.

"I do not pity her and neither should you. She does her best. And I know you look out for her. After all, you could be very disruptive of her life, if you truly wished to. Am I not right?"

"Don't think I haven't considered it."

"So what brings you here today?"

"I've had an abortion."

Roshi sat in stunned silence. She saw tears in his eyes before he brushed them away.

"So you don't always look out for her."

"How can you say that? She's already had one abortion. Her life disappeared after that. She is being punished. If she could not have the first one, then caused the death of the baby's father, why should she have this one and ruin my life, too? She's a coward. Besides, maybe it wasn't Christolphe's anyway."

This time it was Roshi's turn to be taken aback. She stared at him.

"Why are you telling me this?"

"Because you were once my best friend."

Roshi was overwhelmed with emotion. First he was told he had just been deprived of a grandchild. Now he was being offered the other Anais in friendship. It was one of the most bizarre situations he had ever encountered, and he was a man not easily shocked.

"Yes, of course, I'll always be your friend. Before you became two people, I loved the young Anais. If it means accepting the different sides of her, I am still her friend. I would never abandon either of you. Let me think some more about how we can accomplish this without hurting either of you."

"Thank you, Roshi. I've missed you." Anais sat in his study and cried. Her shoulders shook, and her head was bowed beneath her brimmed hat. For once, for this precious moment, it looked like he had the two of them sitting there together. He shook his head at the mess. Yes, he would need some time to consider their options.

"Do you need anything?"

She shook her head, no.

"Then I will let Jean-Paul take you wherever you need to go, and you can tell him to fetch you and return here next week at this time. I must be in Munich for a few days, but we will talk, when I return."

He rang for Jean-Paul who appeared in the doorway, instantly. He must speak to the man about eavesdropping.

"Will you drive Anais home, Jean-Paul? She will give you directions."

As she sat in the car on the way back to her studio, she wondered for a moment what she had gotten herself into, when she revealed herself to Roshi. He was the only one beside Lily who knew there was two of her, and Lily was either not interested or did not believe both personalities existed. Right now, her confession made her feel terribly vulnerable. Maybe it was the hormones after the abortion, she reflected. What else could have prompted her to expose herself?

***

Roshi spent the week in Munich quite distracted. There must be a solution to such a disturbing situation. He prided himself on his ability to come up with solutions, but now he was at a loss to reconcile the fractured Anais. She didn't deserve this chaos. It was not until he sat alone in his first class train compartment and watched the countryside slide by the window, as the window blurred in the rain and he wished to cry, that an impossible idea took shape in his mind.

As for the deception between Anais and Christolphe in their marriage, there was not much that could be done. Angela was the side of Anais that was the most wounded. She need never know about the abortion. Christolphe loved her enough to keep her in a protective cocoon, and it benefited him to keep her safe and sheltered.

As for the emerging Anais, she had now entered his life, totally. Perhaps, on that truthful basis, she could also be useful in the war restoration efforts. She was perfectly trained, and she knew the score. She was somewhat jaded, but wasn't that the perfect quality for a spy? Heavens only knew they could easily replace some of the naïve ones out there, chosen simply because they came from prominent families and wore patriotism on their sleeves. They were the pampered Joel Seaborns of this world. What he had seen on his doorstep was two women inhabiting one body.

Chapter 34
Roshi Recruits Anais as a Spy

If music could be trapped, if a musical instrument could be trapped without the destruction of its music, there would be no reason for sadness. But it wasn't true. Books could burn; violins could burn; music could grow more and more sad until it evaporated like water. Joy and song existed for the sake of music. Notes belonged to no one except the stars and the spirit. When they were burned and destroyed, music had to find another way to appear.

Right now, Anais felt bereft of music. Joy was for children who did not know its ephemeral nature. Joy was for good people and the innocent, not for ugly young women who were shameless and angry. She wanted to kick and scream like a two- year-old, but what good would that do her beside make her a spectacle on the street? Where could this bitterness go? She wanted to light a fire with it and dance with glee as it burned. She was a witch, a two-faced witch, and there was absolutely nothing she could do about it. It hurt more than she could admit. She couldn't even kill herself without killing her other half, the one who was good and precious. She could never redeem her sins for anyone, and her heart felt broken.

***

That afternoon, Anais walked all the way to Roshi's apartment. The week had dragged along so slowly, and Christolphe, gone for long hours at the bank, had barely noticed her state of mind. Angela the frail, as her bold half had cynically come to label her housewife half, had been protected from any knowledge of the abortion. The prescription for heavy menstrual discomfort that she carried after her miscarriage barely worked and, she realized, she should have stayed at home with her feet up today. Last evening, she had been hostess to another dinner party, dressed in a subdued Oriental robe that blended with her surroundings. She told Christolphe after the party that she considered going to the city to her little apartment to rest from the hormonal turmoil and stress of the miscarriage. The center of Paris uplifted her spirits, she told him. Fortunately, he told her he would be away on a business trip most of the coming week. She was such a good sport, he thought. If only she had a few more women friends. She assured him she loved her life the way it was, and he believed her. Why wouldn't he? He couldn't have asked for a more docile and uncomplaining companion.

So Anais slowly walked the distance to Roshi's apartment. The September weather was gorgeous, one of those sensuous Paris afternoons, when couples fell in love all over again. She was nearly healed, physically, though she realized she would never want a child of her own for as long as she lived. This was a cruel world where parents did evil things to each other, their children, and themselves. If something ever happened to a child of hers, she would die of grief. Rather the unborn child, a new spirit, wait in line for another mother. She was honest enough to know she was damaged in ways that would require her to keep certain aspects of life from intruding on her peace of mind. She had taken to writing again, during this long and lonely week. The text had turned into a short novel that she considered showing to Roshi when it was done.

As vulnerable as she felt, she was glad she had gone to Roshi with her predicament. Since her other half had not a clue what was going on, Anais had decided to share her burden with him. He was someone she could trust, someone who cared and eased the isolation she felt.

***

Roshi sat with his back to the fire, something he liked to do more and more. The warmth penetrated his porous bones and warded off winter illnesses. As he got older, he liked to think of the heat as a mother, sheltering him from harm. From the story Anais had told him, he was sure she had not experienced that kind of warmth in her life. She sought lovers for the warmth of their arms, but they were a temporary and shallow substitute.

He had asked her to go back and try to remember her life and its traumas. Then, he had asked when she thought this true split had occurred. He now knew as many details as she did. Descriptions of sexual and emotional abuse, abandonment, abortions and love, suicide and guilt, lovers and promiscuous behavior; he had heard it all and more than he suspected. He wanted to wrap her in warm quilts and nurse her to health. Instead, he sat there in a sphinx pose for long moments and prayed in his contemplative way, wherein he made himself a channel of wisdom. He could do no more. It was divine wisdom that was required to untwist such a history. By himself, he would have had no idea how to begin.

It would seem the complete and final split had come with the first abortion and been truly sealed with the second. But what had led up to those abortions had laid the foundation. In his channeling of light, he asked for the next step to become clear. He focused on repair to her soul just as he did in his prayers to heal global miseries and was not surprised, when an answer came to him. The solution: recruit Anais in his spy network. Use her as an instrument of good, so she would not end up working for the devil. Therefore, it was with confidence that he laid out a plan for her life.

***

It was their third meeting since the abortion.

"You need a purpose in your life, my dear."

She listened intently, feeling that the next few minutes would change her circumstance forever.

"I propose a goal and an actual job that engages your heart and mind, a larger purpose that overcomes these divisions you must endure and uses them for the good of the world."

Whatever it was she had braced herself to hear, this was not it. In some very deep reservoir of her mind she had expected to be judged and pronounced ugly. His statement did not come close. His words made her ears open wider and her heart listen in gratitude. How, she wondered, had she ever deserved to meet this man, to have him in her life, and now, to have him change the direction of her life. In her most hidden self she agreed that her greatest fear was a turn to evil. Though she was not yet privy to the details of her new life direction and its tasks, she knew she had just avoided the dreaded pit of hate. She had once read that evil entered the soul when love departed. This good and excellent man had chosen to love her and fill her life with a kind of love she had never known. It was the true love of a good father. It made her spirit, that had been so burdened, soar with hope.

"What do you think?"

"You have not told me what this path would entail."

She knew she could not simply change her focus without information.

"I hear the cynic in your voice. You do know the old definition of a cynic, my dear. She is an idealist who has been thwarted and disappointed in her dreams."

"Okay, my answer is yes. Sure. Who wouldn't love to suddenly find a great cause and a worthy life mapped out for them?"

Roshi smiled at her bravado. She showed just enough of a fighting spirit to be an asset in his work.

"So, you know me as the Roshi who keeps secrets. You know me as a diplomat and negotiator. You know, I have spent days and months at peace conferences, and I am sure that, during your stay in my home and our travels together, you have noticed me being approached by wealthy investors, government officials and others who wished to blend in with the backdrop of their surroundings. What do you think many of these men have asked of me? What is it I could possibly offer them?"

She looked bewildered. "I never thought they were other than friends or old acquaintances, wanting to reestablish a connection."

"Ah, that is good. Coming from a close observer, and one who has a fiercely bright intuition, I am flattered."

"Flattered?"

"You see, much of what you observed was just that, but I am also approached more often than not to help correct situations that have gotten out of hand or that the police have not enough intelligence to deal with appropriately. In these post war years, a war continues, Anais."

"You mean you're a spy?"

"For want of a nicer word, yes. I work for no government bureau, no specific individual, no bank, or corporation."

"Then who do you work for?"

"Let's say I work for peace and justice...for the welfare of mankind. I do not work for money or glory. As you know, I am heir to a fortune that mostly looks after itself. I was blessed with this fortunate situation. But one day I awoke and wondered about my soul and its purpose. You see, I live here in Paris, my family gone, my country of birth left behind, and I realize I am a citizen of the world who is more attached to ideas than a country. My loyalty does not seem to stop at a border. My affinities do not dissolve with travel, and my beliefs do not change with my clothes. In other words my allegiance is first and foremost to my own evolution as a human being and, secondly, to my worldly circumstances and the opportunities I have been given. I looked at my talents, my early training and my abilities and came to a conclusion. I am a keeper of secrets. I am also one who discerns truths and lies. I do not need to escape this fate; I need only use it in gratitude. Now, I ask, would you care to join me in my work?"

"How does this come about, Roshi?"

"You would work as my assistant. I can teach you what you need to know. How to be a keeper of secrets is nothing new to you. Already, for years, you have kept the gentle Angela a secret. Telling me of her existence was no mistake; it was a deliberate act on your part. It was, I suspect, a survival mechanism that had come to life. It was also your blessed karma that put you in my hands."

"As my assistant, I would acquaint you with a problem situation that has been brought to my attention. Together we can unmask the truth, and we can help unravel its complex and often distorted path. At times, this information can benefit mankind. Otherwise, the situation must be changed. Every case is unique. Right now, the repercussions of the Great War have created loss and hatred. Everyone wishes recompense for his or her own sorry involvement, however, not everyone deserves redemption; some are trying to use the war to satisfy their own greed; certain parties love the fact that the war opened a new and horrible means for them to satisfy their ambitions. The first thing I must teach you is how to listen to a story or a tale of woe."

"It seems we will be spending a lot of time together."

"True. There is much I must teach you, once again. You must learn to arm yourself for this new role."

"But how can I be a catalyst to better political relations in Europe, when I can barely reconcile the fact that there are two of me?"

"How? Who knows better the bitter results of conflict and sorrow?"

"The fire devoured one more note of the piano and only three notes were left playing. Then two.

"Then one which would not die."

—Nin *Collages*

Chapter 35
Anais Reconciles Her Newfound Purpose

Anais was tired, but she turned down a ride home from Jean-Paul. She needed to clear her head. This was not easy to do while living a double life. Roshi had explained to her that her duality could be turned into an asset. She wanted to believe it more than she had ever wanted anything in her life. It looked like her innocent double would be working for Roshi without her knowledge, while Anais, the courageous, would orchestrate information she might obtain from her unknowing twin. Christolphe, for instance, was in a position of authority at the bank, whereby information passed through him on a daily basis. As well, the art community that she loved so much was rife with information and informants. According to Roshi, she would be his earphone, his vision extended beyond his apartment and beyond the reach of his limbs that were becoming stiff with old age.

She had thought she was tired, but she heard a new ring to her footsteps, a purposeful tone to her steps. Her two personalities, that had kept her a prisoner for the last few years, had metamorphosed. Her vigilance had become eyes and ears for her mentor, and she had not wasted a day of her life. Unknown to her, she had been in training to enter a world she never knew existed. Suddenly, her life in the suburbs of Paris seemed like a refuge, her garden a place to gather and assimilate what she overheard.

"Over here, Jacques. Be careful with those stones. Where is your helper today?"

Angela looked up in time to see the wheelbarrow tip precariously before being righted by Jacques. The work of creating a beautiful garden was fraught with more excitement than she had imagined. Presently, she was creating a small fishpond complete with a short but steep stream that allowed the water to cascade into the pool below. Louveciennes was a full-time job.

"I'll be okay, Madame. This is the last load of rocks. Help is not that easy to find these days. I think someone offered my helper an easier job."

They worked in the garden all morning. At first she had considered a Zen garden, but the sound of water had kept her plans under revision until this new idea had evolved. The sound of water splashing on rocks until it found the goldfish pond had been the incentive to continue. The yard was already surrounded by a high privacy wall and sheltered enough to grow lush leafy plants. Near the water would be a small stone patio for romantic dinners with Christolphe and a lounge chair for reading on sunny afternoons. She could write in her diary out here or paint, if she felt inspired. She needed projects to keep her busy because Christolphe was gone so often on his business trips. She felt a twinge of regret that he did not find her interesting enough to stay home more often. There were times, when she felt so lonely. On those days she reverted to an ugly little girl, abandoned by her father. She would never tell Christolphe, of course. He provided such a good life for them.

There were days, when she wasn't occupied with a project like the garden, that she dreamed of owning a car or a printing press or both. Recently, she had found money in a darling Japanese box that she had owned since childhood. It was actually a great deal of money, though she kept the exact amount to herself. Christolphe wondered how she would pay for the garden renovations, and she simply told him that help was cheap enough these days that she had saved out of the household budget. He believed her and rarely gave much thought to the effort she spent to make their lives so pleasant.

Her favorite color was blue, a shade that included the day sky and night sky, the coastal colors of Coliou in the south of France, and the many shades of blue in Monet's garden. Though she was a married woman, she felt like a virgin in layer after layer of poetic purity; life went on forever like the horizon in a Turner painting or more and more flecks of light in an impressionist landscape. But blue was the color of mystery and elegance that held a secret mirror and drew on unexpected ocean depths. She would fill her garden with blue hydrangea, iris, and Japanese lilies. She would write poetry out in this garden and record her dreams. Graceful elegance would be a part of this garden, as it reached down into the soil and up to the top of the garden fence.

***

Meanwhile, Anais, the wild and unknown, had decided to take dance lessons from a Flamenco instructor. She had met him at a café near the booksellers by the Seine. She bought a flounced flamenco skirt and a ruffled bodice and put her hair up with a red rose, when she practiced at his studio. She loved the black character shoes worn by the dancers, the stomping of feet and the clicking of castanets. The instructor told her she was a natural, and she explained that she had lived in Havana for several years. They spoke in Spanish during the lesson, and thus she was removed to a place of warmth and moisture. She danced for hours until she felt liquid and sensuous. Carlos, her teacher, would gyrate beside her, rub against her, and breathe heavily against her skin. She anticipated that they would, one hot afternoon, consummate their passion on the floor of the studio in time to the music on the gramophone. The anticipation beat through her veins that joined the sinuous curves and motions of her pelvis.

After the lesson she would change behind the screen in Carlo's studio and leave her dance costume hung on a hook. She dressed, thanked him, and took herself out to the automobile Roshi had insisted on buying for her. Roshi said she must drive and become confident with quick reactions and movements. It might save her life one day. She drove out to Louveciennes and parked the car beside the house. It was quite safe there and her double never guessed it belonged to her. Sometimes she wondered whether she showed up by car just to torment the unaware side of herself.

Anais had no problem with the seduction of a dance instructor. Quite frankly, she decided, she had no compunctions about the seduction of anyone. She had recently met a fellow who said she would be a famous writer someday. His name was Miller, an American. His French wasn't good, and his English was vulgar, but he was looking for a good time. He had left his wife and young daughter home in New York in order to live the Bohemian life of a French writer. He used words like fuck, when he was near her. To demonstrate how little such language shocked her, she showed him how it was done. And just to prove that actions speak more boldly than words, he was still reeling from her demonstration. He said he was in love with her, though she knew it was not his mind that spoke but a nether part of his body. He was so easy to seduce.

***

Roshi was teaching her how to listen, but what he didn't know was that she had taken those lessons beyond the listening of ears. Did he realize she listened with her whole body in the unspoken language of music, rhythm and body fluids? All of her senses spoke to her. Her body, that had been abused and shamed as a child, had its own radar system. She had read articles about dolphins and their capabilities and wondered what their history had been or why they had been given such acute hearing. As far as she was concerned, every pore of her body was an auditory receptor.

She had taken up the study of D. H. Lawrence, once again, this time with all her feminine receptors on alert. *Lady Chatterley's Lover* had recently been published. It was 1928 and the book's content excited her enormously. His feminine perceptions, his language that understood every nuance of her own feelings, struck her as the most sensitive writing, when it was, in reality, an understanding of a woman's sensuality. The fact that he had run away with his wife before they were married was romantic in the extreme. How had he come to know a woman's body better than most women? As far as she was concerned, he was in full possession of feelings that should be the natural understanding of every woman, and yet was not.

She was transported through her reflections back to the garden of her own childhood, when too early, much too early, she had been introduced to sexual experiences that had made her neurotic. She read Freud endlessly these days and her goal, when she studied Lawrence, was to take full control of her own body and lead it out of a chaos where half of her soul was trapped in a child's sensibility. She became a literary spy, when she read between the pages of a Lawrence novel. She was hungry for the unknown, obsessed with information about other lives and a virtual voyeur through their experiences.

Beneath all of this hunger she was a child, a daughter whose needs were not met, a daughter obsessed with incest and abandonment deep within, somewhere beyond the lives of Angela and Anais in the realm of life lived on the edge. Time was distorted in the diary. It was fiction without officially being called fiction. Its relationship to time evoked the past and present, simultaneously. Relationships continued after being broken off, smells from the past reappeared and ugliness disappeared. Flaws were forgiven and perfection was found in everyone. Yet, death and loss were continuous.

Though it was Roshi who had introduced the word spy, and Roshi who taught her concentration and observation skills, it was also Roshi who unknowingly brought back images from her childhood, disturbing memories of being bathed and soaped within every inch and crevasse of her life, of being stimulated and penetrated until she shook in every nerve ending, hearing words like dirty, ugly little girl in a caressing tone, hearing whispers in the dark that entered her dreams until one became indistinguishable from the other.

In a perverse way these dreams made her powerful and responsible for the power she had manufactured. She was a spy who penetrated her own past, a little girl in a woman's body who wanted more and more until hunger had turned sex into an addiction.

***

Freud called it hysteria. Did he know what he was talking about? The Hindus said all of life was made up of three simple parts: birth, sex, and death. So the entire middle years were devoted to that organ that caused pleasure and pain. She had experienced them both. Recently, she had read of yoga, an Eastern concept purported to be thousands of years old. The most mysterious branch of this philosophy or science, as some would call it, was tantric yoga. Apparently, it was about withholding the little death experience until pleasure was unbearable. It had to do with sacrifice, fire and the ability to control sexuality. It certainly put the notion that men could not control their natures into the category of nonsense. Self-control, that was the key. It was too bad her generation had not yet learned this wisdom. Now, when she was on a case with Roshi, control and discipline were paramount.

One day, Roshi told her that her training was complete. Her areas of expertise were the worlds of art and banking. These were power spots that few had access to, especially the arts. No one suspected artists, writers, playwrights like Antonin Artaud, newcomers like Henry Miller, women artists like Rebecca West or Djuna Barnes. No one gave them a second thought because artists were reputed to be happy and contained in their own little worlds, impervious to the politics of failure. Their only true and common denominator was food on the table, a roof overhead and a winter coat to ward off the cold. Competition left them lean and mean to each other. They spent most of their time practicing for parts, looking for parts or producing art in song, sculpture, or painting and, if there was a moment or two left over, they slept with each other to reduce existential anxiety. Nothing was so uncertain as the career of an artist.

As for the banking world, Roshi had plans for her first assignment that would put Angela in an advantageous and naïve, though valuable, position. The plan was this. Angela would listen carefully at the many dinner parties she so graciously gave. When the parties were over, she would stay awake and record everything that had been discussed. Since she and Christolphe did not sleep in the same room, she was free to keep the lights on until she had exhausted her observations. These would be prompted by questions in the journal. Answers to where, when, why, what, and who could produce descriptions of great value. Under the illusion that she was merely remembering for the sake of being a gracious hostess at future events, she would use all her newfound skills to be useful. If anything unusual went on at these evening affairs, Angela would be the first to know and the last to be suspected of knowing anything.

Chapter 36
Anais Reveals Herself to Roshi

It was with regard to her second assignment that Anais rented the houseboat. In 1928 she gave up her apartment on the left bank for the unique exposure of the Seine. The move put her on the circuit of places to stop for gossip or for the possibility of booking a gallery show. Anais was no longer considered an impoverished writer; the houseboat art gallery put her on the map as a desirable connection. The place was like a pot of honey to bears, a sip of nectar to bees. The object was to make her gallery all the rage. With a bit of mystery behind her, enough money to create an interesting venue and her ability to keep secrets, the houseboat would be a perfect destination to swap stories and tell secrets, to gossip and share. She would be witness to the art world at every level.

If villains intended to exploit her beloved art community for something that might deprive artists of freedom of expression, guilt of the soul or impoverishment of vision, she would be there to observe. Would an artistic community ever again have such a pure-hearted protectress? She could not do enough for this community that had given her an identity and a purpose to live at least half of her life fully.

***

Yves tidied up the deck on his boat then looked in on the houseboat. Anais had left it in perfect order, but it helped to memorize that order just in case he needed to remember clues. The latch on the door was a significant but fragile token of safety. Anyone could walk right in. He had just finished his rounds and was at the back of the houseboat to see what she had done with the balcony, when he felt a slight dip to the deck and heard the rattling of the lock. His back was up against the wall, as he listened. Soon he heard footsteps inside the gallery and the sound of a man climbing the stairs to the bedroom. Quickly, he slid around to the front and stayed undercover.

***

In truth, Yves owed his post war life to Roshi, and it was his own little secret. It was Roshi who had found him, when he was destitute and struggling to survive the trauma of war; it was Roshi who had convinced him there was hope in the world, then Roshi who had trained him to be an observer. It was another word for agent in Yves' mind, but an agent with a different attitude. When he proposed that Yves work on the quay near his parents' old barge, Yves was not only grateful but honored to work for such a wise man. So he had become the official bodyguard of the houseboat and the illusive Anais whenever she stayed on board. Now, he had been hired by her to be the bartender on the night of her party, which would put him in the perfect position to watch over the guests.

***

Angela got dressed. May was a glorious month with a bit of rain and patches of the cleanest sunlight, when primroses spread and grew all over the garden. The smells lifted her heels as she walked. Nearly anywhere she wanted to go could be reached on foot. Today, she preferred not to take the train underground for any reason and carried her bright fuchsia umbrella. Her shoes were a comfortable but fashionable soft leather to match her bag. Her light spring coat was cocoa brown with bursts of the same fuchsia, but it was her eyes that she had taken the most time to fix. They were geisha eyes, heavily made up with black ink and an underlying matte of pale blue as background to her thick lashes. Just a slight outward tilt bewitched most men. Her coat was short and her stockings silken. They felt lovely to walk in, and reminded her that she was among the fortunate. Silk stockings were impossible to find and their cost was prohibitive. She stepped onto the pier just as Yves was stepping on deck the *Hilaire* while yawning and scratching himself. He was tousled and sleepy, but startled, when he heard her footsteps. She was a vision.

Anais stopped beside his boat. "Good morning, Yves"

He looked around. "Good morning, Madame. You have chosen a fine day to walk.

"Remind me, there is something I wish to discuss with you this week. Will you be around?"

"*Bien sure.*"

"Good. *A bientôt.*"

Today, she walked briskly but no less elegantly for all that. After a change of clothes she was on a bus, heading for the Marais, close enough to the apartments of some of her artist friends that she might be able to invite them in person to the opening of the gallery. Perhaps she would have time to view the *Bird in Space* by Constantin Brancusi or visit Marcel Duchamp who still lived in the area. On her way back to *La Belle Aurore* she would detour to rue des Artes and visit a few of the ateliers with her last invitations. She longed to see Duchamp's *Nude Descending a Staircase* because, for some time now, completed in 1912, it represented to her the dissociation she felt from her other half, the half that she protected and kept safely hidden from her friends in the art world.

At her innermost core, Anais was born to be a surrealist and a child of the times. The nude that descended the Duchamp staircase was her several selves. The woman was naked and vulnerable, hurt, and split into layers of lost and lonely personalities. War had happened on many battlefields; its effect spread like a spider's web, and its victims bitten in their sleep. The nude was a sleepwalker, and her sleep protected her body while her spirit escaped in search of a safe place. As Anais got off the bus, she walked with brave steps, now dressed more like an artist than a banker's wife. At this moment she felt profound gratitude for the means and ability to protect her several selves.

***

The next morning, she listened to the sound of her own voice, as she intoned the mantra *OM*. Its resonance hovered longer here on the river than at home. Water held the notes until they swirled in eddies through her mind. She loved this time of morning, the river and her meditation practice. She knew that, when she folded her legs and bowed down to Amitabha, she would feel suffused with life. She gave thanks on her next breath and refocused on the sound, the way it penetrated the space around her in concentric circles, outward ever outward, until it circled back within her own heart.

Years ago, Roshi had explained to her that she must learn to direct her gifts through the practice of spiritual exercises. To that end, while she studied with Roshi, she had done two things in line with his teachings. She practiced a mantra and kept her faithful diary.

Today, she looked forward to further lessons with an archery teacher. Each spiritual practice taught her to focus, to concentrate, and to go to the center of her mind and body, the place where she was at peace with her watery nature. It was the place of truth. There, she often found that what so often appeared to be true was not the center and not quite what she wished to pursue. Thus, redirected, she would patiently carry on and refocus.

She got up from her meditation mat, changed into exercise clothes and began another essential practice. She stretched up in a sun salutation, a practice to become strong and aware of each new day. She preferred, however, to do lunar salutations that were developed especially for women. Mostly, they were comprised of balance poses and, for her, balance was most important. Her two personalities balanced each other but needed maintenance and support. In the moon asanas these two aspects of herself were woven and connected. Neither could afford to become vague or invisible.

Anais knew she would always need to make time for these practices. She was quite alone in the world, and they were the glue that not only held her together, they gave her access to her dreams. She knew she would receive a note from Christolphe soon, telling her he would be back from his business trips to Geneva and Zürich. Then, she would leave this paradise she had created over the deep currents of the Seine and return to entertain Christolphe's guests.

***

There were always detailed preparations for a party.

"Yves, let's go over to the café and hire them to cater the event."

"That's genius. They could sure use the income."

"I figure they can get family and friends to do the *hors d'oeuvre.*"

"Brilliant."

"Let's go. We'll have an espresso while we're there."

Yves watched, as she got her purse, crossed a strap from shoulder to hip and was ready."

"You're ready? Women don't get ready so fast."

"Well, we don't want to scare our caterers. These are artists we're entertaining."

"By the way, I've never been a bartender before."

"In this case it means pouring wine. Bad wine. None of them care, just so long as it's free. What we need is lots of food. You've never seen anyone eat like starving artists."

"Should I walk around with little plates of finger food?"

"Those are *hor d'oeuvres*. When you aren't filling glasses, you can offer more food. That way you hear more conversations."

"I should listen?"

"You should listen very carefully."

Chapter 37
The Party

It was nearly time for the party to begin. The artists, writers, and musicians she knew were growing impatient to christen her gallery and invade her space. She planned to give a surrealist sendoff to her floating gallery. The event had grown with expectation because it would be compared to a surreal celebration. The war, and the fearful closed off states of mind that resulted from its invasion, had left everyone frayed and edgy. Laughter was more subdued; colors were more violent; spaces were disconnected and focus fragmented. Artists needed a focus, but no one knew where to turn in such unrest. A party would help, and a masquerade might be a catalyst to inspire new thoughts. Life was one wave of transition after another, but the transition after war left wounds of bewilderment. Right now, hope was at a low ebb.

***

The evening of the gallery opening was full of surprises. Ernest Hemmingway showed up late in the evening. His was a new presence on the literary circuit. He had come alone and stood in his own uncomfortable aura of vulnerability while she handed him a drink and asked if he had visited the Gotham Book Mart, since his arrival in Paris. He ignored her question.

"I like your houseboat. Thought about owning one myself once." He sipped his drink and continued to look around. "It's a great idea."

Always gracious, Anais beckoned to Djuna Barnes and introduced her to Ernest. Djuna loved to talk, though most of what she had to say was untrue and whispered in the greatest of confidential tones. Maybe I'll introduce him to Miller later, she thought mischievously, after he has another drink. Henry might not like it, but he was a grownup, wasn't he? She smiled with a fey curve of her lips behind her birdcage headdress. After all, what was fiction but lies, and who could recount them better than Miller. Hemingway was getting a reputation for harsh honesty, a fact as unreliable and subjective as truth these days.

Anais slid from group to group, sensitive to shyness, lack of social skills and assorted ineptitudes. She elicited a laugh here and a story there. It seemed that everyone loved her costume and much speculation was involved, trying to figure out what she wanted to portray inside her birdcage. It covered her head and gave her a glimpse of what it might be like to live behind bars. It was certainly a party warmer. To all inquiries she answered evasively, "It's why caged birds sing." From inside the cage her eyes shone full of wonder, as if she expected some kind of miracle to free her at any moment.

Yves watched carefully, as guests arrived. Masquerades gave people the opportunity to be someone else, to act out of character or release inhibitions. Kiki of Montparnasse had arrived and made a sensation, wearing only a frame that depicted her as Modigliani's model. Anais knew better than anyone that the artist's personality, contrary to common opinion, was not naturally uninhibited. Instead, she viewed the artist's naked stance toward the world as courageous. Most of them were hard working, gentle and impoverished. They were also quite introverted. Their extroversion was saved for performances.

She had just delivered a tray of drinks and finger food to the musicians who seemed perpetually hungry and was about to return to the party room, when a guest stepped out from the shadows of the balcony. She knew before he spoke that he was someone suspect. His mask gave him the look of a wolf. Nearby, the musicians were eating, making it a little too quiet on deck, so her mind raced. Disturbance filled the air.

Then, the small jazz combo she had hired for the evening started to play. They were out on the open deck and had chosen the spot themselves. It wasn't often they got to play in the open air with a river flowing all around them as background. It was a unique experience, and they seemed to be enjoying the sounds they put together.

Fortunately, at that moment somebody walked by and told her that Henry Miller was looking for her. She stepped back into the gallery and watched Henry from across the room, as he looked furtively for her while June was occupied in conversation. Anais suspected that June had come to Paris for a surprise visit because she did not trust Henry's motives for being there, and she had good reason to feel the way she did. Tonight, June was dressed as the seductive Scheherazade, a half veil across her face to cover up an eye tick and hatred, as she spoke to the woman beside her. June was alluring and beautiful in a cruel way. Perhaps, she should be introduced to Antonin Artaud who was present, looking perfectly suited to his Roman Nero costume. Anais waited for Yves to approach to take a tray of finger food from her.

"I see it's a night for capes." He grinned. "I have to serve Parsifal over there." He pointed to the shadows. "Seems he's an opera singer, a baritone. Says he was hired to play the role in Beyruth, Germany. Isn't that some kind of big deal?"

"It is, actually, but I don't know the fellow. Did you see who he came with?"

"The jazz singer waiting to sing with the combo. They seem an unlikely pair, split up as soon as they came in. He's been bragging about his good luck to anyone whose ear he can bend."

"I wonder. I'll just introduce myself." She wandered over to the singer, during a pause between his stories, extended her hand, and introduced herself. "Your hostess, Anais, *Monsieur*."

"I finally meet the mysterious lady. Holtz Gratzer, *enchanté.*"

He reached out and overwhelmed her with the strength of his handshake.

"You are German?"

"No, no, Alsatian. Does that make me a German Frenchman?" His laugh revealed an edge.

"It has been brought to my attention that your costume represents the role you will soon play at Bayreuth. You are a Wagnerian and Alsatian. That is quite a feat."

"You understand. It was not easy to land a part there, and Parsifal is beyond my wildest dreams. I have colleagues who would give their right arm for the part."

"I believe you. Do you suspect you are being used by the Germans as a measure of their good intentions toward us?"

"I have no idea. I just want to do a good job and get out." He seemed suddenly nervous.

"I'm sure you'll be fine, if your speaking voice is anything to go by. Come, I'll introduce you to June."

She saw June looking in their direction and led Holtz to her.

"Enjoy the evening. Welcome to Paris and my party."

She drifted out to the balcony again and sat down to listen to Holtz' date, who looked Ethiopian, as she sang with the jazz group that sounded like it came from Addis. They featured an Ethiopian saxophonist with the haunting Amharic sounds that Anais considered to be the first true jazz to arrive in Europe. The music had travelled far, but this evening it clung to the deck and the river in a caress. The notes rippled beyond familiar Western octaves and undulated in movements as old as man and woman. They combined the sounds of Ethiopia with the jazz that was

216

being imported from New Orleans. The sounds completed each other, weaving between riffs of cultural difference and tolerance, exploring and enjoying each other, as the musicians improvised.

As she stood in the shadows on deck, she sensed Raphael's presence before she saw him. He stood behind her and found her waist where he rested his hand. She sighed and felt tension leave her.

"It's a wonderful party. You've done a great job." He chuckled. "I found Hemingway by himself on the foredeck. We talked about Montana and how he would like to build a cabin and live there someday. I can't imagine anyone less suited to Paris society."

They held hands and made a circle of the room. He had dressed like an American cowboy.

"You look like you could rob a stagecoach."

"Right now, I would settle for a beer. Look over your shoulder."

***

Then, as if she had conjured him, her path was intercepted by Roshi. She could never mistake him for anything but himself, but his disguise this evening was endearing. He was Merlin complete with star-studded robe and hat, stage face, warts, wrinkles and a twinkle in his eyes. Raphael slipped away and disappeared into the crowd.

"Where is your wand? I feel like I made a wish and you appeared."

"What concerns you, my dear?"

"Let's go upstairs."

They walked upstairs to the balcony off of her bedroom.

"You are the perfect spy, Anais. Between your two personas, you are apt to learn twice as much as anyone else. You are trusted here, and the artists of Paris know more than they realize. You will not need to betray them; you are to extract their insights and pass them on. No names, just insights."

"Right now, I am concerned about one of my guests, the fellow who is dressed as Parsifal. Something about him makes me uncomfortable, but I have no basis for my suspicions. If you talk to him, I would be interested to hear your feelings. Seriously, what could a young singer contribute to our problems? I feel somewhat foolish for pointing a finger."

"Do not doubt your intuition. We know that bad things are coming. The economy and the evil that has gone underground to fester these last ten years, these are gaining momentum and will erupt in violence. Jews are being targeted. They are among those opposed to the spread of evil. You saw the Marais, the litmus paper of Paris, and knew something was encroaching on every narrow street. Your suspicions are important, so let go of fear."

"This is all so new to me, Roshi."

"Just share a diary with your other half. Leave hints for her, and she will write. That's enough. She does not need to be involved any more than that. If you were only one person, you would still be able to help tremendously. That you are two and discrete is a bonus. When the party is over, you will make your own observations."

"But who are we working for, Roshi? I am always filled with doubts."

"Anyone on the side of goodness, my dear. Can you doubt it? It doesn't matter if it is the Americans, the French, the bankers or concerned Jews. I know you will give yourself wholeheartedly to this cause, now that you know I am by your side. I trust your abilities, as you trust mine. Breathe. Let go of your fears."

"Thank you, Merlin."

"You are welcome, my uncaged bird. I stopped by to see how you were doing, and you are doing splendidly."

Anais smiled and realized her birdcage had slipped. Roshi disappeared as suddenly as he had appeared, but his magical whispers had dispelled doubts about the value of their mission.

She circulated among her guests and evaded just enough questions to cause a stir among the curious. By the end of the next hour, a rumor had circulated that there was a new man in her life, tall and mysterious. She was keeping him hidden, it was said, and that was another cause for talk. How artists loved to speculate and gossip and dramatize. It was who they were, and it colored their otherwise dull lives. Drama was their bread and butter, and from it they thrived.

It was very late and some of the guests were about to leave. Henry's glances were somewhat hostile, as though he had the right to exclusivity. Their little sexual adventure recently might not have taught him enough manners. She said goodbye to him and June as they left, then made herself invisible. She asked Yves if he intended to stay till the end of the party and whether he would lock up. He looked intrigued but didn't ask personal questions. There was something very trustworthy about him, she decided. He would make a good friend as well as landlord.

There was a lot of subtle and not so subtle speculation, as to who had financed the reconstruction of the boat. It was understandable. Most of her guests wanted to believe that Paris was visibly rising out of the muck, that whatever was good for Paris bode well for them, but there were the usual few who were envious. There was always that contingent at any gathering, the ones who were full of pretense and made Yves's skin crawl with their insincerity. Then, there was Parsifal who just didn't fit in somehow and, if he wasn't mistaken, possessed the heavy tread that had climbed the steps to her bedroom that afternoon.

Chapter 38
A Bit of History

The next morning, Yves was at his usual chores on deck. He appeared to clean and paint and varnish his boat in a never-ending round of tidiness. He doffed his hat to Anais, as she passed him on the pier. He would give her a few minutes on board before he made his report on the fellow who said he was an opera singer.

***

Several years had gone by since Adolf Hitler had circulated through political spheres in Germany. Since Hitler had joined the German Workers' Party, it had become openly anti-Semitic, anti-capitalist, anti-democratic, anti-Marxist and anti-liberal. Even tobacco sales had soared in Europe, since 1920, because the packages were now labeled anti-Semite. Just the previous year, after violent attacks on other parties, when the Versailles Treaty was opposed, Hitler had been jailed. It simply gave the man an opportunity to write about his struggles. *Mein Kampf* was published as soon as Hitler got out of jail. The book glorified him and his identification with the people of Germany, their offended pride and insulted culture. Already licking their wounds from their defeat, during the Great War, Hitler added a scalding wound to their anger. Though the Nazi party had been banned in favor of the German Volkisch Freedom

Party, once Hitler was out of jail in 1924 and after the publication and distribution of his book, the New Nazi Party came to power and the freed Hitler became its undisputed leader. Meanwhile, the Paris Exposition created a stir of imagination, and the Art Deco movement flourished. In 1925 the world of finance and reparation had floundered and could not be revived. Despite hard times, Picasso's *Three Dancers* was completed, Franz Kafka wrote *The Trial*, and Virginia Woolf wrote *Mrs. Dalloway*. In the minds of those who wished to move on and into the future, nothing was settled.

***

The Bayreuth Festival had come to life in 1876 under the patronage of King Ludwig. For decades its operatic performances had taken place in that sleepy town in strict compliance with the traditions initiated by Wagner, himself. Wagner's beautiful music had eventually become surrounded by a slavish cult with the inclusion of long and ponderous performances and the exclusion of all that was not Germanic in origin or language. In addition to writing music, during his lifetime Wagner shared his racist opinions. In 1850 he published *The Nature of Race against Jewishness in Music.* At that point even Nietzsche broke off his friendship with Wagner. Hitler, however, had no such reservations.

By 1920 Hitler had become a fan of Wagner's music and friend to his granddaughter Winifred Wagner who then became Hitler's ardent supporter. Modern music and Hitler's fear of change, the unknown and degenerate artists caused new music to be excluded from the Bayreuth Festival. From that moment the festival provided a venue for a unique form of cultural prejudice, orchestrated by the Nazi state.

The summer of 1926 would witness the second performance of the German Worker's Handel Festival. Through opera and oratorio performances, the cult of high culture in Germany would pass on to the masses, a people's voice. Through this special Handelerian preference, German romanticism and love songs that had proliferated since the Middle Ages were being cast off, along with Wagner, in favor of the musical dictates of Nazi ideologue Alfred Rosenberg. Most Jewish musicians and foreign singers had already been banned from performances across Germany. Since the dye was cast, the Handel Festival was handed over to the Nazi Party as it distributed free tickets to wounded soldiers and staged proselytizing talks about the new demagogy that was an integral part of the German Reich. Everyone was exhorted to toughen up and listen with new ears.

How did a non-German opera singer, who did not wish to starve, land a role at Bayreuth these days? The answer: it didn't happen. Ergo, Holtz was a German.

Actually, Holtz had been born and grew up in the town of Gratz of pious Catholic parents. His father was the town miller and, as such, did very well for himself. He was a particularly cruel man, though the village folk considered him an invaluable and upstanding member of the community. He often took to throwing furniture, when he was in a sour mood, and had once thrown Holtz's mother out in the snow because she disagreed with an insignificant comment he made. He often made insignificant comments and droned on and on with opinions that had all of them asleep on their feet. The first time Holtz remembered his mother being jettisoned from the house, he was only six. He could still see her slippers in the snow and the blood, where she had hit her head on a rock, during her fall. He had watched out the window and wondered why she didn't get up. He watched for a long time because she had no coat on, and it was cold. That evening he was sent to bed hungry because his mother was not able to make dinner.

He wondered, if that was the reason she died a year later. She seemed frail after that day, could never seem to get warm, and always wore several sweaters to comfort herself. It took her a year to die, physically, but the light had gone

222

out of her eyes by the time he woke up that next morning to find his oatmeal, waiting for him. He ate it all and the cheese and brown bread on the table. His older brothers were already at the mill, working, his father was gone, and his youngest brother was in the highchair, playing with his food.

It seemed they ate a lot of food in those days but never so much or so well as when his mother was alive. He was six feet five inches tall, pretty much like his brother, the youngest who was still alive. The two eldest had been killed in battle. The youngest had been needed to run the mill for the soldiers and now for the Reich. Somehow, God or the devil had given Holtz a rich and talented voice, and he was expected to use that talent in service to his country. It was a miracle he had landed the part of Parsifal for next season. It wasn't Handel; it was Wagner, but it was a beautiful role, one most singers would give their right arm to sing. He suspected it was because of his looks. He had seen Winifred Wagner in the audience in Vienna the year before and knew she had been attracted to him, when he was backstage after the show. He was the perfect Aryan German: tall, blond and handsome. His voice was officially baritone, but he could sing whatever was required of him.

His rent had not been paid in months and, if it lasted much longer, he would join his younger brother as a miller, anything to feel warm and full again. Funny how, on days like this, his memories of his mother returned to haunt him.

He went back to his music and his studies. It was mentioned in intellectual circles that the new psychoanalysis propounded by a man named Sigmund Freud, a Jew, had triggered the revival of such operas as Tristan and Isolde. His theories of love and death, Amour, Eros and Thanatos, had piqued the interest of Hitler who attended the opera at Bayreuth even if the occasional Jew was in the cast. Holtz did not understand what all the commotion was about, when it came to Jews. He had had Jewish friends ever since he studied music. Knowing Winifred had put him on the map.

At least, until he sang the part and proved himself. In the meantime she had asked him to come to Paris and keep his eyes and ears open. He was certainly not averse to Paris though his brothers were killed by the French or Brits or Americans; he didn't know, but he was sure Carl and Hans had done their share of killing, too. What he was uncertain of was his task. He had been asked to keep an eye on the art world. Just because he was a singer didn't mean he knew other kinds of artists and was unsure what it was he was meant to discover, but here he was in the right place and, hopefully, at the right time.

Specifically, he was told, he was to report anti-German and undesirable sentiments that had infiltrated the world of galleries and publishers: homosexuality, blacks, Jews or the mentally and physically handicapped. Politically hated ideologies that might infiltrate historical awareness were unacceptable. He knew the Nazis were in the process of actively destroying what they referred to as degenerate artifacts. Even certain musical scores were deemed unacceptable. The National Fascist Party had recently come to power in Italy under Benito Mussolini, but Holtz wondered what the difference was between the Italian dictator and Hitler. It seemed that no matter what the Reich did to erase art monuments, new tributes would appear to mock their efforts. The cabarets of sensual nightclubs flourished along with degenerate jazz and swing that were particularly offensive to the Party. Homosexual men may have gone into hiding, but aggressive lesbians were making more blatant and frequent appearances in their mockery of male authority.

After the gallery party on the houseboat, Holtz was mostly concerned about how to begin his report to Winifred. No one in the gallery world and not one of the writers he had met had anything good to say about the new Germany.

Chapter 39
Freudian Psychoanalysis

"Rene, is it true that each of us can, to a great extent control our destiny? Do you believe it's true?"

Anais was halfway through a session of psychoanalysis. She had heard of Freud, was fascinated with his work on dream interpretations, and sought out Doctor Rene Allendy to experience these new perceptions about the mind. Now, it was beginning to wear thin in her estimation. She was required to lie on a sofa and do all the talking while this man held himself aloof and silent for the fifty-minute hour. He never failed to collect his fee, which was steep, but so far it was a mystery to her how he was of any help. Besides, she thought him stuffy, arrogant and possessed of delusions of grandeur. He was the doctor; she was the patient; therefore, he was somehow superior to her. He needed to be taught a lesson.

"Yes, I do. Why do you ask this question today, Anais?"

She shrugged and thought for a few moments.

"I'm not sure, doctor. There are days when my need to reveal the truth is an obsession."

"In what way, my dear?"

He watched intently as she crossed her knees and the short dress she wore slid farther up her thighs on silken sheer stockings. He had not seen such elegant silk, since before the war, and the way her thighs rubbed and whispered together had him crossing his own legs in discomfort. By God, she was flirting with him, and he was old enough to be her father.

"I was gazing at a Matisse painting of three red fish in a bowl at the museum this week and thought of his cleverness. Here is the glass and within, separated from me by a glass wall, are fish swimming in water. I thought, 'How can this fish create its own destiny?' I want to be able to control my own destiny. I do not wish to be trapped by my father and his hold over my childhood. Can I do that?"

"I suppose anything is possible. How would you go about this task?"

"I would find a substitute father, and whatever happened between us could be consensual. I would be in control and no longer a child. I could even reject him, if I wished."

"That is certainly one way to go about it, I suppose. I've never heard of such a deliberate plan, so I don't know what its success rate might be."

She stood up and walked across the distance between them.

"Let me sit on your lap. You can be my father today."

Without his permission she sat on his lap and curled against his chest. It seemed innocent and peaceful for about a minute, but then he felt heat coming from his lap and her bottom. It was molten, and he was nearly beside himself in his unexpected and unplanned desire. He put his arms around her to prevent her from slipping off his lap and movement became uncontrollable, urgent. The surprise, the shock, was so great that he exploded as she continued to rock against him like a child.

***

As Anaïs walked back to the houseboat, she felt relieved. Allendy had been rather arrogant until this afternoon. He had acted superior, and her question about destiny had been answered, when he couldn't even control a sexual advance made by a patient. She thought it was rather dear, when he had blustered and tried to pretend the interlude had not happened. In the future she would make him overcome his scruples again and again, until he learned a lesson. Life was not as easily controlled, as he would like to believe. She thought she had demonstrated that fact quite effectively this afternoon. In a way she felt sorry for him, for his arrogance that never looked at the suffering in the eyes of a client and the idea that he could talk away their sins and his own. He lived in his head. She lived in her body. Their only meeting place was in her secret darkness. Did he meet his old wife in that place or in his head? She left thoughts of him behind, as she started down the pier.

Psychoanalysis was not something to play with, she acknowledged. For some time now she had been known to remark that it was equivalent to a "scientific tampering with emotions." In truth she was quite afraid to embark on such a path or to let it out of its protective book covers. There were good reasons for her fears, and it was understandable. The right analyst and the right fit were necessary in her case because of subjects she had never discussed with anyone except her diary. It was a big step towards exposure and lack of control.

***

After the gallery party on the houseboat Holtz was mostly concerned about his report to Winifred. Back in Gratz, where blame was the order of the day, he never had to consider other points of view. What did he truly know of the international art scene? If artists were the antennae of culture and the keepers of finer values, then nothing he had seen in the Reich approached an artistic attitude. The Paris art scene intrigued him and evoked thoughts that were unheard of in his village.

Because she was the center of her own houseboat party and a most unique woman who obviously promoted artists and their free-thinking agendas, Holtz found Anais to be the most disarming person he had met since his arrival in Paris. He had never known a woman like her. When he had broken into her gallery, the most offensive thing he had found was a stack of her personal journals. Written in English, he thought their ideas were subversive. Beliefs, for instance, that a woman was necessarily as free to engage in a sexual rendezvous as a man, were contrary to folk tradition and the German culture. She talked of abortions and bankers and sensuality all on the same page. None of it was acceptable. Worse than that was the fact that she was married to a respectable banker and pretended to be a docile housewife when, in reality, she was a chameleon and spied on her own husband. In any case it would appear that their marriage was abnormal, an abomination really. Such a degenerate couple could easily be disposed of in his opinion. Winifred, who was a very good friend of Hitler, would find this kind of duplicity quite interesting. Maybe, when this gig was finished, he would get more jobs, enough to pay for the rent and groceries.

Holtz did not understand what all the commotion was about when it came to Jews. They were musicians, the finest. Everyone knew that a person had to eat, and in the music world it was largely who you knew that got you a gig.

If love and death were such motivating factors in a relationship, Holtz figured this Freud fellow from Vienna had the right idea. Sex and death were similar. Since Holtz had never seen love in action, and sex was rampant wherever he turned, he surmised that they were linked. Tristan and Isolde were no exception. The little death that came with orgasm was not unknown to Holtz, but Eros and Thanatos were a different story. It negated life, this longing for death. That death should be welcomed and love denied could only be imagined, as attitudes belonging to those who suffered terribly. Yet those such as the impoverished in ghettos did not long for death. It made no sense to him. In effect, with his theories of sexuality, Freud was a nihilist just like Wagner. He was also a Jew. His hero and heroine rush toward their end as though there was only death to look forward to without each other. Holtz felt very confused but glad to be Parsifal. He studied the musical score and libretto and tried to understand more each day.

"The song wafted past her and over the hedge, lingeringly.

Inside of her it penetrated sweetly and painfully. Something was worth crying for; something in the song."

—Nin *Timelessness*

Chapter 40
Yves's Suspicions

When Anais returned to the houseboat the next afternoon, Yves was waiting for her.

"I turned away two tourists and a gentleman who looked suspicious, *Madame*."

"Suspicious? In what way?"

"I do not know, *Madame*. It is second nature with me. Since the war and all the action I saw in Normandy, I am a changed man and just know when someone seems off."

She nodded at him in understanding.

"I think I must hire you to be a guard. Does that interest you?"

"It does, *Madame*. I would be getting paid for what I do naturally. That's not bad." He grinned.

"Well, you must begin by calling me Anais since I call you, Yves."

"*D'accord,* Anais."

***

The next week, Yves questioned whether this was the best time to approach Anais or if he should wait to tell her more about the intruder. There appeared to be no movement on board. What if he woke her from an afternoon nap? Come to think of it, what did she do on any given afternoon on the boat by herself? He did not even consider a gentleman caller because he had been aboard *Hilaire* all day and no one got past him, not even the rats. Yves stood at the door and listened once again. She had to be upstairs in her bedroom. He knocked rather tentatively then got up his courage and rang the bell. Anais called down the stairs.

"One minute, I'll be down in a minute."

She nearly skipped down the stairs.

"Oh, Yves, it's you. Come in. Come in. For a minute there I thought it was a gallery visitor, and I didn't feel quite up to it."

"I can come another time, if you're tired or busy."

"No, no. Come right in."

She wore an at-home kind of outfit, pants that were loose and a long tunic shirt. She looked comfortable and approachable, her hair tied back in something the Americans called a ponytail. She looked young. While he was only thirty, to him she seemed younger, or maybe he just felt old. She bustled around and made small talk while making coffee and setting a small dish of wafers in front of him. One didn't see much of sugar these days, and he looked longingly at the plate.

"Go ahead. They're for you."

He tried not to eat them like a starving man, but it was damn hard. One bite was equal to one wafer, and several were gone before he looked up. God, he had been raised better than this.

"I feel like I've been gone forever instead of a week. Has everything been okay while I was gone?"

"Except for one visitor. I'm not sure if you remember him. It was that German type, the opera singer. He went right inside and looked around with a purpose, if you know what I mean. Tried to tell me the door was open, so he just walked in, but it's not true. He even went upstairs. I caught him on his way down. I looked upstairs, when he had gone, but nothing looks disrupted, and maybe he was just nosy."

She could tell he was upset to make such a report.

"You're not to be upset, Yves. You've done your job. Nothing was vandalized, and if he ever comes back, I'll take matter in my own hands. It seems these Germans have no boundaries. They still like to think they won the war. That's their problem."

Yves nodded in relief.

"I could have fetched the police, but instead I just let him know I had seen him and would not tolerate more snooping."

"You did just fine. Tell me, do you think the fellow is truly an opera singer?"

Yves shrugged. "Do they have a special look? To me he looks like a soldier, but that could be just the size of him."

"He does look like a soldier, doesn't he? A typical German soldier, and he looks hungry like everyone else, so that doesn't mean much."

"His French is definitely not Alsatian."

"I've heard opera isn't doing so well in Germany, the land of the Meistersinger."

"Why is that?"

"The Germans have some notion that they have been too soft and sentimental. They say it's the reason the allies walked all over them and managed to defeat them. They believe the working man is too much of a romantic and needs to be toughened up."

"Maybe he *is* here for a job."

"Doesn't make sense does it?"

The opera here has barely reopened its doors. German music is not a favorite at the moment nor are Italian composers. French opera houses need to hire their own right now."

"I would not like to be a German in Paris auditioning for a part," Anais mused.

They sat in companionable silence, sipping coffee.

"Yves, how would you like a bigger job?"

"Bigger?"

"More responsibility. You seem surprised. I can pay you, if that's what worries you."

"What kind of job? I'm already your security guard."

"My assistant."

"You mean, like watching the houseboat while you're away? I already do that. I would never take money for watching my own property. Besides…"

"I know. You wish to be friends. Don't worry, I suspect we will be very good friends one day. In the meantime, I need an assistant as well as a guard, and I have just come to the conclusion you would be perfect. Besides, it would make me feel safer."

She was quite smart to appeal to his protective side, he thought. And though he felt he was being played, he was smart enough to admire her and quite intrigued at the prospect of assisting her with anything.

"Okay, I accept. What is my job description?"

For the moment, it is to keep an eye out for the German or anyone else who might sneak around. I don't trust him, but I'm not sure why."

"That's it?"

"Believe me, in the future, when I ask you to run errands all over the city, to be my eyes and ears, you might wish you had not agreed. You will earn your money, trust me."

They shook hands and decided on a regular salary after which Anais felt calm and knew she had been wise to hire Yves to watch her back.

"Now I must ask you some personal questions, if I am to be an effective assistant."

"I will answer what I can."

"First, are you married?"

"Yes."

"Where is your ring?"

"My husband and I have a very loose arrangement. I do what I do, and he carries on with his life. He is a banker. That was your next question, *n'est pas?*"

"Yes. But where do you live when you leave here?"

"I live in a lovely home in Louvecienne. It is my other life. I go back and forth between them, but you have been hired to assist with my houseboat life."

"So these lives are completely separate?"

"Yes, as a matter of fact. When you see me dressed like a society woman and banker's wife, just pretend you don't know me, because I will pretend I do not know you. Is that understood?"

"Perfectly. When do we begin?"

"In the morning. Come here for coffee and your first assignment.

***

Tomorrow, he would go from security guard to personal assistant. He liked the sound of assistant to a mysterious woman who owned an art gallery and rubbed shoulders with famous artists. Once, in his youth he had had aspirations to be a musician. Now he kept a guitar on the boat and strummed a classical piece from time to time. He had been tempted for a while to carry his guitar to cafés to play in public. In fact, he had even tried a few times until people dropped coins in his guitar case, and the café owners asked him to move along or play on the sidewalk rather than occupy space at one of their better tables. That was not how he wished to play music. The young German opera singer flashed through his thoughts. What a miserable life. He noticed the guy's shoes were nearly worn out. Well, in truth, nearly all the artists at the gallery party were a bit run down, shabby, if one looked closely, living from hand to mouth.

He thought of the war poet Edward Thomas who laughed at war one day and was dead the next.

…salted was my food, and my response,

Salted and sobered, too, by the bird's voice

Speaking for all who lay under the stars,

Soldiers and poor, unable to rejoice.

Yves thought of victory and a whole country's inability to rejoice. It seemed to him that the war continued in the dark corners of men's hearts.

Chapter 41
Anais Meets Danger

Anais rang the bell to Roshi's apartment. It was early evening and Christolphe would be gone for a few more days. She needed to shed more of her doubts, and she needed to trust her own powers of observation, but this was an important assignment. She still wasn't sure what questions to ask. She understood that secrecy was the key to the success of this work, but she didn't know if she could be of much use unless she had more information. For instance, being followed to Louveciennes, being spied on in her garden and being broken into on the houseboat, once seemed disconnected. However, recent news that the German opera singer had moved into the Marais could not be overlooked.

Then, there was the hiring of Yves as her assistant. Should she have done that? Would their mission be compromised, if he learned too much? And why was the opera singer leafing through her journals as though in search of information? As for information, the fact that Christolphe was in the middle of Swiss and French banking secrets must mean that he could conceivably collude with bank managers across Europe. Why was their work so secretive? She prayed that Christolphe had not backed himself into a world from which he could not escape. As for herself, Anais needed to know more. It was one thing to know nothing and be protected; it was entirely another matter to miss something because she was not well enough informed. She had put off a visit to Roshi, hoping to come to conclusions on her own, but it was time to be more forthright.

Just how did coincidence enter this business? How would Roshi view all these simultaneous occurrences?

***

Jean-Paul answered the door in a timely fashion and let her in quickly.

"This way, please."

In his usual efficient but enigmatic manner he led her to Roshi's study and left quietly, shutting the door behind him.

"Anais, come in, come in. I was just sitting here thinking of you."

He came from behind his desk to give her the traditional kisses on alternate cheeks and an extra for good luck.

"Sit here by the fire. I'm sure Jean-Paul is already getting us a café crème and will return shortly."

They sat and looked each other in the eye for a moment. It was like coming home for her. It was like the return of a beloved child to him.

"You have questions for me. I can tell by that look."

"I do, Roshi. Many questions."

"I wondered when it would come to this."

"You did?"

"Yes, of course. You are too intelligent and too curious to let the situation continue without knowing where you stand."

"You're right. I'm also feeling vulnerable without more information. It may be getting dangerous, and I don't know why."

She proceeded to tell him the list of unexplained events that ended with the hiring of Yves as her assistant.

"Let me begin at the end. As for Yves, you show great promise in hiring him as your assistant. He is a reliable and good person to have at your back. He saw a lot of action in the war, lost his parents and brothers, and has been strong-minded enough to survive and keep his values intact. Do not worry about him. Believe it or not, he is already one of my agents. You have noted certain facts, but there are a few you have missed. It is to be expected on a first assignment.

"So many people are walking the streets of Paris who look like the wounded after battle. I was not here for the war, Roshi. Maybe I was also too young, but when will the pain and suffering leave the faces of the survivors? Can I understand, if I have never been through it?"

"You understand well enough, my dear. You lost the love of your life and his child because of this war. You understand more than you realize. What cannot be condoned is the willful continuation of this pain. Too many are profiting from the destruction of others. The Germans have not forgotten, nor are they about to forgive the fact that they lost the war. As we speak there is movement, agitation if you will, to resurrect the spirit of revenge. Your observations can help us connect the dots and find those who profit from the suffering of others."

"Am I to suspect Christolphe, too? What must I do, if he is involved?"

"If he is somehow involved, Anais, then we suspect he may be blackmailed. Do you understand why?"

"I had no idea until last week. I think he has been meeting a lover, another man. Could it be because of his sexual preferences?"

"Yes, my dear. I am afraid that would be precisely the hold someone may have over him."

"But Roshi, he is such a gentle man, a loving person. Who would do this to him?"

"Someone who needs leverage. Our private lives can always be used against us, and the Germans have been quite two-faced, when it comes to this kind of prejudice."

**

Anais left Roshi's apartment that afternoon, glad to have admitted her need for his continued help. She was not happy, however, about the possibility that Christolph could be implicated. Aside from his work at the bank, she knew he was very interested in film and planned to produce a documentary himself one day. What if she offered to help? It could bring them together more often. Who were these people who thought themselves above reproach and thought they could torment him with blackmail about his sexuality? Let he who was perfect throw the first stone, she thought. What would her double do if this so-called scandal came to light? She walked back to the boat, lost in thought, forgetful of her need to keep watch, worried about Christolphe and inattentive to her surroundings.

The next thing she knew she was lying on the sidewalk and could dimly hear shouts and running feet, then nothing.

**

The first face she saw as she regained consciousness was Yves.

"Ah, you are conscious at last?"

"It's so good to see your face. What happened? Where am I?"

"You're in hospital for observation. The bookseller on the quay saw it happen. Someone called for an ambulance, but he ran back to the pier to let me know, when he saw the ambulance arrive. So here I am, your assistant, a bit late but in person. How are you feeling?"

"Like it has been a long day. I want you to take a message to this apartment to let Roshi know where I am."

"Is it your own address? Will I meet your husband?"

"No my husband is still out of town. Go and come back, okay?"

240

"Done. I will return soon."

Chapter 42
Hospital Visitors

The hospital might have been described as an event catcher or certainly as a space for the occurrence of synchronistic events to take place. As Anais would later write in her diary, she had nothing to do but sit in bed and let the world come to her.

No sooner had Yves left to tell Roshi where she was than the nurse arrived, telling her of another visitor. This time the nurse nodded knowingly. Who could it be? A minute later Holtz entered the room with a bouquet of roses. They were her favorites, bold reds and coral, vivid and fragrant. Her surprise was evident.

"My goodness, how did you know I was here?"

"Well, it's all over the streets by the quay, even at the café. Everyone is talking about an attack on the beautiful Anais who lives on the houseboat. There is talk of intrigue, spy rings, the underworld and all things romantic. You have captured the imagination of those who live near the river."

"You make me sound like a celebrity."

"I am a singer and an actor, *Madame*. What else do you expect, if not drama?"

"Well, thank you for coming. And thank you for the lovely flowers. Please ask the nurse to put them in a vase for me."

He left the room with the bouquet while Anais composed her thoughts and a small plan of action. When he returned a few minutes later, she felt more prepared. In this spy business it was the sudden and unexpected that left her speechless and uncertain. She was sure she would improve with more experience.

"So on the streets, are they saying who attacked me?"

"Only that he was a big fellow and some say he has been hanging around near the pier for several days. A few say they would recognize him, if they saw him again."

"I can't imagine what it's all about, can you?"

"Maybe it was someone you forgot to invite to the party."

She frowned.

"I'm joking."

"Forgive me, I have a headache. The doctor says I will be released in the morning, but I may have headaches for a while."

"I have an idea. Why don't you come and stay at my new apartment for a few days. It's safe there, and you can wait for your husband to get home."

She tried to remember if she had mentioned Christolphe being gone and for how long.

"That's a lovely idea, Holtz. I appreciate it because I must admit this whole situation leaves me feeling vulnerable. But why do you not come and stay on the houseboat, instead."

"Probably because I am so pleased to have my own place, privacy, and the chance to do something for you. Please say you'll stay with me for a while. I feel that you need more protection than that houseboat. Why, anyone could walk right in at any time."

"You're right. There have been intruders there already. So yes, I may take you up on your kind offer."

He smiled his wide stage smile that charmed opera audiences.

"What time does the doctor say you can be picked up tomorrow?"

"I'll be ready soon after breakfast. Come at ten."

She took a deep breath, when he had left. Tomorrow it would begin.

When Yves returned, he handed her a cryptic message from Roshi.

"Take care," it said. "Remember your angels are always nearby." He also sent flowers.

Yves hung around most of the day. He seemed to take his assistant position quite seriously. In the morning she would be gone, but she gave him Holtz' address just in case he needed to contact her.

***

The next day started with overcast skies, heavy with grey clouds. Her overnight bag was packed, and she was dressed and waiting, when Holtz arrived, looking eager and young.

"My dear Holtz, I hate to tell you that I must exercise a woman's prerogative to change her mind. I have decided to return to the houseboat instead of taking you up on your kind offer."

"I am *désolé, Madame.* I wish to be your knight in armor as they say."

"Well, you can make yourself useful by accompanying me there. I need help with my bag and these flowers, and you can turn on the heat and make me a coffee, when we get there. It will help with this headache."

She watched, as he changed his plans and became helpful. He might be German, but she thought him too naïve to be involved in international intrigue.

Roshi put down his pen and stared into the fire. Maybe it wasn't such a good idea to recruit Anais as one of his own agents. If he worried this much every time something like this happened, he would die before his fated time. So this is what it was like to have a child and care so much for every breath and every hair on her head. When had he truly become her father? Was this how his own father felt, when he had gone? Had he caused so much pain and concern, too?

Everyone had been alerted. Raphael and Yves were on their guard. There was no more he could do. Roshi had questioned Yves, when he arrived with the bad news of the attack and was truly impressed with his loyalty and concern.

Over the years, Roshi had kept an eye on Yves, trained him from time to time, but had never actually used his services on an assignment. Until now, his services had never been required. He had several agents in Yves' category, those who had never been tested. In the future he would consider him more carefully. Anais, he knew, had a sixth sense about men, and she had trusted him enough to hire him. Yes, he thought, he would be seeing a lot more of Yves Gauger.

***

"Anais, you're a mess. I don't understand why you continue to tip-toe around on behalf of an old Oriental grandfather. Because he has been good to you is no reason to put yourself in danger. Whatever you're involved in must be dangerous. Someone obviously wants to be rid of you.

"I agree."

"So, what, you have a death wish?"

"Lily, I owe him everything. And he…well, he's a special person. He finds ways to keep people from destroying themselves, and on some very deep level I need that chance at redemption. My shame, my guilt, and my unworthiness drive me on."

"Anais, you are one of the most loving and worthy people I know."

"You and Roshi know all there is to know about me, Lily. Don't you find some of my actions completely reprehensible? Sadly, I have become a total escape artist.

"You are being excessively hard on yourself this afternoon."

"That's why I love you, Lily. You find the best in me. You ask me to continue to be happy with all that I have been given. It's true, isn't it? We have this one life and the circumstances we were given. Now it's up to us to accept our own destiny, to recognize that destiny and embrace it wholeheartedly."

"I guess you have answered your own question. That's why we live the lives we do, my dear."

"You are sincerely an antidote to existentialism. Roshi is my friend, a father to me, an undefiled love in my life, and I would risk everything, if he asked it of me. Do you think, sometimes, we look at each other without truly seeing?"

"Oh, it happens to me all the time. That's why I love to come to our café and sit and watch people. It's a life lesson without leaving this table."

"It's a fishbowl, life, and we are in the bowl as Matisse would say."

They were at their favorite café in the Marais hidden in the maze that made up their old neighborhood. Anais remembered it all so well.

"You know, I think the answer to this mystery has to do with the banker I saw talking to Christolphe at our last dinner party. I had breakfast with Christolphe this morning before he left for work. I do not think he is mixed up in anything but his job, getting ahead and keeping gossip at bay. And yet, there is a connection."

"Did you ask him?"

"No. Angela the frail is too sheltered to ask such questions. She hasn't a clue. But she did hear Christolphe mention that Herr Dietrich, his boss, seemed to be previously acquainted with a number of artists in our city.

Apparently, the German banks, the Austrian banks, *and* the Swiss banks have a philanthropic interest in the arts. It turns out that Herr Dietrich's bank supports the Bayreuth Opera Festival. With a little snooping I discovered that someone by the name of Winifred Wagner, who is in charge there, is sleeping with Herr Hitler, who is a little demigod in Germany right now. He loves opera and Winifred is his personal *volksbank*."

"Goodness, I knew you were starting to make connections."

"True. Are those banks trying to infiltrate the lives of our friends, Lily?"

They sat in silence for a while. The implications of what she heard herself saying seemed so far-fetched yet not impossible.

Anais thought of the surrealists. They exposed their work everywhere they could. What were they trying to say? Theirs was the upside-down, right-side-up depiction of crazy and contorted visions, until wrong became right and right was subtly ridiculed. She was close, very close to something, like the corner of a surrealist painting. She felt she was floating in a night sky and Chagall's world was floating around her.

"Lily, I think it's time to get something done. I'll see you soon, okay?"

"You know where I live. I'm always here for you. Good luck, and I'll pay for the coffee this time."

"Thanks, Lily. See you soon."

She nearly ran out of the café, excited and disturbed at the same time. The whole incident of being hit on the head had shaken her and clarified certain connections. She wondered whether the concussion had helped make them. Now, she needed to calm down and take a deep breath.

Chapter 43
More About Holtz

She knocked on the door of Holtz' apartment. Music played on a gramophone inside, shaky and loud. She knocked again, harder this time, and the door opened a crack of its own accord. There, dancing in the living room was Holtz. He was wrapped in the arms of a beautiful woman, and it was June, the erstwhile partner of Henry Miller. She was the first to see Anais.

"Come dance with us," she beckoned. "Or perhaps you would be interested in a little more than that. Holtz here is quite the stud. But I suppose you already know that."

"Excuse me, I'll come back another time."

She closed the door and walked down the corridor to the foyer as quickly as was dignified. She heard Holtz call down the stairwell, but she continued to walk. By the time he caught up with her she was already on the street where lover's quarrels were common events in the Marais.

"Anais, stop. She doesn't mean a thing to me. She invited herself to the new apartment."

"I'm sure that's true."

She stared at him with his jacket half unbuttoned.

"Let's step into this café for a small chat. Then you can go back to her, if she waits for you."

They stepped inside a warm café.

"Now Holtz, I have a few questions I must ask you."

"Sure. I'll try to answer them."

"How long have you lived in Paris?"

He seemed momentarily disoriented by the wide jump the conversation had just taken.

"You mean how could I have met June? I only met her at your party."

"Why do you rent an apartment in Paris?"

"I intend to spend a lot of time auditioning here."

"Really. How do you expect to land a job, when it is obvious you are German?"

"But I am Alsatian."

He stood silently, looking guilty.

"I think you should join your friend before she leaves.

"Will we see each other, again?"

"Of course. And you are still invited to my home for dinner. That has not changed. Neither has the fact that you'll make a wonderful Parsifal."

So she had been mistaken. He *was* up to no good. What that mischief was she could not fathom. Surely, artists had nothing to contribute to the kind of information that would foster war efforts. Fortunately, she would be able to watch him at the dinner party tomorrow.

She chuckled. His plans to get her into his bed had backfired the day she left the hospital. If he was the one who had knocked her out, he had done a good job. As the doctor had predicted, she had a headache and would feel drowsy for several days. Instead of a demonstration of male machismo, he acted like a small boy, and it was obvious he was disturbed. She had kindly feelings about him and wished him well. June, however, was a nasty bed choice, a woman who was unstable and likely to cause him more trouble than he needed. *C'est la vie.* It was nothing to her. She owed him nothing. As far as her intuition was concerned, he was just a harmless artist, trying to succeed at his art. Misguided. *Point finale.*

***

Yves strolled down the pier. He walked by his own boat and entered the houseboat to check its security. All seemed exactly the same, as the last time he had checked. In the manner of Sherlock Holmes, he had taken to putting small tell tails in doorways and strategic spots. Nothing had been disturbed. He opened the companionway to his own boat and unfolded a deck chair. He would make himself a café crème and sit out on the deck to relax and take in some sun. The weather was getting chillier each day, and he was happy to catch a last few rays. As he sipped his coffee, he watched the trawler that had tied up to the pier late yesterday afternoon. Its flag was German, its hull made of metal and its insignia Bavarian. The crew was fastidious. Funny, how Germanic types kept turning up in his scope these days. Since he didn't believe in coincidence, Yves decided to keep an eye on them. This was the first time he had come across an Austrian boat and decided they were more Germanic than the Germans. After all, they hailed from Hitler's homeland.

***

Angela arrived home with plenty of time to organize another dinner party, then dismiss the help. She checked the garden and dressed for the evening before Christolphe arrived home on time, as he had said he would. He seemed inordinately happy to see her. After getting ready for the dinner party, he had come to her room to tell her about his trip, to drink his bourbon and to acquaint her with profiles on some of the guests who would be at the dinner party. He embraced her, kissed her on the forehead and said he love her and missed her. Yes, she had missed him, too. She told him she had added an opera singer to the guest list, and he was delighted. Soon the bell was ringing, guests arriving and drinks were being poured to make everyone comfortable.

It was as she adjusted some lovely Zen chimes in the garden outside on the patio that Holtz arrived and joined the party. He fit in smoothly, and soon the guests were speaking in two languages accompanied by much laughter. Everyone was honored to meet the future Parsifal, a celebrity in the opera world.

As Angela watched the guests, she eventually began to notice a particular rapport between Holtz and Herr Dietrich, head of the German Swiss bank. To her, it seemed they must have met previously but, because she spoke no German, it was impossible to be sure. Certainly, they became quite friendly during dinner and after, when port and cognac were being served in the living room.

***

That evening, Angela wrote all these observations in her diary and immediately forgot about them. Holtz was a lovely young man who acted too familiar, when they happened to be alone, but she accepted this as an overly extraverted mannerism. She had been doing a lot of reading in her spare time and wrote of philosophical musings. For instance, she had heard of an extraordinary young woman and budding philosopher who was German, writing about the human condition in such a unique fashion that she was becoming known by word of mouth, and what she had to say was unpopular. She was a protégée of Martin Heidegger, and her name was Hannah Arendt. Lately, defending Jews was an unpopular pastime, and Arendt was a Jew. It shocked Angela to the core that Jews were unwelcome in Europe. France was turning into an unrecognizable place. Arendt's thesis dealt with the formation of character, love and Augustin, that of men and women, equally, and fate in regard to starting anew, leaving behind the nihilistic trend that had become quite the rage since the war. Quite frankly, she was so caught up in Arendt's antidote to existentialism that she had not paid much attention to her guests that evening. The young fellow,

Holtz, approached her and asked, when they might get together, which seemed rather forward and odd. He implied that they had met before tonight and knew each other well. In any case she simply ignored him and the guests who were all speaking German. Angela, the perfect hostess, quietly absorbed the atmosphere, listened with a different antenna, and scanned the room, alert to the needs of her guests.

***

She spent the rest of the week in her garden like someone hypnotized by the harmony of rose trellises, pruning as she snipped and shaped the bushes for next spring. Autumn was her favorite season. It was surprisingly refreshing to be rid of the dead and weak branches, to inhale the musk of fallen leaves and to rake and clear space for next year. While many people she knew felt saddened by autumn or the thought of endings, she felt energized. She covered the plants that would need shelter in the winter and looked forward to the dreams of a sleeping garden just as she looked forward to her own dreams.

She and Christolphe spent their evenings reading or sharing information about their day; for they led a quiet life when not entertaining. That afternoon, they had taken a walk in the Bois de Vincenne. When it started to rain, they took a cab to Saint Germain, where they stopped at Café de Flore and ordered hot chocolate and cakes. Everyone had disappeared from the glassy streets, when the rain started, into the warmth of bistros or cabs to look out on glistening streets and air that oozed mystery. Birds twittered, enlivened by their love of rain; living in the moment, the sparrows had forgotten the war much faster than humans.

It was a time to be together in the quiet softness of the afternoon, time to reflect as they walked back to the train station. They stayed under their umbrellas, listened to the rain and smelled its fragrance. This was something they shared, the ability to be open together, in love with nature, in love as friends who were comfortable in the peace of their friendship. They also walked from the station to their home in Louveciennes and understood why their guests loved to make this trip that took them so quickly outside the city. During the ride, the worries and problems of post war Paris fell aside, and they sighed in relief.

When they walked together, holding hands, Anais let herself absorb her commitment to this one man. Her multiple selves existed together like the colors of the rainbow, when he held her. To be whole was to experience an uncomplicated knowledge of herself, instead of seeing lips, eyes and hands, separately. She wanted to find a coherent language with which to write, one that would not limit or isolate, one that would connect them more deeply than marriage, one that would point the way to self-realization. She gazed at Christolphe and wondered, if it was possible to help each other.

"My love, I have been thinking."

"That sounds serious." He chuckled.

"It is serious."

"What is it, Anais?"

"I've been thinking that I would like to help you with the film work."

"Where did those thoughts come from?"

"It occurs to me that you must see life quite differently through the lens of a camera."

"That is certainly true."

"Would you mind teaching me?"

"Well, there isn't much time for film these days. You may have noticed my extra hours at the bank. Maybe, we could start your instruction on our holidays this winter."

"Really?"

"Yes, really."

"We could be a film team."

"We could, yes."

They strolled through the park, thinking separate thoughts that afternoon, as Anais smiled contentedly.

Chapter 44
Anais and Yves Prepare for the Party

Anais stopped by to invite Yves to come by in an hour or so for a coffee. She carried small cakes that Angela had baked. Yves would love them. She sat on her upstairs balcony just outside her bedroom and day dreamed, as the water of the Seine flowed beneath her and out to sea. The mind has its precious defenses and its labyrinthine traps, she mused, but one could be lost forever in a maze, deep within the unconscious. There the Minotaur was a bully, free to torment, to shame and to hold hostage any desire for redemption.

She recalled years ago, when the ship she and her mother and brothers had taken to New York City took them across the Atlantic. She was only eleven but each day she walked on deck along the ship's rail, and each day the waves seemed the same. Sometimes they were bigger; other times they were more calm, but the depths were endless, deeper and darker, as the surface was left behind. She was only eleven, but she had wanted to die. She knew in her deepest self that she would never see her father again, but she was unable to deal with such a never-ending thought. Forever was a long time. That is when she started to write in her diary.

That is the moment her diary became her best friend. Dr. Allendy recommended she give up such a childish pastime, but he was simply jealous of the way she confided in her diary, instead of him. It made her smile. Honesty was reserved for her kindred soul. The poor man was ruined. He had some kind of father complex that gave him a God-like attitude, which she considered abhorrent in a psychoanalyst. She had seriously taught him a lesson.

She remembered writing in her diary one day on the ship, sitting in an armchair, wrapped in a warm blanket. The captain walked by, then stopped.

"What are you doing, my dear, writing a letter?"

"I'm writing in my diary."

He laughed. "Really? And what do you tell your diary at your young age? Do you have secrets?"

"Yes, secrets. It's my best friend."

"Well, carry on. When you get to New York, you'll make lots of real friends."

But I'll never abandon my best friend, she thought. The captain walked off, muttering to himself, getting on with the more important business of checking his ship. She wondered, if he would abandon his ship as it sank.

The captain had been wrong, of course. There were no friends in New York until Roshi had come along. But, of course, he was a grownup and felt sorry for her. She had never been able to tell anyone the secrets she told her kindred diary. Linotte, she called her diary persona, when she finally decided to give her a name. It was the most beautiful name she could imagine. Was that the moment, the real moment, when Linotte came into being, when she was given a name?

Anais thought of her gentle Angela side: the Piscean woman of harmony and peace, Angela who lived in Louveciennes with an innocence and purity that needed protection. She was innocent Linotte, married to a man who would never challenge her. She supposed he loved her in his own way, and it suited Angela who loved being cared for and protected.

Truth. Anais had always thought that knowing the truth was essential. However, she realized that knowing about a situation did nothing to change it. Roshi had seen the truth in her, the beautiful truth he called it, and had helped her to cultivate her talents. But even Roshi had not seen the ugliness or accepted her the way her diary did. If the world knew the truth about war, how it got started and how it escalated, would it change anything?

***

Yves rang the bell to the gallery and called upstairs.

"Yes, come upstairs, Yves. I'm on the balcony."

"You've been gone over a week."

"I have. Just resting, getting my thoughts together."

"And have you? Have you come up with anything you wish to share?"

"How's this? Truth is what everyone seeks. It comes in the form of love. The truth is that life can be changed by a single act of love. Do you believe that, Yves?"

"Well I do, and I don't."

"Meaning?"

He sat there gazing out over the water.

"I suppose it can change the way we feel about something, you know, change our attitude. For instance, there is a lot of love that happens in the middle of war. You see men, putting themselves in grave danger to save their comrades. Then, someone shoots them. Maybe that person, the one who sacrificed himself, will return to life on earth as a more self-actualized individual. That's what those who believe in karma will tell you. The change is an inner change. The one who survives has a chance to become a better person."

"Do you believe it? As my assistant, you need to know that I'll be working as an agent of truth. I know that sounds vague and maybe bizarre. I work with others who are not exactly trying to catch bad guys or bring them in for punishment but to subvert their efforts. I am saying this aloud so I can figure out what I actually do. In short, I observe. At times, I might expose what I have observed. In doing so, there is the hope that perpetrators will find that they are confronted with more obstacles than makes it worth the effort they expend. For example, are they willing to be caught? Is it worth getting caught? In effect, I help to ward off evil actions through exposure or by derailing a train that might be heading for a collision."

"You mean you are working for Roshi."

She stared at him in shocked silence for a moment. He went on.

"I met Roshi years ago, just after the war. Then, I met him again. We talked, and he invited me back. I like him. I would add, as your assistant, that our boss is a most unique person. He is someone who has seen the war and not allowed it to break his spirit. I am proud to be a part of these efforts, Anais, and I will do whatever I can to help."

They sat in comfortable silence. It was cool but sunny, and the water coursing beneath them was soothing.

"I guess truth can give you courage, Yves."

"Yes, it makes sense. If courage comes from the heart and so does love, then the truth is that they are connected. The soldier who sacrifices himself for love does it because he has courage and knows it is the right thing to do."

"When I was quite young, I started my search for truth. My father bought me my first lovely diary, then left me and my mother and brothers. He gave me a gift before he abandoned me. I ask myself, why would he do that, but I never get an answer."

"This job we have working with Roshi will be a bit like that, Anais. Just because we keep our eyes open does not mean we can always come to understand motives. You will never know what was going through your father's head."

"Do you think it would make any difference if I did?"

"That is another issue. Now you speak of forgiveness. And who hands out forgiveness? Can the allies forgive the Germans? Can the Germans forgive themselves? I say no to both of those questions."

"Then how does forgiveness come about, Yves?"

"Somehow, forgiveness must come from God, Anais."

"Does God do such a thing, or does he make us suffer first?"

"This I do not know. I truly do not know. We can only carry on and accept our destiny or fate, whatever it may be. At the same time we must pray that we do not fall into the hands of the devil."

"For out of the dictionary each one of us chooses a particular vocabulary with insistent repeated words which are the keys to our psychic life…

"There is not one big cosmic meaning for all, there is only the meaning we each give to our life, an individual meaning, an individual plot, like an individual novel, a book for each person…

"We tried our best to annihilate the individual life, but it is only a well-integrated individual who knows something to offer to collective life…

"The worse the state of the world grows, the more intensely I seek to create an inner and intimate world in which certain qualities may be preserved…

"And I ask myself if the artist who creates a world of beauty to sustain and transmute suffering is wiser than those who believe a revolution will remove the cause of suffering…"

—Nin *Diary*

Chapter 45
Stock Market Crash

It was 1929, a decade since the war ended, but all around her were signs of a prelude to more war: thwarted desires, fears of the future, frustration, always the daily frustration that nothing was the way it used to be.

For as long as she could remember, beauty was a thing she strove for, a goal somewhat like the announcement of peace that hadn't happened. Without beauty she imagined a stained and impure world, riddled with fear and confusion, and worse, fear, dread and terror. Without beauty lives were empty and dark. War was the ultimate ugliness.

She knew there were different kinds of war, as many kinds as there were individuals, and by this she meant inner wars. That kind of war led to self-destruction and the battle between demons and daimons. Artists went through this battle every day of their lives. Creation, after all, was the foe of destruction.

For Anais, the diaries she wrote were written to combat separation and disconnection between spirit and soul. She applauded the war memorials that were being built and the reminders that war exiled individuals from their homes and friends. Loneliness, isolation and fear grew. Children were abandoned. Inside, she had an exquisite mental image of the beauty around her, which seemed equivalent to the battle of good against evil. The search for love, truth, and beauty was a search for God and father.

The fathers of war, however, did not inspire these values. Roshi hoped to change consciousness at a time, when awareness had gone deeply underground. Artists, he noted, were the keepers of consciousness. They may or may not have been ahead of their time, and they were often wounded as well as gifted, but one thing was a certainty, artists rarely succumbed to psychic illnesses. Somehow, their creator had exempted them, so their clarity would remain unobstructed. In this they were blessed.

Anais knew that Roshi was a great philanthropist. She had only to examine her own good fortune. Right now, his request of her was the use of her vision, her eyes and her imagination. As a gatherer of insights and observations, she felt at sea, regarding the usefulness of her contributions, but Roshi had assured her this was the residue of selfless service, the not-knowing how or if that service had been received or been used to further good. For his guidance in this tenuous world, she was grateful.

Her reverie was interrupted, when the bell at the gate rang, followed by an impatient and rather loud knock. Hurrying to the door, she opened it to find Lily standing there. She looked distraught and frightened.

"Good heavens, Lily. What's wrong?"

"Oh Anais, you have no idea. It's tragic, simply tragic."

Anais felt a sinking in her stomach. Had something happened once again to disrupt her fragile world?

"It's the stock market. The stock market has crashed."

"Here, sit down. What does it mean?"

"It means the world economy has failed. As we speak, hundreds of thousands of people are being ruined. For the old, savings will be gone in a blink. For the young, there will be no jobs because parents must keep working to feed themselves. It means many institutions will close. It means artists will not get patrons. It means the ugliness of poverty has returned. It is not a good thing, Anais."

Lily started to cry. "What will I do? All my income was in stocks my parents had left me. Now I hear they are worthless, and banks are closing their doors. Bankrupt! How can I be bankrupt?

They sat there, imagining the collapse of their world as they knew it. War was a dreadful experience and, after nearly a decade, most people had not yet recovered. Poverty had prevailed during the Great War, too. Back then, there was hope that it would soon be over. None of them understood the intricacies of finance, therefore it left them feeling helpless. Anais intended to have a long talk with Christolphe this evening. In the meantime she would talk to Roshi.

***

When she let herself into his study, he was seated in his usual place at his desk.

"Roshi, I'm sure you've heard."

"Indeed. I have spent most of the morning in meditation. The balance has tipped and spills over. It will take years to correct the balance, but there is much to be done. For the very poor, not much will change. For the self-sufficient the wait will be long and the times sparse, but they will be all right in the end. It is the rest. For those who have never had to worry about where their next meal came from, there will be great suffering. Already, I have heard of such despair in the face of financial loss. There have been suicides. Men have left their families. Women cry. The wheel of life turns in an unstoppable circle. No one escapes."

"And you, Roshi, have you lost everything?"

"No, Anais. I would never have played with the stock market in this disturbing climate. As for the banks, the Orient is not so connected to Europe and North America to be affected. Someday, it will happen in Japan and even in China, but not this turn of the wheel. The Orient has other problems. Our work will continue more intensely than ever. Thank God you now have some experience to draw upon. I have just received grim information about the Germans and their clandestine activities. We now know that they are using the banker artist connection to track down wealthy Jews. They hope to confiscate fortunes to finance the future war they have in mind to wage. They intend to hide much of the art they want to confiscate until they can redeem it for themselves.

She could only flinch, and she wanted to hide in a hard shell.

"Yes, it's shocking. But more and more I'm getting very close to the source of this diabolical plan. It seems there is a relatively naïve, angry and ambitious young man named Adolf Hitler who is being groomed to lead this merciless onslaught. The real tragedy of the stock market crash is the weakening of the allies to fight a future war. They do not want to get involved, just as the Germans predicted."

In those minutes, listening to Roshi, understanding that the Western World was in real trouble, she felt her resolve strengthening. No longer did she feel confused or wonder if her contribution was enough. She would do whatever she could and never question her contribution.

Roshi saw emotions flicker across her face. He nodded. Here was the spirit that he suspected underlay the Anais he had known as a child, and he gazed at her inner courage in awe.

Chapter 46
Rendezvous with Raphael

Anais had another early morning meeting with Raphael. At the moment there did not seem to be much going on in the spy network that she could detect. The stock market crash in the United States that followed the crash in London caused most Americans to go home. Who could afford to study art in Paris? Money flow that had once crossed the Atlantic was at a standstill. Bankers were holding their breath; farmers could not afford next year's crop; storeowners could not stock their shelves. The rest of the world had stormed the banks to remove their savings, and tellers had been shot. But more often than not savings were gone, and howls of despair could be heard around the globe.

In Paris, *Les Halles* did a quiet but steady business. Roshi had been right. The poor would not suffer, as much as those who had been comfortable with their finances. Because it was an ancient and diverse market, the stalls and vendors had always gathered their produce directly from their farms or boats. They arrived from their mills and gardens. Night was day for those who frequented the market. Those who sold their goods left home in the early hours of the morning and by 3 AM the stalls unfolded their richness. Everyone was awake.

As for the night life of Paris, it often ended up at *Les Halles*. Affairs, clandestine meetings, nefarious transactions, the black market and every other transaction, existed beneath the table and transpired in the winding streets of the endless marketplace. By 8 AM it was finished, the produce gone with trucks packed and carts empty until the next morning. Anything was for sale in *Les Halles*, including sex and sadism. Name your addiction, and it could be found. For those who needed privacy or just a place to meet, it too was for sale. The excitement was palpable. Transactions were cash only, and banks never tried to infringe on this lawless territory. This was a Paris that did not change with the fluctuations of stock dividends. Many considered it the impregnable heart of Paris that would exist as long as the city.

Her plan was to rendezvous with Raphael at midnight.

Anais wore a black cape beneath which her night attire was mostly lace and satin. She carried a rose, and her beaded purse held only the necessities for the meeting. Raphael would be dressed to surprise, but he assured her she would recognize him.

"*Ma chérie*, it's me."

He came from behind her and held a hand on her shoulder. She was startled for a moment by his voice in the darkness. It was deeper than during the day, and for a moment she thought she had been discovered and unmasked.

"I did not consider that an American might be able to fit in with this charade."

"Oh, but there is so much you do not know about American men."

"You're right. I was still an adolescent when I left there."

He took her arm and led her through the narrow alleys, as though he had been born on the streets. Before she knew what he was about, they had entered a rooming house where he had paid for a room for the night.

"It would seem that you have done this before," she commented.

"I never share secrets. I am a spy, after all. And so are you. You learn not to ask."

She thought this over for a minute.

"Then how do you learn anything?"

"Roshi would tell you to watch and listen. There is so much more that you can discover in silence. So now, be quiet and I will demonstrate."

Slowly, Raphael slipped the cape from her shoulders and caressed her neck and arms. He breathed into her mouth and kissed her gently at first, then passionately, as he worked his way across the silken drape of her negligee. Every fold revealed more passion. He was right. There was no need for talk, though she could not control the sounds of her love in these embraces of discovery, for he held her arms down, ready long before her. His arousal had been building, since they made this assignation, and they both knew it would be like this, far more intense than their imagination. The heat, the smells, the night shadows in a room with only a bed on which he had paid extra for clean linen, the sound of his breath and the rhythm of his thrusts took her up and up and left her there, waiting for more. As spies, they were both subject to emotions they normally had to keep to themselves. This night they were free to let go and revel in sensation. She was a married woman; he was married to his work, but this night they would share their secrets.

After the little death and the lazy drowsiness had passed, they talked. In this secluded room they whispered to each other. He had suspicions about Holtz, the fake German they called him, and his associations with Herr Dietrich. Even Christolphe and her cousin Ernesto, he discovered, once knew each other in Cuba. Thus, he and Ernesto were also suspect. Ernesto had been to Paris and Switzerland on a number of trips, but she was most surprised to hear that Ernesto had met Christolphe. Now she would have to follow these trains of evidence somewhat deeper. Raphael shared his information about Winifred Wagner and Holtz. He knew about the transport of artwork to Germany. There, he believed, they were sealed and inventoried for future use. The Germans were nothing if not organized and obsessive about records and files.

By 5 AM they were ravenous and dressed each other with great tenderness. They went to breakfast in Les Halles mixing with other lovers, venders and truck drivers, as the first light of day brightened the sky. Anais looked forward to many such meetings with Raphael. Theirs was a deep connection, timeless and rare to the world of spies.

She didn't know why she had so recently been afraid of intimacy with another spy, despite the fact that Roshi had given her his name. Involvement. She felt committed to the spy business now that she knew it through Raphael and had become his lover. It was exciting, arousing, but not as dangerous as she had imagined. She had once heard that a vivid imagination was like a razor's edge. On one side was the bigger-than-life image, and on the other side was fear. Too much, too little, both created a false and deceptive reality.

Had she found a new *cher ami*? Was she now in the thrall of a new persona created to win Raphael's love? Seduction saturated the air she breathed. She wanted to cry out, "Please, fill the empty spaces in my heart." Here was a real flesh and bold lover who knew her secret spy self and had seen through her invisible side. He was not repulsed, but watched her intently, as she lay naked on the bed before him.

Chapter 47
Lily's Panic

Lily sat in her living room, trying to quiet the panic that was devouring her. She felt so alone and vulnerable. It must have started many years ago, when her best friend Anais had suddenly left the country, when Mama had died and Papa could not live without Mama. Why did neither of them consider her? How was she to survive without either of them? Nanny had hung in there longer than the others, but she had finally died of heartbreak, when her son was killed in the war. Last year, her dog Daisy had died, and now this. This was about more than attachments and loneliness; the stock market crash was about survival. She simply could not afford the grocer.

What was she trained to do? Art history did not put food on the table. It was a gentile study for someone who did not need money. The art world was dominated by men and wealthy patrons. Of course, she knew them; they knew her, too. It was the perfect milieu, if need was not a factor. It was exciting to know artists, but no one would seriously wish to have their lives. Poverty was not glamorous; hunger was painful. She felt like she was being punished for being useless, for having grown up with all her basic needs cared for. Now this, too. Yesterday, on her way home from the atelier, she found herself walking beside a handsome fellow who appeared to be one of those horrible Germans, but he said he was an opera singer. He walked her all the way to her foyer and said he had just moved in two buildings away.

This afternoon they planned to meet at a café. He was classically handsome and did not know her. Therefore, he would not know she was destitute nor would he need to feel sorry for her, a stranger. His company could be a pleasant interlude in otherwise miserable circumstances. Why was it she felt so private and proud, too proud to let on how badly she needed help?

Lily loved Paris; she loved the Marais, which had become part of her as she grew up. The harder the people of Paris tried to find a way to create beauty and art, the more modern life devoured its citizens. She thought of her city that had so recently attempted to return to pre-war prosperity, as a laboratory of great ideas. Fashion, literature, theatre, ballet, art and philosophy flourished. Just this year Bergson had been awarded the Nobel Prize and Josephine Baker starred in the *Revue Nègre* with her startling and free association of body liberation and choreography. Yet people froze, starved and walked the streets lost in their desire to escape cruel fate. Lily imagined herself on the street beside those others and shuddered in fear. She still owned her apartment, but that would be the final devastation, if ever she had to give it up. In a city that had defied death scenarios for two thousand years, Paris chose life, but wealth was a different story. Wealth was subjected to political solutions, tradition, and envy that could not be changed. Money was the subject of much deceit and dissimulation carried on by many who were weak in character.

If it came down to it, Lily would sell her body or her erstwhile values to survive. She did not deceive herself into thinking she would be any different from so many women before her who had done the same. French women were the best in the world at that kind of redefinition. Pulling herself together, Lily gathered her energy to dress for the café. Like most *Parisiennes*, she dressed for the occasion, and it was important to look whatever part she had to play. In this instance the dilemma was the occasion. What did she expect the outcome to be? What did Holtz expect from the encounter? She decided that chic and artsy was always an option and, quite frankly, today she could not pretend to be other than who she was. What she did not want to portray was desperation. Hopefully, he would buy her a patisserie with her coffee. To that end she applied makeup, trying to minimize the freckle spots and concentrating on her eyes with their wide, sincere innocence. Then, she decided that high heels were perfectly acceptable with such a tall male specimen. In truth, despite the fact that she was sure he was German, she was attracted to him. She stared into her own blue eyes, adjusted her collar and was ready to leave.

Chapter 48
Ernesto

Angela opened the mailbox at her gate and looked with surprise at a letter from Cuba. The return address was from Ernesto. She hadn't heard from him in the years since she had left Havana. She was curious.

To her surprise the letter informed her that Ernesto was arriving in Paris any day now. He had followed in the family business and accepted his role as eldest son. The Coca Cola business, from a banker's perspective, was crucial to the economy of Cuba. Ernesto said he was coming to Paris on business as well as pleasure. He hoped for an entrée to the art world for his personal interests and an introduction to the banking world to take up where his retired father had left off. This visit was quite important to him, so she would certainly hostess a diner party while he was in the city in order to introduce him to Christolphe and his colleagues.

***

It was time to spend days on the houseboat again. Spring had blossomed, and Paris was in her glory. Anais planned to mount several consecutive art shows in the next while. Man Ray's photography and his film *L'Étoile de mer* would be shown at her gallery along with the *Passion of Joan of Arc* on alternate evenings. She, herself, was busy writing a book about the work of D. H. Lawrence that she intended to call

An Unprofessional Study. It was something she had wanted to do for years and had handed over to Angela to edit and finish. As well, she and Christolphe had found their way to Morocco in the winter. True to his promise, he had taught her use a camera and praised her fresh eyes that saw photographic possibility in the most unexpected scenes.

"Bonjour, Yves. Surprised to see me?"

"Bonjour, Anais. Welcome back."

Once they returned from their holidays, it was easier to spend the rest of the winter in her cozy house. She was reluctant to admit it was the shadowy figure that had followed her and caused her to lose courage and to stay in more often. With the economy the way it was, there was more violence on the streets, more men out of jobs and faces of desolation on every corner. She was also worried about Lily, and one of the reasons she came into town today was to visit her. Dismay about Ernesto's visit was also a concern. Why was he here now?

***

Another strange letter had arrived recently. Anais had received notification from the estate of Joel Seaborn of an inheritance left to her by Joel before he died. Included was a letter from his parents who wanted her to know how sorry they were, when they heard of the loss of their grandchild. It was all she could do to finish the letter. Memories welled up in places she had thought were stored away forever. They simply refused to be banished. Angela would have been shocked had she read the letter. Ernesto, Joel, and Christolphe; it was as though the universe had conspired to expose traitorous thoughts. Lily was on her mind as well as Raphael who had secreted his way into her heart. Winter had been made warm and loving by their clandestine meetings, their whispers and heated caresses. Too many confluences of the stars and planets and too much conflict seemed to reach into the lives of everyone in Paris this year. If a stock market across the ocean could crash against the shores of France, she couldn't imagine what other news might be exposed. She wanted to run away.

***

Yves made coffee and put it on a tray with a few biscuits. The Lulu brand was his favorite. He could now afford just a taste to enhance an afternoon. It looked like rain, and he wondered what it was like in Anais' boudoir with rain, hitting the roof and running onto the balcony before joining the flow of the Seine. He imagined her in a warm and comfortable outfit, sitting at her desk with the heater in the corner. He rang the nautical bell on the gate.

She leaned out the window.

"Just come upstairs, Yves. It's nice and warm up here. It's like a bird's nest."

He made his way slowly, balancing the tray in anticipation of their meeting.

"How are you, Yves? It's been a while."

"I can't complain. Life has been good."

He watched her drink coffee and bite into a biscuit. Everything she did seemed to fascinate him. He hoped he had not begun to fall in love. She was quite the handful, he suspected. Besides, she was a married woman.

"Yves, I had some unusual correspondence today. A letter from Cuba in particular. My cousin Ernesto says he will be arriving in Paris soon."

"Is there something wrong with that?"

"I don't know. It's one of those uneasy feelings I get. It might not feel so strange except he mentioned Christolphe, as though he knew him already. Now why would Christolphe have never mentioned him? And why come to Paris now with the banking world so closed off? Cuba is a long way from here.

274

"Do you have any plans for his visit?"

"I was hoping you could show him around. I will pay for the taxis and such. He mentioned something about the art scene, and that set up a few more red flags. I'm sure my gallery show will be open while he's here. He may want to hang around and get to know some of the artists who are sure to stop by. Other than that, I begin to wonder, if I am getting suspicious of my own shadow. Everything that has converged upon my life to this day makes me wary."

"It's the dark side of the spy, I'm sure."

"And what about you? No suspicions, nothing to report?"

"No, but that's probably a good thing."

"True."

They sat quietly, each sunk in their own thoughts, Yves wishing he could express his feelings but at the same time afraid to expose them.

"I suspect, if you go through with the art shows, we'll see more of our opera singer."

"That's quite possible. Funny that he is living in the Marais close to Lily as well as Raphael. Is this too much coincidence?"

Yves shrugged. He had heard about Raphael and felt a twinge of jealousy. What he heard detracted from his attention to their conversation, so he shrugged once again.

Chapter 49
Evil Gains an Upper Hand

Anais had plans to stop in to visit Raphael before the gallery shows began. Strange, that all her acquaintances lived in the Marais. Raphael, it would appear, was located only a block from Lily's apartment, but wasn't it the same building where Holtz lived? La rue des Falconniees was quiet, an empty shell of what it once was. Ancient echoes of children playing whispered at every cross street and alleyway, in the empty playground and the Lycée, as if the stones of the cobbled roads and arches remembered each child, recorded laughter and listened to taunts. It created a sad music to her ears. Kick this ball, catch another, run, dodge and block the ball: she would have liked to sit on a raised sidewalk to watch the games. Suddenly, she stood before the building Raphael rented, amazed that an American cared to involve himself with post-war Paris. Roshi, it seemed, collected the most amazingly disenfranchised group of individuals, each with a story to rival the next.

She looked up the front of the building toward the third floor, but the curtains were drawn and motionless. Hopefully, Raphael was at home. Though she had tried to stay away, she had been drawn back. It was not her normal behavior to seek out a lover time and again. But this felt different. Her attraction to Raphael had penetrated to the area of her lonely four-chambered heart and settled in where secrets dwelled. Perhaps, because of Raphael's connection to Roshi, she trusted him and, because she trusted him, she had briefly lifted the veil that covered her face. Once that veil was raised, he had acknowledged her immediately. Hopefully, they would continue to explore this relationship. If only he knew how much she desired such exposure but dreaded its intimacy.

In the foyer she rang the doorbell to his apartment and waited. Maybe it was not wise to arrive unannounced. She waited several minutes and decided to walk upstairs. Most likely the bell in this old building didn't work? She hesitated, worried about being seen by Holtz, and noticed his name had already been posted on the list of occupants.

She made her way quietly on foot up the stairs. At Raphael's door she knocked, then knocked again. Obviously, he was not home. Disappointed, she stood there for a moment, lost, wishing he were home, when the doorknob clicked and the door slowly cracked open.

Now she felt a chill. Apprehension crawled up her spine. Something was wrong. Was someone inside? Surely, Raphael had not gone out without locking the door. If he was home, he would have answered the knock, but she could not leave. Was he ill? Was there a problem?

She pushed gently against the door and watched, as it swung open. It was silent, the air motionless and stagnant. Nothing was out of place in the foyer or the hall, so she stepped inside and hoped she was not making a big mistake or about to embarrass herself. Carefully, she closed the door behind her. She should simply turn around and leave, but her feet, with a mind of their own, drew her forward like a sleepwalker. There was no sense in turning back now. She called his name again, feeling like a voyeur as she walked toward the back bedroom, but something was definitely wrong. She didn't know how she knew this. The bedroom door was ajar and she pushed against it, then watched it swing open, and there on the floor was Raphael.

She knew he was dead. His essence was gone. The Raphael she had come to visit had already taken his spirit and departed. Blood pooled on the floor near his head, but it was impossible to see the damage. Oh, God, here was one of the most beautiful men she had ever known, dead. A special man was gone, and in his wake was violence. She froze, heart pounding, unable to take in the crime scene, her powers of observation drained. All she could feel was blank, empty loss and abandonment.

Slowly, she came to herself as the air crackled with clarity, so clear and magnified that details emerged in three dimensions. He was unarmed, but she was certain a bullet had killed him. He had been ambushed in his bedroom last night, as he was getting ready for bed. Slippers had fallen from his feet. He fell, and the duvet had been dragged to the foot of the bed. She walked around the room and noted how tidy it was, as though a cleaning lady had been there earlier in the day. There was nothing else in the bedroom, so she made her way through the apartment, searching for clues to this disaster.

In the kitchen were the remains of a light meal: a sandwich before bed, a cup of tea emptied, tea leaves in the teapot, the *Paris Match* spread out on the counter and beneath its pages, undetected and overlooked, a journal. She certainly understood journals, so it didn't surprise her that Raphael had kept one. He was lonely, living in Paris apart from his family. She knew all that, as she picked up the thin moleskin covered book and tucked it in her purse to read and, perhaps, to understand. She could not phone the police, but she must report this to Roshi.

As the clear atmosphere faded, fear and anger replaced it. Who did this? Had Raphael found important information? Who also knew of his work and focus? She needed to read the journal for hints, and she needed to tell Roshi. First, she needed to be calm and take herself to a safe and public place. If she had been seen arriving here or was suspected of being more than Raphael's mistress, she was in great danger. She backed out of the apartment, feeling that she had seen as much as she was capable of seeing.

At a café half way to Roshi's apartment, she stopped and ordered a coffee. She started to read Raphael's journal from the back. He had not kept it for long and talked of their relationship. She felt her public persona disappear, as she continued to read. Her eyes blurred until she was afraid she could not see the handwriting and stopped to catch her breath, blow her nose and wipe away tears that streamed down her face. She had abruptly thawed though it had taken her a moment to realize what was happening. She had not let anyone into her heart for such a long time; she hardly recognized the loss and grief that nearly overwhelmed her. She needed to take a deep breath and hurry to Roshi's. To that end she left money near her cup and exited the café with head lowered. What she didn't notice was the person who sat, and watched and followed her as she left the café.

"The piano started to burn slowly, and as it burned the notes played wistfully out of tune, unreal, like a pianola. The flames consumed the wood but not the notes and not the wires. The notes played like the cry of trapped music, hollow, expiring."

—Nin *Collages*

Chapter 50
Roshi's Wisdom

Roshi opened the door himself.

"Come in, my dear. You've heard what happened."

"How did you find out so soon?"

"It happened last night and was reported just a few minutes ago. Another agent found him, but we could not be directly implicated. The landlord called it in."

"Oh, God, Roshi. Who knew our work would be so dangerous."

"It has been known from the beginning, Anais. When money is involved, there is always danger."

"I was in love with him, you know. I don't know how it happened. It was all so fast...and I'm married. How could this have happened?"

"The heart does not need a reason, my dear. And this is a great lesson for you, learned on your first big assignment. It is possible to feel exceptionally close to a colleague because of the danger and the secret nature of our work. Oftentimes, it is necessary to be exclusive, during an investigation, when we are open to ideas and intuitions that would not otherwise be considered. It forces two people into intimate contact and is a different kind of love, if love can be so categorized.

"Someone has been following me, Roshi. I should have told you long before now. But I did not recognize it as something connected with our work. I shrugged it off in denial. Now, I realize, I didn't want to believe it could be more than my imagination. You know how comfortable I find my inner fantasy life."

"So this is another important lesson. Shadows, the sound of footsteps, street violence, and the occasional recognition of a figure in a crowd: nothing can be taken for granted. I'm sure you're being followed. We need to sit down and put together information and analyze patterns, time factors and locations, then define what it is we actually know and what remains hidden.

"We have Holtz, Herr Dietrich, and your cousin Ernesto. Christolphe is suspect and Raphael is gone. Yves has seen a voyeur; you have been followed and attacked. All of these people have circled you as though you are the center of their interests."

"But why me?"

"That is the big question. Why you?"

"All these people are involved with banks or need money in the case of Holtz. Although with Holtz there could be a more direct connection to the bank world. After all, you did have a sense that he knew Herr Dietrich."

"What about Raphael?"

"He was very close to you, too. Did you share something with him that he may have suspected needed to be followed up? Think, my dear."

"I shared my suspicions about Holtz, who conveniently lives in the same apartment building. But honestly, I don't think Holtz has followed me. I would recognize him easily. It would be hard for him to remain hidden."

"That's still a very important lead. Do you know, if Raphael found out more about Holtz?

"He must have moved into the same building, but we'll never know."

"Never give up on any lead. There is always hope, always a detail or small clue left behind. Raphael was one of my most experienced men. He would have left something for us."

"He may not have wanted us to read it, but he left a journal on the kitchen counter. The murderer missed it because it was underneath the newspaper."

Roshi reached into his packet and handed her a folded note.

"And this was found in Raphael's clutched fist."

She reached for the note and unfolded it.

"No. No, I can't believe this."

Roshi sat back and watched her reaction. This was real grief. He had no doubt that she had felt very close to Raphael, but this was different. He understood. Tears filled her eyes. She tried to brush them away, but they overflowed rapidly and refused to go away. No one said this was an easy job, and here was an example of betrayal, disbelief and denial. She would have to believe, if it turned out to be true. It was a distinctly distasteful part of their work, unearthing truth, no matter the strong desire to brush it away.

"Will you look into this? Can I ask you to see with honest eyes? This goes beyond your personal attachments. We must see and hear like lie detectors or cameras. Then we must put together the reality that presents itself. Remember, this may not be what it seems."

Anais closed her eyes for a moment and breathed deeply.

"I will do what I can, but I need to go out to Louveciennes to recover for a few days. Angela is good for me that way."

Chapter 51
Retreat

The days at Louvecienne passed in a blur of flowers and water lilies, spring sunshine and memories. Every fruit tree in the garden was in heavenly bloom. From her chair in the garden she felt draped in lace and the gentle covering of forgetfulness. Despite the blossoming of spring, she felt listless and hollow. She could not understand why life seemed to slip away from her, when everything around her was being rejuvenated.

She closed her eyes and let the beauty of the garden envelop her. She let beauty take her to better times. The books she had read, the people she had known, especially the artists who started out with a vision and a desire to promote beauty she allowed to file through her mind in an array of inspiration. She concentrated on all she had been given and for that which she was immeasurably grateful. Flowers in her garden grew and bloomed and went to sleep until it was their time to grow. Their purpose was to glow with color, to help the bees, to spread their irresistible scent. They did not ask why they were subject to rain or inclement weather. They survived or they died, and then they revived, when the season was right. She, too, would survive and blossom and find inspiration.

On the fourth day, she came out of her reverie to get ready for another dinner party. It was Angela's job to be Christolphe's partner, and Friday would arrive soon enough. This time she intended to invite Lily. With her desperate financial situation and her great beauty, maybe she would meet one of the single men at her party. Maybe she would get to know Lily somewhat better. After all, she had been in New York, during all those formative years, when Lily was not only in the Marais but had been there when the Great War had raged in the French countryside. She was there when the Germans moved closer and closer to Paris. She sensed that much of the Lily she thought she had become reacquainted with was submerged beneath the fears that only loneliness can expose.

So an invitation was delivered to Lily, while the evening was planned and organized. Flower arrangements overflowed with blossoms from her garden, and a water lily floated in a glass bowl at the center of the table. Her kimono was painted with lush spring blossoms, and her diary was ready to record conversations, clandestine glances, irrelevant asides and the group mood. All her senses were tuned in, as she waited for her guests to arrive. She wondered who would be attracted to Lily and whether Lily would find one of the guests interesting.

The doorbell chimed in a delightful ripple of sound. It put her in a receptive hostess frame of mind, as she opened the door. Lily was the first to arrive, and that was a good sign. It was her first time in Louveciennes, so Angela wanted to show her the garden before the others arrived.

"My goodness, Anais. I had no idea you lived in such comfort."

"Well, normally it is Angela who lives here and Angela will hostess the dinner party, but I wanted to be here to explain that to you before the other guests arrive. Thank you for coming. I thought you might find at least one of the men personally attractive. Besides, I needed a female guest this evening to liven up the conversations."

They wandered into the garden.

"The garden is so beautiful and makes me think of your connection to Roshi. No wonder you have learned to speak Japanese."

They re-entered the house just as Christolphe came downstairs.

"Hello. So you are the famous Lily of Anais' childhood. It's good to meet you at last. Welcome. Scotch? I'm fixing myself one."

"Sure. On ice, please."

"Ah, a woman after my own heart. Wait till you try the food that Anais had the cook prepare. You'll feel like you're in Japan."

Anais smiled, about to say something polite just as the chimes rang again.

"Oh, I love the chimes," she heard Lily comment.

The evening routine had begun, and Angela was vaguely aware that Lily was not the same Lily she had played with as a child. How lovely and grown up she looked, how glamorous with her tall and elegant stature, gorgeous blue eyes and a sprinkling of disarming freckles along her cheekbones.

***

The evening was a success. The ambiance changed with the addition of a woman. Many conversations were meant to include her, and much more French was suddenly taken out and brushed off to accommodate Lily. It wasn't until well into the evening, when the sake, warm and fragrant, was set on the table and poured into tiny cups, that Lily was noticed speaking German. Now the whole evening changed, and echoes of surprise turned into appreciation. Everyone wanted to speak to her in German and, as she grew more confident, she explained that she had learned German years before, when she was very young and her parents had taken her with them to live in Germany. By the end of the evening she appeared quite fluent, which was another surprise for Anais.

Angela watched and listened carefully. She was the perfect hostess, anticipating everyone's needs, while she noted that more than one of the single men was quite attracted to Lily, especially when she switched to German, for this allowed everyone at the table to relax and feel at home. She made note of the two most attracted young men, so she could ask Christolphe, about their backgrounds and if it was possible to follow up on these introductions. With her model-like height, blue eyes and blond hair, the Irish Lily could pass for a Scandinavian or even a German. No wonder the men swarmed around her. They must have felt that they were back home. And how could anyone have known she spoke German? It shone a new light on her friend.

Chapter 52
Diary Reveries

After everyone had left and the house was put in order she sat at her bedroom desk by the open window over the back garden and opened her journal. The greatest surprise had been Lily. Who would have guessed? Her beauty, her sophistication, her intimate knowledge of the art world and fluency in German made for a big hit. Herr Dietrich had hovered for most of the evening, but Lily seemed more attracted to the young men her own age. Christolphe could not stop his praise of her old friend and insisted she be part of their evenings on a more regular basis. The guests concurred. Angela recorded nuances and blatant jokes, gestures and covert glances. She felt programmed to notice so many details and wondered how she could use these descriptions in her fiction writing. Her diary was taking on certain themes such as that of dinner parties, social events, or private moments, when she and Christolphe talked together. She found it rather odd that she gravitated to narration and character when, in real life, she considered herself an introvert who tired easily of people and their chatter. She was like Constantin Brancusi who remarked that his studio was his garden where he was happy, when he was alone. She never minded being alone. Such peaceful moments helped her feel centered. Occasionally, such as today, she and Lily would meet at a café to discuss romantic prospects from the party though she didn't think Lily needed much help in that direction.

Anais and Lily met at La Coupole, half expecting to see Hemingway at the next table. His second book had just been published to great acclaim. *A Farewell to Arms* embraced the Italian war front and depicted the world of the soldier, love, death and finer emotions with which the average person on the street could empathize. Suddenly, everyone wanted to read his first novel, and *The Sun Also Rises* could be seen in every bookstore window.

Anais arrived before Lily who was late, as usual. It was comforting to know some things never changed. She had read the diary entries from the weekend party and didn't know what to make of them. Why had Lily never mentioned her fluency in German or her early years in Berlin?

"There you are."

Anais was startled out of her reverie, as Lily came up behind her and hugged her enthusiastically. Every male at the sidewalk café and half of the women had turned their heads at her arrival. She wore a stunning outfit with a pink headscarf that piled her curly hair higher on her head and made her look even taller. Pink and blue in all shades melted on her dress and matched her leather purse and shoes. She did not look like a woman in financial difficulty, but Anais knew that French women were exceptionally skilled at this cover up. Old clothes could be rearranged endlessly to fool the unknowing. It was a matter of pride. Since the Great War, hunger and privation had been the norm in Montparnasse and the Marais. They had learned many of these couturier tricks in the last decade. Now, with the financial crash in the United States, Parisians were braced for a repeat of austerity. It was not uncommon a few years ago to find someone frozen to death in a studio apartment, starved, every piece of furniture gone into the stove before they succumbed.

She was certainly given to morose reverie today and needed to pay attention to their conversation.

"I had a wonderful time at your place."

"Oh, we enjoyed your company tremendously. Christolphe says you are the talk of his department at the bank."

"The men were charming. I had the feeling there was a lot of money in that room."

"That's partly true. Those men are in charge of huge estates and foreign investments. Yes, I guess you could say they certainly are close to wealth. Which ones were you attracted to?"

"Well, I certainly liked Hans. He's from Switzerland, and we have a lot in common. His parents may even have been acquainted with mine. He was very sweet, and I've already gotten a note and flowers from him. He wants to go dancing at the Rotunde this weekend."

"Wow, that was fast work. Who else took your fancy?"

"Max. I adored Max. He seems a bit dangerous, if you know what I mean. Kind of exciting…the kind one's mother would not approve of."

"Where does he hail from?"

"He's from Berlin and that's a wild place these days. Cabarets, lots of nightlife, drugs, shady underworld stuff: I suspect Max is acquainted with some of it. Certainly, he's not an innocent like Hans. Of course, I haven't heard a word from him."

"It seems rather soon. Would you like me to find out what he does at the bank?"

"Sure."

"I'll get Christolphe right on it."

"By the way, your Angela self is quite the lady. Who would have guessed that my dearest childhood friend would turn into two friends? It's weird."

"I don't care to discuss her, if you don't mind. Did you learn anything else at the dinner party?"

"Well, I heard that Max is being groomed by Herr Dietrich to take over his position one day. He says he loves artists and might like to have a tour of the art hot spots one evening."

"Really?"

"Oh, yes, but there are complications at the moment. You know, I'm seeing someone else, right? It's gotten pretty heavy and, for the moment, I'm in lust."

"Oh, no, I didn't know. Do I know him?"

"He did mention your name. He's gorgeous, an opera singer, and he just moved in a few blocks away."

"Not Holtz!"

"Why yes. How did you guess?"

"Well, it isn't every day one meets an opera singer."

Anais felt a sinking sensation in her stomach. Her *pain au chocolat* looked indigestible, and her *café au lait* sat in its cup, getting cold.

"I'll have that croissant, if you're not going to eat it."

"Sure. I've no appetite today for some reason."

Lily grabbed the chocolate croissant and finished it quickly.

"There's not much to eat at my place," she explained.

So it was hard times for Lily, much worse than she had let on. Roshi had told her to keep an open mind, but this was getting worse each day. Lily certainly had a motive to get involved and easily had the opportunity to pass on sensitive information. She found it difficult to see her best friend in such a light? Surely, there was someone else she could investigate?

Chapter 53
Behind Appearances

Ernesto had been in Paris for nearly a week this time. The trip from Cuba, the time zone changes and the weather did not particularly agree with him, as he was not a good traveler. He was also out of touch with the art world. When he was in school, he was too young, and now he was living so far away. He had just absorbed the Dada Manifesto of 1918, ten years after the fact. "Dada means nothing," he recited. "After the carnage, we hold out hope for a purified humanity…everything we look at is false."

As soon as he had absorbed these words, they were old and used. The Surrealist Manifesto of 1924 took up where the Dadaists left off. They believed in "pure psychic automatism through which (they) proposed to express verbally, in writing, or by any other means, the real function of thought." These views of war cancelled themselves out, and now, half a decade later nihilists were obsolete. He would really love to meet Andre Breton or Tristan Tzara to discuss all the reasons for their opposing views.

Last night, he was invited to something more exciting. He had met Robert Desnos, who knew his cousin Anais and asked him to join a few people this evening for a session with a medium. Never would this have been an option in Cuba. Some called it the big sleep, but in reality it was hypnotic trance. There were "dream poems" that had come out of these sessions. It could not be underestimated and fit well with the new psychoanalysis begun by Freud, now taken up by Carl Jung of Zürich.

Ernesto's plan was to travel between Zürich and Paris. With the turn in the world economy, Cuba was in trouble. His father was getting old and, after Anais left Cuba in such a hurry, Ernesto had taken over most of the bank's affairs. It had been a grueling apprenticeship this last decade. He felt that his entire being had been put on hold. Finally, he had had to seek out a few life experiences for himself. Either that or lose his mind. Damian had drifted away years ago. Who could blame him? He told Ernesto he was in a solid relationship these days, and Ernesto tried to forget him. It did not help that there was no possibility of any kind of relationship in Cuba. He would die of suffocation, if it continued. So this trip, which was one of several he had made over the years, was a life-saving foray into his soul, a time to combine bank work with his passion to find himself. To this end he had begun Jungian psychoanalysis in Zürich.

Maybe he would meet someone special this evening. His only social obligation was to see Anais before he left. The family would be quite upset if he didn't. It wasn't as though he hadn't enjoyed her company for the short time they had known each other; it was simply the fact that she was family, a bit naïve and an obligation. Tonight, he would have a session with the psychic, and it was the first time he could remember being this excited in years.

***

Christolphe stepped off the train in Zürich and stood under the dome of the train station. A few blocks to walk up Bahnhofstrasse and he would arrive at his destination. Private banks in Switzerland were harder to find than a good woman. He was still pleased by the dinner party his Anais had pulled together on the weekend. He was just about the luckiest fellow he knew: a life of health, wealth and a fine wife. It didn't get any better.

As he day dreamed, he almost missed his destination. There it was, the smallest brass plaque on a door to a three-story building that could pass for a private residence. No one would suspect it was a Swiss bank. Discretion and a doorbell, a code for the doorman and a moment of scrutiny from the security guard, when he was admitted beyond the front door: the banks were all alike. Privacy was their most valuable asset. Who would have it any other way? Christolphe was recognized and welcomed these days. He felt privileged and important, when he came to work, and each day was an adventure. He pitied those who considered work to be dull or boring. He was born to this life and loved every minute.

There was a lot happening lately. Everyone wanted to secret away family wealth in keeping with such times, when security was threatened. Those who prepared for war in small or large countries around the world needed Swiss banks, as repositories until their troubles moved on, and it was safe to resume activity. Switzerland was synonymous with the mountains, a place where danger resided beside neutrality. There were the heights and inspirations, the avalanches and deep forests, where one could become lost. But in the center of those mountains were tunnels and safe havens. Some said there were dwarves and misshapen elves who dwelled deep in the mountains and guarded bank assets. They were greedy hoarders, and they maintained hidden caches of gold. It was believed that they were the official keepers of darkness, so necessary if light was to exist.

The Swiss were famous for ancient alchemists who knew about these treasures and whose greatest desire was to be able to transform ordinary metals into gold. They lived on the mountainsides in little towns like Einsiedeln that Christolphe had visited and found so charming. The Swiss psychologist, Carl Jung, had recently begun to interpret the activity of those alchemists and to study the formulas of Paracelsus. In the limited boundaries of the human mind the greatest transformation of ordinary metals to gold was in the transformation of body to spirit. Christolphe thought it was a lovely pipe dream. He was nothing if not practical. Wealth was not a dream or an alchemical formula; it was real and obtained through hard work, diligence, imagination, and organizational skills. Dreamers were rarely successful people in his estimation.

"Good morning, Herr Guiller. Can we get you an espresso to start your day?"

"Ah, you read my mind, sir."

"This way. I'll take you to the director's office."

He loved it when his every need was anticipated. He and the director would sit, have their breakfast together, then get down to work. Quite civilized.

To his astonishment, this meeting was full of surprises. Already seated in Herr Dietrich's office were several other bankers and investors who were introduced, in turn, to Christolphe. One of them looked familiar, but it wasn't until he was introduced that he recognized his wife's cousin.

"But you are the cousin of Anais."

"I am. All the way from Cuba."

The others stopped to listen to their conversation.

"This is such a surprise, a complete surprise. I believe we met, only once, before Anais and I were married. Welcome. Welcome."

They got up to embrace in a Swiss greeting.

"When she hears you are in Zürich, she will insist on a special evening together. We live in Paris, you know."

All of this was a façade and a front for the others in the room.

"Yes, I know, and I was told not to return to Cuba until I had seen her. Her mother and aunt are well and anticipate hearing that she is in good spirits."

"Well, gentlemen, please excuse us. Ernesto is my wife's first cousin, and we will take up our re-acquaintance this evening, when today's work is done."

They all nodded approvingly and got down to work. At lunch Ernesto quietly informed Christolphe that he had a business meeting to attend that evening, but he would look forward to visiting with Christolphe soon. He had decided there was no way he intended to cancel with the medium for bank business just to see his cousin. At 5 PM he intended to take the train to Paris. If the evening went on too long, he could overnight in Paris and return early in the morning to attend a second bank meeting. Life was too short to waste it any longer on that which did not touch his heart.

Chapter 54
The Dinner Party

Giving parties, this seemed to be the theme and purpose of her life. Angela went downstairs to speak to Camille. She and Jacques had been working for her household since they arrived in Louvecienne, and she did not think she could manage without them. Camille had already bought everything they might need from the grocer, and Jacques had done the housekeeping on the main floor. He was now in the garden, sweeping, cutting and weeding.

Angela was in her bedroom that was also her study. She was at her desk, finishing her journal entry from yesterday, when she had been quite disturbed and couldn't fathom why. This morning she had read last evening's diary entries and wondered, if she was on the verge of paranoia. Suspicion filled the pages; questions and dark conjectures were crammed into a penmanship that she did not recognize as her own. These were not dreams because they were written before she went to bed, but they had caused her to sleep badly and awaken to more ominous forebodings. This evening, the dinner guests were an unlikely group, and for the life of her she could not understand why they were invited. It made her feel that she was losing her mind. Lily was invited as well as Ernesto, Holtz, Yves, Christolphe, and Herr Dietrich. Seven people sitting around the table, brought together ostensibly to welcome Ernesto, the cousin she hadn't seen in years? And who was Yves? Lily had been to a recent dinner at their home with Christolphe's colleagues.

She had been a delightful and refreshing guest. Maybe she was to be here to balance energies. Maybe the guest list was simply ingenuous, a mix of personalities for a non-business meeting of possible friendships. Who knew? She was ready to give up attempts to understand motives these days. Nothing seemed to make a lot of sense to her. Maybe, she concluded, she needed to get out more, make more friends, expand her world view, and take more responsibility for her own well-being. The next moment a great fear seized her until she felt cold, worried about war, fearful of violence, and immersed in loss and sadness. Where these strong feelings came from she didn't know.

She did believe, however, that oversensitivity was a curse and a lack of self-control. She needed to straighten her spine, breathe deeply, and believe that everything would be okay. On that note, she took herself downstairs to help with dinner plans.

The guests arrived one at a time somewhat bemused. Christolphe, especially, wondered what to do with them. He was accustomed to business dinners and somewhat at a loss, when it was a matter of friends or family.

"No business talk this evening," she told him.

Then what would he discuss?

Lily was the first and, fortunately, their common ground was the bank people she had met. She was just telling Christolphe that she had had dates with two of the young men at the last party, when the door chimes rang. It was Ernesto.

"Anais, you look beautiful. How are you? It would seem that Paris suits you."

"Goodness, it has been such a long time. I couldn't believe it, when Christolphe said he had met you in Zürich. How are Mama and the boys? And what about Aunt Evaline?"

The chimes rang, as he started to pass on greetings from the family. It was Holtz. Angela noticed a strangely familiar glance of greeting between him and Lily. Maybe it was another fluke of her imagination. Holtz was directed to Christolphe who, of course, remembered him from their previous dinner party, while Lily moved over to continue her talk with Ernesto. The last guest to ring was Yves. He recognized Holtz but, diplomatically, said nothing about their encounter. He suspected he was not recognized, dressed in a jacket and grey flannel pants, buffed shoes and a tie, his hair nicely trimmed and demeanor quite different. Holtz was so self-centered he would never remember a security guard on the pier. Besides, he immediately noted the energy between Holtz and Lily.

Yves looked around and introduced himself to Angela, the serene version of his Anais. His Anais. He heard the descriptor in his mind. Now, where had that come from? She kissed him on both cheeks after a handshake and led him further into the parlor. So this was the beautiful home in the suburbs, the gracious banker's wife and the banker himself, who approached Yves with hand extended, looking for an introduction. Yves quickly introduced himself to save Angela the embarrassment of not knowing a guest.

"I'm delighted to meet you, sir. I am a friend of Lily's," he lied. "We go back a long way."

Angela drifted away while Lily was across the room engrossed in a *tête-à-tête* with Holtz. As Angela served wine on a tray, she moved from guest to guest, the perfect hostess.

"Let me finish up here, Ernesto. I am so delighted to see you. I'll be right back."

Ernesto waited patiently, watching Christolphe. He was sure he had seen him at a few social functions in Havana. They had never been introduced, but Ernesto never forgot a face. He was certain Christolphe had been accompanied by someone that Ernesto was certain was homosexual. Not possible, right? Anything was possible, he supposed. In his circles at home he kept as far away from reproach as he could.

Yves was on his own for the moment and wandered over to introduce himself to Ernesto.

"Ah, Anais' cousin. So good to meet you. She has described you as her best friend in Havana."

Ernesto nodded.

"Yes, we are cousins, but we were very good friends."

"Where are you staying? Will you be here long?"

"I want to explore some art film, take in the art side of Paris, maybe travel back and forth to Geneva, Paris, and Zürich. There is a lot of bank work to do for the family while I am here, but the art scene is an opportunity I crave when I am back home. There is nothing like it."

He was a serious fellow, thought Yves.

"Your little cousin must seem quite grown up, since you last saw her."

"She is, and so much more sedate."

Yves noted that he did not reveal where he lodged.

"I love him with my mind, admire him. I love him gratefully for his wide understanding, his love of me. I *want* to love him, because he *ought* to be loved. I hate myself for whatever I make him suffer for I have moments when I know that no multiple lives or loves can be worth his love, when I desire desperately to be able to control the overflow of my excessive nature and imagination."

—Nin *Diary* August 11, 1929

Chapter 55
Yves Joins the Party

That evening, Angela wrote in her journal. What a strange evening we had at the house; apparently, no one is as they appear. Lily arrived first and spent most of the evening flirting with Holtz; Ernesto spent his time flirting with Christolphe; Christolphe circled the group asking questions about Yves; and Yves was completely inscrutable. I cannot be sure, but he seemed to follow several conversations not meant for his ears, including the quiet ones between Lily and Holtz. The minutes before we sat at the table felt like a caricature of that childhood whisper game, whereby a phrase is passed around a circle and ends up incomprehensible and unrecognizable back at the beginning.

Once the guests were seated, the turn of conversation became a puzzle. Indirect comments were made to each other that seemed meant for another. Yves, for instance, asked questions aloud that seemed to hold the whole group in suspense.

"Christolphe, I did not realize you had lived in Cuba. Ernesto tells me he remembers you there, years ago."

"I don't believe I met Ernesto there."

"Darling, you never told me you had once lived in Cuba. What years were you there?"

Angela seemed completely perplexed.

"It has simply never come up in our busy lives. I believe I was there after you left. Believe me, if you had been there, I'd have found you."

That caused a jovial laugh from the table.

Holtz asked Christolphe, "Have you always done bank work, sir? In Cuba, were you there on bank work?"

"Oh, yes. Banks and their intricate interactions with other communities has long been my specialty."

"And now that the war is over, is that still the case?"

"You sound like you need a banker's advice, young man. Even opera singers occasionally need to meet with their bank manager. Come see me on Monday morning. We'll talk."

Christolphe appeared to shrug off the conversation, but Yves watched him carefully, as he nodded to Holtz. This was an actual appointment and not just small talk that had transpired.

"What will happen to us now that the United States is in such a predicament?"

"To tell you the truth, Lily, the worst of times is over. It is what has led up to this crash that is of the greatest concern. Day by day, from here on, the situation will get better. It took the crash to alert everyone of the actual standing of the world economies to each other. Now, we at the banks can get to work on repairs. It's hard to make reparations, when one is in the dark about the extent of the problem."

"Are you saying it will get better?" asked Holtz.

"That's it in a nutshell. Hang in there my friends. We have turned the corner."

"What if we have no stocks, but other valuable assets?"

"That is why we will talk on Monday. Each one is unique. Many assets are for sale these days. Only a few are desirable. We'll talk."

Ernesto looked between Holtz and Lily.

"What of countries that have assets to sell?"

Yves had been waiting patiently to hear this vague question asked.

"It sounds like everyone is lining up for appointments on Monday."

Everyone laughed, but there was a tension behind the laughter.

"How about you, Lily? Do you need an appointment?"

"Oh, Anais and I already have an appointment to meet for coffee on Monday."

More chuckles.

"What about you, Yves? It's not every day I offer free consultations to friends and family."

"My affairs are in real estate, *Monsieur*. My father always said I could not go wrong to stay with the land, and so I have done. This is not to say I do not take an interest in the investments of others or the banks. As for me, I can wait for years if necessary."

"Spoken as a true Frenchman. You are lucky you can eat your assets, my friend. Most are not so fortunate as to be able to wait."

"It is a long view into the future, a perspective that relies on hope and positive projections into the unknown."

"Farmers have always taken chances on the next season and the one beyond, *Monsieur*. It has made them strong and steadfast. One forgets that they are the true backbone of any country."

There was a moment of silence at the table, as everyone tried to remember when such an attitude truly existed. For Lily, it seemed like an illusion. Holtz was reminded of the mill of his youth and the farmers who arrived season after season with the fruits of their labor. It was a blur from the past. Yves gave tribute to his own family as he spoke, yet Ernesto found it impossible to connect with what Yves said. *Who still thought in such an archaic way?* he wondered. He had never been close to the land or the workings of the seasons. Cuba was not in touch with its laborers or farmers. Companies like Coca-Cola and plantations with enslaved workers dotted the hinterland. Those in his social set went to Switzerland, to school or England to learn the language of diplomacy. Banks dealt with hoarded money. They needed investments and bank vaults to secure ill-gained and portable cash. He felt like he was three times removed from this conversation. He squirmed uncomfortably in his seat. He had not truly come to Paris on business and hated the whole discussion. He really wanted to find like-minded fellowship and delve into the whole art culture, maybe even bring some of it back to Cuba.

Chapter 56
Lily's Mistake

Lily hurried along the street to a secret meeting with Holtz. She was embarrassed. Of all the artists in all the ateliers she found herself in a passionate affair with a German opera singer. Seriously, she did not know how it had come about. When she saw him at Anais' home, she had nearly wept. Yes, Anais could understand the strange physical hold he had over her, but she hadn't seen her all week to explain. Surely, she wasn't so desperate that she needed these complications. Besides, the guy was impoverished, the same as every other artist. All her friends, certainly, were artists, but they were friends and did not cross the line into her more staid and secure life. She liked the Marais; she loved Montparnasse and the artist's insights, but never ever had she wanted an intimate relationship with one of these impoverished souls. They were different. She admitted it. She was not an artist, but an art historian and a lover of the arts. Artists needed support; what they sacrificed every day was dinner at the table for the future, the unknown and everyman's fears. She loved every one of them, but this was different. Holtz was so handsome and confident, so earthy and irreverent that she had succumbed to his charms in a moment of temptation. It was the beginning of her demise. Now he felt that blackmail, for that is basically what it was, was necessary. She had told him about buyers and benefactors, ateliers and on-going profits. At first, it had seemed harmless, but the dinner party had brought home some realistic truths. This precious and apparently innocent information was the kind that wicked people were willing to buy. With a look at herself that felt clear for the first time, since the financial crisis, she realized there was danger in what she had done.

She and Holtz were meeting in his apartment this afternoon, and she planned to keep her head about her. Two could play this game of deceit. She opened the front foyer door to his building and rang the doorbell to his apartment. He would be down to fetch her in a moment. She sighed. Truly, theirs was the best sexual experience she had ever known. What a shame. She was not naïve enough to believe it was love, but it was wonderful while it lasted. He appeared at her side, suddenly, like a cat, she thought.

"You frightened me. How can such a big guy walk without making a sound?"

"I used to practice, when I was a kid, before I got big. You had to meet my father to understand."

She could see a shadow cross his eyes before he smiled cheerfully.

"Let me take your bag. Are you planning to cook me a lunch?"

He looked so hopeful, like a hungry little boy.

"I might, if you're good to me."

They could tease and spar with each other all afternoon. The embraces and kisses to follow always fired in her an intense response. How did he do it? He carried her grocery bag up to the third floor.

"Someone told me there was a murder in this building not so long ago."

"True. Apparently, it happened to some guy just after I moved in. Don't worry, it wasn't my apartment. It was the one above me on the third floor. They cleaned it up, but no one has rented it yet."

She shuddered.

"People will forget in time. Right now, people consider it just too much bad luck to rent such a place, especially since the war."

They listened to opera that afternoon, especially Wagner. She made a special lunch of steak and *frites,* and watched as Holtz ate like a starving man. Not many people could afford meat these days and, quite frankly, neither could she, but in the back of her mind she knew it was her farewell to Holtz. There was no sense letting an affair end on a tragic note. She knew he would not be terribly hurt; missing good sex was not the same as losing love. She knew this with her mind, yet the ache of loneliness was there. This hateful war had caused so much destruction on so many fronts. Battle lines were constantly being reenacted. She would be more prudent in the future. She realized just then how lonely she had to have been to fall for a handsome smile and blue eyes. She envied Anais her two lives, not just one, but two, wherein she could come and go and always have a backup plan with a man who adored her. Fortunately, she had a good plan for the rest of the afternoon: sex, incredible sex and a role-reversal. She, too, could get information with blackmail.

"So my dear, have you had enough to eat? Would you like to lie down for a while and make yourself comfortable? I shall change the record; I don't want you to exert a single muscle."

Holtz lay back on the bed, arms behind his head, locked in anticipation. He watched her tall and elegant body change the record to *Carmen* and lower the sound, so it wasn't the main attraction in the room. She unwrapped her dress and let it slide down her arms, then leaned over to unbutton the front of his pants. He shot up beneath his trousers, instantly on alert and painfully aroused.

"Now, relax my dear, there is so much more to come."

God, he didn't know if he could handle it.

As though reading his mind, she whispered, "Oh, you'll be fine; I know how to make this last all afternoon."

She bent down to breathe on him in the hottest wave of moisture he had ever known. Much later, she whispered again.

"You're like a work of art. I can't imagine where I would secret you away, if I didn't want anyone to steal you from me."

He groaned as she raised the level of sensation beyond his realm of experience.

"Now, take a breath. Where could I put you?"

She held the next caress; so close, so exquisite he wasn't sure if he was in a dream state.

"You know where."

"I do?"

"Lily, please."

"I just thought I could treat you like a painting, my treasure."

His laughter ended in a groan.

"There's always the Swiss Bank National vault in Fribourg."

"And here?"

She bent down again and his spasm nearly took them off the mattress.

"I see now," she whispered. "Where else?"

He whispered back, secrets, a game, a little game that led to more and more favors until he could no longer go on, and they both fell asleep. She put a blanket over them and held him close for an hour, thinking of the things he had told her. This had been a meaningful goodbye, indeed.

Chapter 57
Lily's Confession

Lily approached *La Belle Aurore* that afternoon low in spirits, embarrassed and contrite. She didn't know how she would find the courage to tell Anais about Holtz and the fiasco that had turned out to be her relationship to him. Now, that she had walked away from his apartment, sat alone in a café for an hour and taken stock of her life, she acknowledged her loneliness and her fear. She was not just sad, she was afraid; she was alone in Paris and in the world. Her parents and Nanny were gone. There were no brothers or sisters to fall back on. There were no cousins or relations who would care what happened to her, and she was desolate. It was no excuse, but it felt like it. She needed more backbone, a new outlook on her future, more education and a wider scope of friends. Befriending artists would not be enough; they had too many of their own problems. She needed to let go of false pride and ask for help. First, she had to confess what she had done, but it was an awful, wrenching feeling. To that end she had walked all the way to the houseboat to see Anais. Without telling her she would be stopping by she could only hope she found her at home. Otherwise, she might lose her courage.

As she walked down the pier she saw her friend on her balcony, watering the plants she loved. She called out and waved. Startled, Anais called to her.

"I'll be right down to open the door."

Lily stood at the gallery door and stilled her quickly beating heart. It felt like she had been running. The door opened wide.

"Lily, what a wonderful surprise. Come in. Come in."

Lily stood there, awkwardly.

"I must talk to you, Anais."

"Well, this sounds serious, and you are quite pale. Are you okay?"

"I'm not sure."

"Come. We'll go up to my private space. It is just where you need to be with a nice cup of tea or coffee."

"Just a glass of water, please."

"I have a better idea."

Anais led her to a lovely chair near her desk and asked her to wait, then returned with a glass of water and a cognac."

"It's nearly the end of the day and you look like you could use this."

They sat silently, sipping their cognac, and Anais waited for the storm. What could be so awful to cause her friend such upset?

"I have a confession, Anais."

She nodded.

"It's a fright, really. I don't know how to begin."

"I'm listening."

"Remember that fellow Holtz at your dinner party? Well, I've been having very passionate affair with him."

"And is that a problem?"

"Oh, Anais, he's really a German, and I have told him things that make me wonder, if I need my head examined."

"I'm not sure what you mean. What could you possibly say to him that might be wrong or inappropriate? After all, we are no longer at war with the Germans. Someone has to reach out a forgiving hand. I don't blame you for being with a German, you know. He's quite a handsome fellow and apparently talented. Is that so bad?"

"There's more. I think he's up to something sinister."

On alert, Anais nodded and listened.

"He has gotten information from me about the artists I know, their current and past work, who they have sold to and who they intend to sell to in the future. I have told him all about their dire circumstances and where they live. In fact, this is mostly information anyone can glean, but I am the one who has sold out, so to speak. I think he is a thief or working with the German government to steal. I don't really know, but I'm afraid. And worse, I have done it to pretend someone cared what I had to say or know. It was wrong."

Lily took out her handkerchief and wiped her eyes. She was distraught and inconsolable. Anais let her cry until the tears stopped and the sobs had calmed.

"I think you should stay with me tonight. Does Holtz realize how much you have come to your senses?"

"No. I don't think so, although I just came from his apartment. We had lunch. I bought the food and prepared it, and then I seduced him to within an inch of his life. I'm surprised he's still alive. It's the least I could do. I managed to get some information of my own. It's only fair, I thought."

Anais tried not to look too surprised.

"My God, Lily. That might have been dangerous. What if he is truly a criminal, despite the blond beauty and the Wagnerian talent? After all that effort I hope the information you got was worth it."

Anais prepared a pot of coffee, as they listened to the hum of the river beneath them, and they slowly began to share the details of Holtz's life and current activities. For an innocent-looking bystander, Holtz had gathered quite a bit of information.

Chapter 58
Ernesto Visits the Gallery

Yves watched Lily leave *La Belle Aurore,* looking better than when she arrived. Such a beautiful woman. Yves sighed. Maybe he should consider looking for a good woman. It had been a long time, since he'd appreciated a pair of legs or high cheekbones. What woman would want to live on a trawler on the Seine? He sighed, again, and images of Anais appeared: boat cleaning, writing at her little desk, leaving the pier with heels and an elegant coat. He was spoiled for any other woman, his sighs endless today.

***

Several hours later, he heard footsteps on the pier and looked through a porthole in his salon. He recognized Ernesto from the party. Now, this was interesting. Ernesto looked bewildered, and Yves could tell he couldn't believe he had found the right address. There was only one houseboat on the pier, but Yves did not want to reveal his presence. He watched.

Ernesto finally went through the gate and rang the bell. He saw Anais look out the window in surprise, before she opened the gallery door in welcome.

"My dear Anais, I hope I'm not intruding."

She welcomed him inside and closed the door, leaving Yves curiously unsettled. There was something about the guy that did not sit well with him. Maybe it was the Cuban Spanish arrogance or that suave handsome wealthy intelligent something. He listened to the voice in his head and recognized jealousy when he heard it. These thoughts were not acceptable. Where had they come from? They seemed to appear often since the party in Louvecienne and the meeting with Christolphe. He didn't feel completely comfortable with him, either. If this continued, he would question his own ability to discern between fact and fiction, valuable assets he had honed sharply for years. He and his boss needed to sit down and compare notes.

"Please, come upstairs."

Ernesto nodded and tried to take in his surroundings while she went ahead of him, expecting him to follow her upstairs.

"This place is surprisingly comfortable," he commented.

He entered her boudoir on the second floor and caught his breath. Now this was a woman he had never known. How we all grow up, he thought. She motioned to a chair and took her place on the love seat.

"Can I get you a coffee?"

"I wouldn't want to put you to any trouble."

He noticed two empty glasses and the pillows in disarray on the love seat.

"You just had guests?"

"Oh, of course. Some days *La Belle Aurore* feels like a mini salon."

He nodded, his head empty of connections.

"So how are you enjoying Paris, my dear cousin? We didn't get much time to talk at the party, and I was hoping to see you again. I sensed that you and Christolphe knew each other. Surprising, that he had forgotten to mention he once lived in Havana."

His brain felt blocked. Where were his social skills? This was his own cousin, but he didn't know this person.

"Anais, I want to tell you something. We once shared secrets, and I am so overwhelmed right now I don't know a good way to say this."

"Are you sick? Is the business okay?"

"It's nothing like that. I'm a homosexual. Do you know what that is?"

She started to laugh.

"I'm so sorry, Ernesto. I'm not laughing at you or the levity of your circumstances. This is Paris, *mon cousin*; of course I know the definition of homosexual. Some of my best friends are of such persuasion. If you wish, I can introduce you to a few of them."

He listened in astonishment as she talked. Embarrassed and more light-hearted, he felt a thaw beginning between his shoulder blades. Was she the nether side of his heart?

"I don't know what to say. All these years this essential part of my being has been hidden. Never, have I told anyone. I have had to travel across the Atlantic Ocean to hear words of reassurance. It is as though my whole life has been overturned, like a rock, and the belly you see is now exposed to the light."

"Yes, but think of all that has lain dormant. When you go home, you will dream dreams of creation, the new and the adventure of exploration. Themes will appear that were once buried and suppressed. A new life awaits you, Ernesto. I am glad I could have been a catalyst. But tell me, not to so abruptly change the subject, what is it you have come to Europe to do? Since you never expected, in your wildest imaginings, to expose your underbelly, what is it you truly expected to find here?"

"Well, artists, I guess."

"But that isn't true, is it? You once told me you would stay in Havana and live out your life there in charge of the bank, eventually."

"Times change. We all change."

"Yes, I understand more than most. You can barely recognize the young person you taught to swim in Havana. So, of course, I understand change. How have you changed, Ernesto?"

He hung his head, but she waited quietly.

"I have become bitter, and I wear a mask. Every day I grow more and more opaque so no one can see me. My mind is clouded in despair, and the family business is failing. The military is gaining, the old families are slowly, inexorably being deposed. The Havana of the country club is quiet and very subdued. I believe everyone is looking for an escape route, but for most it will not come."

"Are you planning to move to Paris?"

"I doubt it. I want to go somewhere I can speak my own language, somewhere I can be myself. I can still liquidate our assets, if I am wise, but the family will never understand. Father is old and infirm and will consider it a betrayal of all he has worked for. However, he will die soon, and I need to have a life."

"How desperate you are, my cousin? What are your plans?" *Would you be desperate enough to kill for your plans?* she wondered.

"So far, I have no plans. This is a scouting expedition."

She did not believe him. He was very uncomfortable, now, sweating with a light sheen across his forehead.

"Well, I hope you will find what you seek in this beautiful city. I look from my balcony, during the day, from the windows in the evening, and I never fail to be inspired. Something in the earth beneath Paris rises up to meet the light. The artists feel it, feed on it, would never leave it. May it find you and guide you to a new life."

They said goodbye soon afterward. It had been an emotional afternoon for her cousin. She sat and practiced her recall, every gesture and glance, every movement of body and switch of attitude. She excelled in this post-interview analysis, free of obstructions and walls. Why had he lied to her? He had been seen in Paris on previous visits. His foray into art and homosexuality were only two reasons for his visit. Money and the desperation of the Havanese political situation now entered the equation. Was that it? Was it all about the family business? He had already admitted that he did not seek a new home in her city. Buenos Aires came to her mind as a place that would suit her cousin; the white washed Paris of South America.

Every piece in this puzzle should have made it easier to see the whole picture. She only wished the suspects were more removed from her life, so she could feel more rational. This business with friends and relatives was a bit of hell, and nothing made sense.

Chapter 59
Christolphe at the Bank

The next suspect in whatever nefarious goings-on that lurked in the Paris world she so cherished was, unfortunately, Christolphe. She had left him for last in a genuine reluctance to know the truth. She, who had wished to devote her life to truth and beauty, might be living with a liar, a thief, or worse, a murderer.

In fact, not only could she not bring herself to be a spy in her own home, she could not figure out how she would go about it or if she could bring herself to do so. How does one spy on a husband, especially, when the desire to do so is missing? She already knew what Roshi's answer to that quandary would be, so there was no reason for a conference. The more she worried about it, the less she liked the idea.

***

The next afternoon, she walked back along the pier and stepped aboard the *Hilaire*.

"Yves, are you down there?"

His head emerged from the engine room where he had been working on the fuel line. It was a full time job just to keep *Hilaire* afloat. He was smudged with grease and sweat and wiped himself off with a hopelessly filthy rag.

"What can I do for you, *Madame*?"

"My God, you scared me; I don't even recognize you in your disguise."

"We assistants are versatile."

"Well, I hope so. Can we talk? I think I have a serious assignment for you."

***

Yves listened carefully as Anais voiced her suspicions. She held nothing back.

"You have been far more busy than I imagined. This gets more and more complicated, and all these people surrounding you are friends and family."

"Except Holtz."

"Yes, except him. Now there lies my main concern."

"How so?"

"First, he is not family or friend. Second his motives are as solid as any of the others. Third, he's German and lied about it."

"I hate to think of any of these people being implicated, Yves. Surely, much desperation is involved in order to kill."

"Yes, it's true. Someone must feel trapped and desperate."

"And that brings me to your assignment. I cannot very well spy on my own husband."

"Who better?"

"I'm serious. I want you to do it. He leaves for Zürich again tomorrow, and I need you to follow him."

"You don't understand. He is not a part of our world. A banker's wife can only make so many observations. I can't manage it, and Angela would be horrified at the thought of following him."

"So far, I don't understand how you think he might be involved."

"He seems to be the common denominator in every instance. He knew.

Ernesto, his boss knows Holtz; he has heard me talk about Lily for years; he handles money and knows many bankers in several countries; and he is in the perfect position to know many artists because I am his wife. I wouldn't be surprised, if he was the one who arranged to have me followed."

"But why? There has to be a motive."

"That's what I need you to find out. It can't be money. Is it ambition? Is it fear of something? I just don't see it. I'm too close to the situation."

"Okay, but I want you to be more careful while I am away on these scouting expeditions. Keep the gallery closed his week. Do not let in visitors. No one, understand?"

"Yes, I know it's getting dangerous. I also know we are about to straighten out this mess. Raphael must have discovered something bad enough to get himself killed. Believe me, I'll be careful."

Yves got up and searched the back of a drawer in the galley.

"This is for your bedroom. Use it if you have to."

It was his service revolver.

"I have another, so don't worry about me. And let's hope none of these dramatic actions are necessary."

Anais sat quietly and held the revolver.

"I was trained in how to use this, but I hope it is not necessary."

"This wonderful life I praise so often seems blank and stupid today. I could do without my mirror, without lovely clothes, without sunshine – none of these things are necessary when I am alone."

—Nin Diary October 17, 1927

Chapter 60
Dismay

Christolphe boarded the Paris train to Zürich. It was his favorite bank trip. Zürich was the city he loved in Switzerland. The vaults, the important deposits that reflected the state of Europe and the Western world, its power plays, the clandestine meetings and the Swiss competence that was a marvel of discipline, focus and discretion. It was a cunning combination that made for a powerful backseat driver. The Swiss moved and shook the world without leaving their mountain tunnels and bank vaults. They were the keepers of world peace and balance. Without their interface with the powers of good and evil, they believed there would be head-on collisions like there were in the Great War. They were intermediaries, and they were a necessary influence in finance. Without the cushion of their staid traditionalism and conservative dealings, Christolphe truly imagined the world would be in a state of continual chaos.

The newspapers were full of stories of the collapse of the public banks and institutions. Although the private Swiss banks and their private customers had been affected, much wealth had been preserved. Reporters listened to the whispers of reconstruction and revival. In reality it was the last decade in which the economy had fallen. With the advent of the so-called crisis, Christolphe, his colleagues and their clients, were well positioned for this coming decade of growing affluence. He was proud to have insider information and to be in the advance guard of the repairs that were inevitable. The general public, he had come to realize, were sheep whose insights lagged many years behind reality. Only when the money growth died would the public think life had improved.

***

Yves sat on the train to Zürich, two rows down and on the other side of the aisle, facing Christolphe who drank coffee, ordered from the breakfast cart, and read the *Zürich Zeitung*. It was a traditional banker's breakfast. Christolphe did not notice Yves who was rather unrecognizable in any case. A master in disguise, Yves now sported a mustache, a beret and glasses. His clothes were not the elegant set he wore to the dinner party at Louvecienne, but he had an unobstructed view of Christolphe, as he enjoyed his morning repast, the train and thoughts of his destination. I feel a bit jealous of him, thought Yves; he is clearly satisfied with his life, this morning commute and thoughts of his work once he arrives there. It is an enviable position to be in.

As for his beautiful wife, waiting docilely for him to return, Yves had no words. It was beyond his comprehension.

At the Zürich end station he followed Christolphe who walked directly to Bahnhofstrasse and, some distance down the street, disappeared through a private doorway. Obviously, there was no other way to enter such a fortress, so Yves found a seat at a nearby café and settled in to watch the entrance to that inner sanctum. True to the punctual Swiss nature, other employees began to arrive for work on time. They were all dressed in their executive bank manager's attire, and Yves guessed that no one worked at this location unless they had achieved a certain reputable status. Patience was the name of the wait, for nearly an hour later who should ring for admittance but Holtz? Now this was getting more interesting. He assuredly knew his way around, and the fact that he was admitted meant he was known. Certainly, he had been here more than once.

So it was true that Christolphe also knew Holtz. This was a circle that tightened and wove like simple basket weaving, thought Yves. A strange thought. The ties we weave, the binds that chaff. Woven deceptions were being slowly and intricately designed, and Yves' thoughts flew in all directions. Thankfully, he could sit here and sort them out. A few more patrons rang the doorbell, and one was turned away.

The fellow shrugged, then made his way to Yves' café to sit and contemplate his predicament. His table was nearby, and they casually struck up a friendly conversation.

"I see you were turned away from the bank. Me, too."

"What was your problem?" "Probably the fact that I had questions and nothing to deposit."

The fellow sat thoughtfully for a few minutes, minding his own business.

"Are you Swiss?"

"No, French. And you?"

"Belgian. You say you had only questions?"

"Yes. I'm looking for some assets of clients who claim their bank account seems quite empty these days. Columns don't seem to add up."

"Really? Are you a detective?"

"Just a concerned citizen. In Paris we seem to have assets disappearing frequently, especially artwork. It's a great place to find art connoisseurs."

"I hear you. I stored a few precious pieces here, and now I want to retrieve one of them for my daughter's wedding. I'm told no one can help me, as the goods have been moved to another location. I must make a written request, and they will begin a search for the piece. It could take a long time, and the wedding is next month."

"That's an interesting problem. Why would they have moved your treasure somewhere else? Where could be more safe? I do not like the sound of that at all."

Both men ordered another coffee and decided to sit together to collect their thoughts.

"What do you really know about this bank?"

"My brother-in-law, who is Swiss, recommended it, said it was just about the most discrete in Zürich."

"Do they have many connections in Germany?"

"That goes without saying. All the Zürich banks are connected to Austria and Germany, even the Scandinavian countries. They keep all they do private and secure. Even Americans bankers are here, those who wish to keep a little aside from the taxman."

"So why did you decide to secure a valuable painting in a vault where no one could see it?"

"Well, *Monsieur*, I am a Jew. Does that make sense now?"

"Not really. Are you saying you have deposited art and deeds and other forms of wealth in this bank simply because you are a Jew?"

"I am not a paranoid man, my friend, just prudent. Something is afoot and my family feels the same squeeze that Jews have felt for centuries. It is tightening around all aspects of our lives. Suddenly, we are not comfortable and believe another war is inevitable. Those who chose not to flee are delusional. It is time to pack up and go somewhere where we can be safe and raise our children in peace."

Just then the bank door opened, and Holtz slipped out, walking up Bahnhofstrasse back toward the train station.

"Do you know that fellow," asked Yves?

"He looks familiar."

"Aside from looking German, have you ever met?"

"No, it's more than that. I feel that I should remember, but I have been too preoccupied lately to remember every face I see."

"Out of curiosity, who was the artist who painted the work you stored with the bank?"

"It was an artist my wife has loved. There were several, actually. There is an early Picasso and two Moise Kisling paintings. But her favorites were George Braque and a small Chagall."

"My God, those are valuable and amazing works."

"You see why I wished to store them safely. Slowly, slowly, *Monsieur*, we are letting go of our life in Belgium, and we will leave for the New World. I must arrange for passports, transportation and the collection of a lifetime that hangs on the walls of our beloved home. People tell me Argentina is a good place to be or maybe even Los Angeles in the United States. But I think there is no love of Jews anywhere in the world. Hopefully, we will not trade one uncomfortable situation for another. It is a dice throw and a matter of fate at this point."

As Yves listened, he was dismayed to think that life was so hard for these people who added so much to the culture of Europe. Just as his thoughts began to coalesce, another customer rang the doorbell on Bahnhofstrasse and was quickly admitted. It was Ernesto. The plot thickens, thought Yves.

"Now, there is a fellow I recognize," his companion pointed out.

"Do you know him?"

"He's from Cuba, big family there, important but in the same straights as the Jews. The rich families have held the people down too long, and it is just a matter of time before they rise up. Believe me, there will be no valuable paintings hanging on anyone's walls when that happens. This fellow was at the last bank meeting I attended, when I was depositing our valuables. Don't know his name."

This had been a most valuable trip for Yves.

"I can only say it was fortunate that we met like this, Isaac. For me, it has been a fruitful day. If you care to share your address with me, I may be able to refer you to someone who would love to help."

They shook hands and parted ways though Yves was certain Isaac expected never to hear from him again. As soon as he returned to Paris, Yves intended to relate this day in its entirety to Roshi who would find it very interesting indeed. As for Anais, it was not the best of news. It appeared that her husband's bank might be involved in underhanded transactions or outright theft. What did Christolphe know of this? Did he have a role in it? Whether or not he took direct part in these affairs, it did not look good or speak well of his character. So, had the self-satisfied banker hardened his heart and compromised his ethics in exchange for favor with the boss? Yves had fought in a war and lost his family in order to keep his morals intact. He would do it again, if it meant saving his soul.

Chapter 61
Roshi Intervenes

That evening, once Yves had returned to Paris, they went to visit Roshi who sat in his study with a robe over his knees. Nothing seemed to keep him warm these days. As Anais and Yves took him through the connections they had made, it seemed they tried to soften their suspicions and the many coincident connections to Anais. What were they to make of such knowledge? Yves told Roshi about Isaac and passed along his address with the list of paintings and assets he had stored with the bank. As they talked, they sat across from each other and the fireplace. Above the mantel was a painting by Fugita Tsuguhara. He, too, was from an old Samurai family of great discipline. In Japan, said Roshi, painting was an old and honorable profession. Apparently, just last year the painter had caught his wife Pink Snow in the arms of his cousin and let her go. It had created a terrible scandal in Tokyo.

The fired cackled and flickered but did not make Roshi look less old or frail. Outside, the leaves of autumn were the brilliant colors of the fire inside. Yves mentioned that the *Salon d'Autome* was advertising a new show, where all the well- known painters and writers would display their newest work. It was rumored that Gertrude Stein would step out that evening with her friend Alice to attend the show. She was a source of knowledge and insider information, when it came to art collectors and dealers, since she possessed one of the finest collections of modern art in Paris. She was a legend in Paris but rarely seen outside her apartment.

Anais intended to be there. Truly, Isaac was right to be concerned about paintings that were suddenly not available. Roshi knew he could get them returned, but the more serious issue was that Isaac's family would be in the path of danger before too much longer. His intuition told him it was paramount to convince Isaac to listen to his inner forebodings. Roshi had friends who could help his family. True to character, the Swiss would never wish to attract international publicity or bring attention to their role in the commission of fraudulent crime.

It would be Anais' task to leak information to the artists she knew about the bank's behavior in their collusion with art confiscation. They would put out a warning that buyers and sellers must beware. Any suggestion that work was disappearing insinuated a collaboration between powerful banks and those who paid them to make the works disappear. Roshi suspected the Germans. Was this what Raphael had discovered? Perhaps, he had discovered where their stolen assets were hidden.

Roshi wanted everyone at his apartment the next week. The guest list would include Herr Dietrich who might very well be implicated in crime. Anais confessed that she was very much afraid for Christolphe. What if his job was compromised even though he might be innocent?

"But if we find the killer and manage to release some of the art work, he will get a promotion, my dear. If he is guilty, he will be punished by more than the loss of his job."

Chapter 62
The Meeting

The purpose of the meeting was to sort out disconnected facts. Oddly enough, every one of those invited showed up, and now, they were all seated in Roshi's living room. The fire burned brightly, but Roshi had not risen to greet anyone. Jean-Paul acted as their host and stood in the doorway with a fellow Anais had never seen before this evening. He and Jean-Paul looked quite formidable, as they stood at attention, ostensibly to see to guest needs. They were all seated with cognacs in hand and invitations in pockets. Few people were invited to his famous apartment, and no one had considered turning down such an invitation.

"As you may well wonder, I have asked each of you here this evening because you are all connected to each other in some manner. Each of you is a link in a chain and one of you is a murderer, but a chain is only as strong as its weakest link."

There was a gasp from Lily.

"If you have come as an innocent suspect, we are sorry for the rude awakening. But at least each one of you will leave here educated in post-war complexities and the sordid details of reality. More people need to be aware of these unhappy events, so injustices might be stopped or at least challenged. You may ask how we have come up with our evidence.

"The problem I will present here goes beyond circumstantial evidence. This evening one of you will confess because one of your acquaintances will point a finger at you, and you will be exposed. Now, let us begin.

"First, Christolphe. Your lovely wife is here this evening, helping to gather evidence. That dinner party at your gracious home was planned by her. You seemed surprised that night and acted like you did not know certain guests, but Ernesto, for instance, you knew quite well. You had met him in Havana where you lived in some comfort for four years."

Christolphe paled but his innate dignity was maintained.

"Ernesto, you recognized Christolphe but chose not to remind him of your acquaintance at the party. One can only ask why?

"Lily you are acquainted in a biblical way with our friend Holtz, here. And Holtz, you conveniently moved into a fairly pricey apartment just one floor below the one rented by our deceased agent Raphael, but perhaps you did not know that the fire escape outside your own bedroom goes up just outside his bedroom window. Perhaps you did not know he was a secret agent. He was shot from that window.

"Herr Dietrich, you are the director of a well-respected private bank in Zürich. You must have made the acquaintance of one Isaac Gold, a Jew. He came to you some time ago, requesting to deposit his art collection, the deeds to his Belgian properties and his Paris home. He is liquidating his assets in a desire to leave Belgium and Paris for re-location in the New World. Unfortunately, when he wanted a certain painting returned to give, as a wedding gift to his daughter, he was met with administrative obstacles. It would seem that his painting had been moved from your Zürich vault. That begs the question, Where is the painting he requested, and why isn't it immediately available to its rightful owner?

"Now, this week, just a few days ago, several of you were observed, as you entered Herr Dietrich's bank. We know Christolphe was already at his desk, but the first visitor was our young Herr Gratzer. What was the purpose of your visit Herr Gratzer?"

Holtz looked like a deer in headlights, but he held himself tall.

"I have my savings at that bank."

"Is that so? How does an impoverished artist like yourself find enough cash to deal with a private Swiss bank? We all know there is a minimum deposit policy in all its branch institutions."

"I have been paid in advance for my up and coming role in Bayreuth."

"Mr. Columell, why were you at the bank that day, allowed in by the guard with no question, as though you were an old friend of the bank?"

Ernesto, too, paled at the direct questioning.

"I am here to negotiate a loan for our family business in Havana, sir. It is not common knowledge."

"It is a small world we have here today. I have it on reliable resources that this is not your first visit to Paris in the last few years. It is a long way to travel to secure a loan, am I correct?"

Roshi glanced around at the tense figures in the room.

"Why is it each of you looks guilty of some crime?"

Anais felt the discomfort in the room like physical pain between her shoulder blades.

"Is it not more correct, Ernesto, to say that your family's bank has been in dire straits for some time and that you are in actual fact here with the last of your ill-begotten gains, to put whatever assets you have managed to get out of Cuba into a Swiss, secure and completely private account?"

Silence.

"I am here for personal reasons. I have considered moving to Europe, making a new home here and studying art. You mistake my motives for being here, sir."

"No. That is not quite true. It is said, and quite accurately, that if you wish to lie, base your facts on truth. They will be harder to discern. But the real facts are different, are they not? Of course, you would like to live in this beautiful city of anonymous characters, where promiscuity and homosexuality, for instance, are quite acceptable because you are homosexual and have hidden that fact for many years. It is nearly impossible to live a lie forever. You would like to study art because you are an artist at heart who has never practiced any art or made an attempt at artistic discipline. Art, you know, is a fantasy until it becomes real. It is said that you must practice your art or it will destroy you. What art have you practiced at all, Ernesto?

"Lastly, there is the question of money. To live here without a job takes a great deal of money, far more cash than is required in Havana where help is cheap, and the class structure imbalanced. You have never wanted for anything, never had to work to provide for yourself. Some would call it spoiled. To spoil, by definition, is to make rotten, decayed. Life for you on this great wheel of existence has come full circle and, when Raphael found your secrets, because he did find them, you killed him. Like a coward, you pointed a gun through his bedroom window and shot him in the back."

"You have no idea what you are talking about. My family business is not in trouble. Where did you get such an idea?"

"Well, sir, what you did not consider was that Raphael did not work alone. When he encountered you on one of your many trips to Paris, he told me, and I had you and your bank dealings investigated."

"He kept a detailed journal *Monsieur*, and a safety deposit box wherein he collected evidence. We have been watching you for some time."

"This is outrageous."

"No, *Monsieur*, it is truth, though I must admit there have been truths I've encountered that have been more

333

surreal than our surrealist artists could ever imagine. That brings me to the next issue we must discuss. Art.

"Holtz, Mr. Gratzer, your considerable talent aside, it is quite a coincidence that you discovered the apartment directly below Raphael's with the connecting fire escape that descends from bedroom to bedroom. One can only assume that you had frequented that bedroom to test the stairs and its convenience and that you have had intimate relations with Ernesto in order for him to have been there, too."

There was a gasp and a cry from Lily.

"Why that is disgusting, Holtz! How could you have made love with me one minute and with him the next?"

"That is a good question, Lily."

"Well, what do you have to say for yourself?"

"You're old enough to know the score."

"That's right, Lily, you are. You have been in this city all your life. This sort of behavior is quite common, especially in the art community, especially when there is a need for money. Your Winifred Wagner was very generous in her gift of the apartment. But she is another wealthy person who never had to fight to survive. What good is a big apartment without money for food or heat or roses or taxis? It was a bit of an insane gift that required you to provide her with information about the arts in return for the rent. You had no idea where or how to begin."

Holtz sat there looking confused and miserable.

"The artist's life is not easy and never was. A singer needs a patron, good food and exercise, musical instruments and plenty of time to practice a role. As well, peace of mind always helps, and you have had none of those. Am I right, Herr Gratzer?"

He nodded, painfully.

"So Ernesto's attentions provided a much needed income. As well, he wanted to know what you knew about the artists you had met, and when you mentioned his very own cousin, whom he had not seen in years, he was intrigued. Little Anais, nearly a full-fledged *saloniere*?"

Chapter 63
Retribution

Roshi paused for a minute and looked carefully at the faces in the room, their concern and their surprise at these revelations.

"I will continue, if you have each absorbed what I am telling you. There is more, of course. There always is.

"Christolphe, you work in Switzerland and Paris. You have the prefect wife and the most open privileges a husband could have.

"Ernesto remembers you from your days in Cuba, when you experimented with life and your sexual preferences. He remembered you well, but could not have known that you would meet his cousin, fall in love and change. Your days of experimentation are most likely over, but this is an unhappy reminder of that past that you would like to have kept in the closet. Ernesto decided, along with Holtz, that you were good for a small extortion payment each month. Now Holtz had two regular cash transactions and both of them were linked to further access to the art world."

"And what about me?"

Lily sat at the far corner of the sofa, crying into her handkerchief. Anais looked from one to the other, trying to assimilate these dreadful connections that she had been too naïve or blind to make.

"You were collateral damage, Lily. When you told Anais you were ruined in the bank crash, I had your finances examined carefully. Holtz, however, saw a beautiful woman who lived only two blocks away, a convenience he could not resist. Your many friends in the ateliers made you the perfect informant. Without any suspicion you told him about your friends, their addresses, their current and past art works, where they had sold and what they considered to be future prospects. He did not need to go anywhere for his information except to bed, and he made sure you were completely on your back."

Lily's light complexion turned red with embarrassment and anger.

"You pig! How dare you?"

"You loved it!"

"Now children, we do not have time for this. It all makes me tired at my age. We are not finished."

They all stopped suddenly. More? How could there be more than this?

"This brings me to Herr Dietrich. Is it not true, sir, that your mother's family is from Austria and that you came from a long line of artists and musicians? I would venture to say you became entirely sick of the whole scene, the poverty, the high drama and the lack of respect afforded to you, when you grew up. I am sure you came to think of the art world, as inhabited by miscreants and outlandish creatures. You do not see any problem in exploiting them for doing only what they love and were born to do, anyway.

Through Ernesto, whose precarious financial situation you had also checked out, you discovered his musician uncle, Anais' father, his cousin the gallery owner and his proclivities, when he paid for sex. What a windfall! As we all know in the financial and political sectors, reparations are being discussed. Herr Hitler, who failed art school, has taken a prurient interest in what he could not achieve. Money for the next war, which will surely happen in our lifetime, must come from somewhere. All you had to do was sit back and give orders. You knew they would be obeyed. So while you haven't committed murder, Herr Dietrich, you are guilty of more deliberate and planned crimes. To steal millions of dollars of art is a crime against culture and refinement. It is a contribution to the lowering of mass awareness, for the artist is a forecaster of the future. Artists do not fabricate art from pure air; they filter and condense the energy left in odd corners and cracks where emotions are either left to fester or to grow in beauty. They sacrifice their wellbeing in order that the rest of us may, hopefully, come to our senses. Through these cracks they transform light and show us true happiness. What are you doing with the art works you have so grievously misappropriated?"

"I have no idea of what you carry on about, sir. I am the director of a private and quite reputable bank. No one has ever accused us of such improper behavior."

"There is always a first time, sir. You have been followed, and your German counterparts have been brought in for questioning. This is now an international offense and, as such, is no longer completely in your hands. I would like to reacquaint you with one of your most prominent clients. Jean-Paul?"

They waited, as Jean-Paul left the room and returned with Isaac Gold. Roshi noted a change in Herr Dietrich's demeanor, as Isaac walked into the room.

"As we speak, arrangements are being set in place to return Herr Gold's property. It will be packaged and shipped to an art dealer in New York City. You see, Herr Dietrich, we are not asking, if you have acted inappropriately. We already know the details and have gone to great lengths to rectify the situation. As for *Monsieur* Gold and any wish he may have to pursue the matter beyond this point, that is up to him. Right now, it has given us all a bad taste for Swiss bank transactions. The purity and righteousness of the Swiss national character is being brought into question, Herr Dietrich. What you do in the future is a reflection of world opinion toward the Swiss. It is one thing to be uninvolved in war or reparation; it is another to be actively involved in unethical and even criminal activity. You are welcome to leave now, sir. Jean-Paul and officer Guillimard of the French Secret Police will see you to the door."

Herr Dietrich stood, and for a moment it seemed that he would defend his behavior, but looking at the faces in the living room, he thought better of it and followed Jean-Paul. His hat and coat were returned and once the door opened, he was gone.

Christolphe sat there, looking stricken. Anais walked over and sat beside him, holding his hand. Neither of them spoke.

"Jean-Paul, you may take care of the next problem."

At that Jean-Paul re-entered the room with detective Guillimard. Anais wanted to cry as she saw her cousin being led away.

"As for you, Holtz, I suggest you vacate your apartment and return to your family mill as you await the curtain call for Parsifal. Be glad we have a certain fondness for the artist and his plight."

Roshi turned to Lily. She, too, looked stricken.

"Anais, I had no idea until I spoke to you last week. I was just so lonely."

"Come here, my dear."

Lily approached Roshi's chair, and he indicated the ottoman in front of him.

"Sit for a moment."

She looked far more affected than the actual murderer.

"We are sorry for your plight, Lily. As Anais' best childhood friend, you are like a second daughter to me. So this is the proposition I am offering you. It is the same one I proposed to Anais many years ago. You are welcome to come here, live in the same little apartment where Anais spent some happy years, and I will try to figure out what the future of your financial affairs might be. I am told they could be a lot worse. We do not want you to be lonely and desperate, Lily. We are your family now, and we love you.

Jean-Paul, please have *Madame* show Lily where she would stay, if she decides to live with us."

Now only Christolphe and Anais sat in the living room as the others were dispersed and given admonitions.

"I will leave you two to work out your problems. Take your time."

They watched as Roshi slowly raised up from the chair before the fire and made his way in the direction of his meditation room. Anais knew he would spend the remainder of the evening in contemplation and meditation, absorbed in the healing values that the universe needed to evolve and balance itself. Christolphe gripped Anais' hand more tightly.

Chapter 64
Redemption

"Can you ever forgive me, my dear? Could you understand something that is so foreign to you and to your entire psyche, your sense of marriage and love?"

"But I do understand, Christolphe. I do understand. You see, I am not the same woman you married. If you can understand the fact that there are two of us, two of me, then why could I not understand that you are the past and present, two in one? All I can say is that for most of us there is duality. I do not mean the derogatory duplicitous category, by which so many refer to that word. Perhaps it was the Great War that taught us to protect ourselves from ourselves but, in this modern new society in which we live, it is rampant. It does not mean I love you less or am naive enough to believe that what I see is all I get. There are days, when I sit and contemplate Brancusi's *Nude Descending a Staircase* and wonder how many more of my selves are scattered about the city of Paris. Christolphe, I do not love you less. Perhaps, if all my selves were gathered up and love could be measured as such, they would add up to more than a single Anais."

"My dear, you are the sweetest, most forgiving wife any man could ask for."

He went on thanking her profusely, but Anais knew then that he was not truly aware of her dilemma. She could never explain her two sides to him in a way that would make him understand. Denial was a great equalizer; it smoothed out what people wished to see and hid those that they wished to deny. It was a great defense mechanism; and while it was in place there were no holes or cracks to allow the light of understanding to enter. She sighed and knew she was just as guilty on some level. After all, she was able to tell one truth while another truth scuttled away safe and sound, unexposed to any light. This house of love, where a spy could live, had to be good enough for her. She was not perfect nor did she expect Christolphe to be perfect. They would continue to struggle, in love, in defiance of the world outside their home, two hearts that managed to work as one whole heart. After all, Roshi had once taught her that redemption was brought on by our choices.

Christolphe gazed at her, more in love than ever. This wonderful woman had seen his other side and was not repulsed. She claimed to understand, and he believed her. Once again, he thanked whatever fortunate star had crossed his path, when he found her. Her outlook on life was generous; that was the only adequate way to describe it. For her, there seemed to be no need for forgiveness, simply an acceptance of who he had once been. How many of us know what parts are still alive and which have already been lived out? It had to do with emotional debts, what had been burned off, and what continued to require attention. Love was a matter of courage. He thought of those gathered by Roshi in the living room that day. Every one of us is guilty, he mused. We are guilty of ignorance; that which we see each day right in front of us is ignored. We are guilty of stupidity, when we remain in a stupor, dull and wishful of other scenarios that do not exist, but that we are too stunned to change in deference to habit. Kant wrote that stupidity was not caused by brain failure but by the wicked heart. Tomorrow he would go to Zürich and hand in his resignation, admit what he had observed all along and find a better place to work.

Chapter 65
The Future

Lily was shown to the room she intended to occupy in the near future. Jean-Paul told her she need only tell them what she wished to be brought over from her apartment. The rest could be put in storage until she felt she wanted it back. He smiled such a welcome that she felt she had found a new home. She was exhausted and, as soon as Jean-Paul left her alone, she fell into that deep rest that restores body and soul. She was certain she saw her parents, smiling down at her. Nanny came by, admonished her for her near descent into hell, then hugged her and said she would be fine now. How insidious was the slope of destruction. Everyone that Roshi had gathered had been an example of banal levels of lost hope, the kind where evil insinuates itself smoothly and slowly into daily habits.

***

Ernesto arrived at the police station in handcuffs. How was it possible he had descended into a hell where he had murdered someone? Was he the person who had done it? He knew better! He had grown up in love and privilege with everything strewn at his feet. He was the favored son, the one with potential and greatness before him. Then, the universe had intervened, and his dark side had gained a hold over him. He had shared his distress with no one, except

343

perhaps with Anais on that lovely day in Havana, driving up the coast. He had felt stifled then, but as he looked back, his youth was highlighted as a time of freedom and wealth, a time to grow up and take responsibility, a time to curb his desire for fun and irresponsibility. No one ever told him that life was a series of stages where we are tested and tested again. Now, he saw that time for what it was, a transition, a test of character, or a crossroad where good and evil offered different paths.

***

Holtz quickly gathered his suitcases. Truly, it was all he had of his own. Why not go home to his brother, the mill, the town where he was known and respected, where the Winifred Wagners of this world were too far away to corrupt and demand their own perverted version of what they considered good for others. He could mind his own business, practice for his role, then show up to sing it. Why should treachery and skulking deception accompany his music, which he realized was attached to his soul? He felt that he had not only closely escaped the clutches of evil, he had learned a lesson about being a true human being. He knew without any doubt that he had just become a better singer, a true spirit and advocate of truth and beauty. If his values were rejected by audiences and patrons, he would find a new place for his voice to be heard. If the Jews were moving away to places like Buenos Aires and Los Angeles, and he liked all the Jews he had met in the music community, maybe he should follow them. With these thoughts he looked around the apartment, locked his bags and carried them down to the street. A taxi would take him to the train station, and from there he would make his way home. He was ready to begin a new life.

***

Yves walked around the corner as Holtz got in a taxi. The young man had certainly been shown a lesson about the meaning of life and art. Not a bad lesson to learn.

Everyone had seen the errors of their crooked paths today, and it made him wonder about his own state of inertia. He felt a stirring in his blood that he hadn't felt in years. It was a thaw, no doubt about it. The question was, what did it mean? He had just been witness to a profound change, a turn of direction and purpose for five individuals that was bound to cause a ripple effect in their lives and his own. There was no such thing as remaining unaffected. He considered that we are all moved by the actions and reactions of those around us, and these five had rubbed along beside him. What was his own destiny that had been a part of his life?

Yves pictured Roshi in his mind, sitting there near the fire, an aging Bodhisattva with a robe covering his legs and a mind as clear as a cloudless sky. Yet age was slowly closing in on him. How much longer could he sustain this work on which so many counted?

It was then that Yves made a decision. He would talk to Roshi about a greater role, more training, more dedication to this cause that had just changed five people into better human beings. Until now, he had been a grateful bystander, somewhat indifferent to all but the fact that he had an income and an interesting employer. The shift inside made him weak on his feet. His heart pounded in his chest, and a heat made its way up his spine. This was definitely not indifference, and he took a deep breath.

Chapter 66

Anais left Christolphe, packing for a last trip to Zürich. He intended to spend as much time in the city as was necessary to clear up the impossible scandal that would destroy the bank, if it were not rectified. And, if nothing was to change, he was finished there.

She walked to the train station, heading into Paris. She wanted to spend the day on *La Belle Aurore*, then visit with Lily in the evening. Life had changed. It felt hollowed out and vulnerable to possibility. It was a feeling that was precious and something to be recognized in awe and gratitude. She felt she had been instrumental in bringing about change. It was the action of consciousness. The hollow space she felt was a place necessary for change. For now, it was a sacred space that one could draw upon in times of spiritual need. It was time for her to make deposits rather than withdrawals.

She walked down the pier and saw Yves standing at the bow of his *Hilaire*. They nodded as she walked by. She knew in that moment that she and Yves would work together in the future and they would do good work.